NORTH RECKONING

NORTH RECKONING

J.T. JERNBERG

DORRANCE PUBLISHING CO., INC.
PITTSBURGH, PENNSYLVANIA 15222

ISBN: 978-0-8059-7665-6

Printed in the United States of America

First Printing

For more information or to order additional books, please contact:
Dorrance Publishing. Co., Inc.
701 Smithfield Street
Third Floor
Pittsburgh, Pennsylvania 15222
U.S.A.
1-800-788-7654
www.dorrancebookstore.com

DEDICATION

This book is dedicated to two important women in my life:
my late mother, Joy, and my wife, Carol.

I appropriately dedicate it to my mother because from the time I was a young boy
until she passed away it was her constant encouragement that I always continue to
create art—whether it be "homemade" comic books, silly satires, or complex poetry
and prose. One of the final things she said to me: "I now hope you have learned that
you must never quit writing." I have tried to heed this excellent advice.

Equally, this book is dedicated to my loving wife. Throughout the years we have
been together she has been the love, inspiration, and civilizing force in my existence.
It was her faith and trust in my abilities and vision that urged me to continue writing
and, in particular, complete this work.

For their belief in me as an artist and even, more to the point,
their unconditional love, I dedicate this novel.

CONTENTS

1

DRINK BEFORE DEATH

A refreshing breeze off the mountain peaks made the ride on the trail more tolerable. It was a warm afternoon, but there was no time for relaxing in the shade — even if it were readily available. The rider felt tempted to take another swig from the canteen, but decided against the impulse. It would be better to conserve water until the supply might be replenished. Rudimentary thoughts of life, meeting basic needs, and enjoying the beauty of the natural surroundings should have been uppermost in the mind of the rider. Instead, the thought of revenge dominated his mind and soul. He had to get across the pass and over to the encampment known as Fortune River. At Fortune River he could find the people who had caused him so much grief. There, revenge would be achieved. It was July, 1875.

The rider got off his horse and walked it up a fairly steep trail. Large clusters of pine trees formed near the summit of the trail. A quick blast of wind arriving from the summit felt comforting. The prospect of the unknown on the other side of that summit did not produce quite so much comfort. He truly did not know what awaited him. Would he survive the day or be killed on the spot? This uncertainty was troubling, yet he scarcely felt inclined to dwell on it.

At the summit, he looked down at what appeared to be a large valley. About a mile or so distant he could clearly see some buildings, and even a few tents. They bordered a swift, flowing river. This had to be Fortune River. The rider remounted, then slowly rode down to the settlement. Soon, the business of the day would be transacted.

He approached a cheap, dirty looking wooden structure resembling a building. It had a window in front brandishing the words, "Sunset Saloon." How appropriate. Someone would be facing a sunset fairly soon.

He tied his weary, black horse at the hitching post near a watering trough. The horse rapidly found the cool treat and quickly thrust down its snout and drank eagerly. The rider climbed up onto the rickety boardwalk and went through the saloon doors.

Inside the saloon, there was a cheap, well-worn, dark brown bar with about six wooden stools in front. Three of the stools were occupied. A bartender was talking to the man sitting on the second stool from the right. The rider glanced around the room. Over to the right, there was a player piano, and it was playing, "Sweet Betsy of Pike."

To the right, there was a round table where three people appeared to be playing draw poker. In general, the facility was dirty, reeking of cheap liquor, and potentially very dangerous. It was a typical whiskey bar of that era.

The saloonkeeper looked at the rider and yelled, "A stranger in town. Hey, mister, what are yuh buyin'?"

"Beer, if you have any."

"Just whiskey."

"Then whiskey."

The fellow in the third chair from the right looked at the rider and smirked. The rider ignored the insolence and chugged his glass of rye.

"Who the hell are you, mister?" the smirking man suddenly asked.

The rider glanced at him, and made an assessment. The man was around thirty-five, heavily bearded, wearing a big floppy hat, a red plaid shirt, and Levis, and holstered a Colt. 45. The man also had a thick lock of black hair hanging from one of his belt loops.

"I didn't say who I was, mister. What difference does it make?"

The man sitting at the first bar stool quickly stood up, smiled, and said, "No need to get cranky, stranger. We really don't see many folks comin' into our settlement these days, so we're natcherly curious. My name is Elijah Johnson, and ah came to Fohtune Rivuh 'bout a month ago. Ah've been trying to pan some gold outta that river, but all I've done is get a big, big chance to study a bunch of wuthless rocks and learn how to count grains uh sand."

The second man cackled and said, "Be damned if yuh didn't find more than I did. At least you edjucated yerself about gee-olo-gee."

"This here is Jake Baker. Yuh might think we're partners, but we ain't. More like competitors. The barkeep is Willard Harrison. Doesn't like tuh talk much, and ah think he might be runnin' low on whiskey. Watch out for what he might charge yuh."

The rider looked at the one called Jake Baker. He wore dirty buckskins, a folded hat, and had a bushy, gray beard and long, stringy hair. He smiled, yet did so from a perspective of cultivated, repressed cruelty. The bartender — although middle aged, balding, mustachioed, and gruff voiced — looked comparatively tough, but not cruel. The old man Elijah appeared to be a rough customer himself, but there was a twinkle in the eyes and a winning smile that separated him from the others. Lastly, the fellow in the red plaid shirt reminded the rider of a coyote sniffing around for weaknesses or spoils to pounce upon.

This man in the red plaid shirt interrupted the rider's thoughts as he addressed Elijah Johnson, "You ain't very polite, you old mountain goat. You didn't interduce me. Stranger, my name is Nate McAvee, and I asked for your handle, stranger."

"I don't care for your tone of voice, Nate McAvee. However, I'm not here to cause new trouble. I am just looking for five people — actually, any of them. One man is an Indian who goes by the name of Blood Hawk. Another one is a strange guy with long, blonde hair, speaks with a southern accent, and is meaner than a mountain cat. A third one is a thin Frenchman who's bald, Eastern-bred, and wears a black suit and string tie."

Elijah said, "I don't reckon I recall any fellers like that, except maybe for the Indian. I think he came here about three days ago — along with a friend."

"Shut up, you old bag of bones," the man in buckskins shouted.

Everyone looked at Jake Baker who simply looked down at his shot glass and said no more. He stared at the bartender and forcefully shoved his thick finger into the glass, demanding a refill.

The rider ignored Baker and said, "The fourth man is a real piece of work. He is southern, educated, has good manners, is supposedly charming to women, but deep down, rotten to the core. He is probably still clean-shaven and wears a black hat with a string of small mirrors wrapped around the hatband. Have you gentlemen seen any of these people?"

"And what if we have, stranger? Why should we tell a migrant character like you? What's in it for us?" McAvee sneered.

"Not much. I don't have much to offer. If I were to find out that anyone was protecting these men, I might not like it."

"Is that a threat, saddle tramp?"

Elijah said, "You said there were five men. You only described four."

"I don't have to describe the fifth one. He is in this saloon."

Abruptly, all talking ceased, and all faces were drawn to the rider. For an instant, nobody moved. One could have heard a bread crumb bounce off the filthy floor.

Suddenly, the man called Jake Baker jumped up from his bar stool and went for his gun. Before he could completely yank it from the holster, the rider drew his Colt .45 and fired at the man. Baker flew backwards and jack-knifed over the bar; his head flipped down as if to greet the bartender in a mocking wave. A bullet had shattered his heart.

The men at the card table quickly got up and ran through the swinging saloon doors. The other men, astonished, gawked at the corpse and then looked at the rider before Elijah spoke.

"What in hell was that all about? Why'd Jake try tuh kill you, mistuh? Ah think you owe us that much! Talk!"

"Since I'm still holding my revolver, I really don't have to tell you jacks-or-better nothing! Just understand that he was the fifth man I was looking for and that he was a cold-blooded killer. He was one of five men responsible for killing some people very dear to me."

McAvee smirked again, and spoke. "It just goes to show, you don't really know who yer drinkin' with half the time." Ostensibly concerned that he not anger the rider, he added, "I- I took this feller to be a nice hombre, but he *did* draw on you first. You was justified!"

"That's what ah say," Elijah reinforced. "If he had nuthin' to hide, he wouldn't 'u gone for his smoke wagon like he did. Mistuh, that was a pretty fast draw. Where did you learn tuh shoot like that?"

"I had to learn to shoot like that. Besides, like a lot of men, I was in the War Between the States."

"So was ah," Elijah said, "But ah usually ended up fightin' Yankees from a distance, or getting up close and usin' the rifle butt or bayonet. E'scuse muh detailin' all that. Ah'm not sure what side you fought on."

"I was one of those 'Yankees,' but so what? That war is over. I don't want to start it again."

"Ah sure as hell agree with you on that, stranger. Tell yuh what, ah'll buy yuh a drink as long as yuh'll take rye — that's all that son-of-a-gun has."

"You have a deal, old timer."

2

---•—

STABLE AND SUPPER TALK

There weren't many businesses in this slap-dash constructed community, but the essential ones were there. In addition to the saloon, there was a small hotel/restaurant and a livery stable. At the latter, the rider was getting his horse brushed down and fed. The aging prospector, Elijah, stood solemnly nearby as the rider cared for the mount.

"One thing puzzles me, stranger," he said. "How did yuh figure that one of them five fellers was in Fohtune Rivuh? Gotta tell yuh — I been in lotsa remote places before, and this is sure one of 'em."

The rider slowly turned and, without smiling, squinted at Elijah and answered, "Since you were kind enough to buy me a drink, I guess I owe you something, old timer. I have been tracking these scoundrels for over three months. I started out in Montana and have just missed these characters in one town after another. On the east side of the pass, there is a town called Grubstake where I played poker with four men who liked to hear themselves talk. I just lost nearly one hundred dollars thinking my three aces wouldn't be topped, when one of the men I called threw down a diamond flush. He guffawed and bragged this was the second time that week he had skinned a greenhorn. I asked who was the other 'lucky player,' and he said a 'smelly, weather-worn man sportin' buckskins, who blathered bad jokes, and smiled like a savage who skinned something alive,' had lost fifty dollars to him in a hand of five card stud four days ago."

"And he was headed up here?"

"The lucky gambler said as much. He told me that the buckskinned loser bid farewell to his fifty dollars, and said, 'That's a crappy way tuh say goodbye to my friends, but what the hell! Anyway, I'm gonna go up to Fortune River and see if my luck holds out better there. I hear folks are still pannin' for gold up there.'"

Elijah shook his head, spit out his tobacco, and said, "Yup. That matches what that character said to me shortly after he came to Fohtune Rivuh. He said he just got fleeced in that 'pig's ass of a town, Grubstake,' and needed to find his fohtune in a new way."

"How well did you get to know this man, this Jake Baker?"

Elijah took a large bite from his tobacco plug, cocked his head, smiled, and asked, "If ah tell yuh, am I gonna be next on your gun smoke menu?"

"I doubt it. Besides, I'm usually not in the habit of gunning down people who are engaging in civilized palaver. Not only that, I owe you a whiskey."

"Glad to hear that," he laughed, accidentally swallowed some tobacco, coughed, laughed again, and was met with the rider's laughter.

"I'm stayin' in my own tent 'bout a half mile up the river. Drop by tomorrow an' I tell yuh all I know. I better get back to my camp before dark. If yuh ain't goin' to stay in the flea bag hotel, yer welcome to put down your bedroll at my camp and eat some beans and fatback tonight."

"Thanks. I'll take my chances with the fleabag hotel. I haven't slept indoors for a while, so I want to remember what it's like. I will make a call in the morning though."

After Elijah Johnson rode away the rider checked into the hotel, secured a room, and considered whether or not he would sleep on the bed. He checked the mattress and found it rife with bedbugs, so he opted to throw his bedroll on the floor. Before turning in, however, he went downstairs to find some supper.

The proprietor of the hotel, as well as the so-called restaurant, was a stocky, middle-aged woman who went by the name Naomi Harrison. Yes, she was related to the bartender, Willard Harrison. She was the man's sister.

Fortunately, Naomi had a pot of jackrabbit stew on the stove and hospitably served a bowl to the rider.

Already seated at the table was the bartender and two of the men who had been playing cards at the round table in the saloon that day.

"Yer in for a treat, stranger," Willard exclaimed. "Sis here is the best cook in the whole Rocky Mountains."

One of the men retorted, "That's 'cause she is probably one of two or three cooks in the entire Rocky Mountains, you oaf."

"Watch your tongue, Phinneas Pleasance, or I'm going to have second thoughts about marrying you!"

Everyone laughed.

Naomi brought a loaf of bread, put it in front of the rider, looked intently at him, and remarked, "You certainly are a fine looking specimen of manhood. If I were just ten years younger I'd forget about that old fart, Phinneas, and set a trap for you. Where you from, good lookin'?"

The rider winced either from the hot stew burning the tip of his tongue or the unsolicited attention form Naomi Harrison.

"Ma'am, you're embarrassing me, but thanks for the flattery. I'm actually from Minnesota. I used to work in a hardware store there with my parents."

"Why aren't you there with them now, Mister...?"

"North. John North. I don't have what I once had but still cherish."

Naomi, a remarkably perceptive woman, had ample experience in reading people. She looked him over intently. John North was twenty-nine or thirty years old, about six feet tall, and clean-shaven. His hair was medium brown, full, but not too long. The eyes were green and steady. She noticed when he addressed someone his eyes appeared to be searching for the inner soul of the listener — as if each person might possess some tiny scrap of truth he was seeking. His smile was sincere, but it shielded some inner sadness she felt he was withholding from observers. Her sensing this was remarkable since North exuded strength, calmness, and, most of all, self-assurance.

Before she could say, "Oh, Mr. North…are they…," John seemed to read her mind and said, "Yes. My parents and kid brother are all dead."

"What happened?" one of the men asked while tilting his stew bowl to his whiskered face.

"I don't want to talk about it here. Let's just say that those five men I said I'm looking for had everything to do with their deaths."

Naomi draped a comforting arm around John's shoulder, tried to pull him toward her, and declared, "You needn't feel obliged to say anything you don't want to, John North. Just keep one thing in mind. Things aren't particularly great here in Fortune River, but it's a town — or at least a place that intends to become a town someday. And if you ever want to settle down in a nice, quiet, beautiful piece of God's country in the mountains, you are welcome to stay."

"Here! Here!" Phinneas echoed. He raised his cup of coffee and toasted, "This is for John North! Hopefully, 'nother new citizen of Fortune River! May you always be happy, never point your fast gun in our direction, and inspire Naomi here to cook good suppers again just to impress you!"

Naomi threw a biscuit at Phinneas, and everyone laughed, including the manifestly serious John North.

3

NO CHANCE TO BE SAVED

John North slept surprisingly well that night. He got up, shaved, put on the shirt he had washed and wrung out before retiring, and went downstairs for breakfast. This time, only Naomi was present. She quickly served John a platter of eggs, ham, and fried potatoes. Like the food last night, it was delicious.

"Naomi, you are enough to make a man want to settle down. Your cooking is fabulous. I think Phinneas is a lucky varmit."

"Flattery will get you anywhere, hansome. Did you sleep well?"

"Yes."

"I hope you didn't use the mattress, though. I'm ashamed to say that there are critters thrivin' in that territory. I mail-ordered some new mattresses from Kansas City fourteen weeks ago, but they haven't arrived yet!"

John swallowed his mouthful of eggs, lifted the cup of coffee to his lips, and stared blankly into the plate of sliced bread.

"I know you don't necessarily want to talk, John North, but I'd be willing to listen if you change your mind. Before I came up to bask in the glory of this glamorous boarding house, I used to be a school teacher back east. I taught reading and writing, but I spent a lot of time listening to a lot of people too."

Oddly enough, John North felt as if he could trust this woman. He really did not know her, and felt generally suspicious and guarded around new people, but the present time, location, and company appeared keenly agreeable for him to open up.

"It — it's difficult for me to talk about things, Naomi."

Naomi sat down next to John, grabbed a slice of bread, started to nibble, then patted him gently on the left hand.

"When I was younger, I had high hopes in life. Fancied myself a businessman. Then the war came along, and I ended up fighting at Gettysburg under the command of Colonel Joshua Lawrence Chamberlain. I ended up at The Wilderness and Petersburg, among other battles. Killing, maiming, coping with disease, hearing the crying, smelling the foul odors, and waiting for the end of the war was all I knew for nearly two years. I'm sorry to paint such a picture, but I'm sure you've heard this sort of stuff before from others."

"I have, sir."

"After the war, I went southwest and joined a cattle drive in progress moving up from Indian Territory just north of Texas. In Nebraska, we got in a fight with a Pawnee raiding party, and it was like the war all over again. Most of us made it up to Montana.

"I later found work when Grenville Dodge worked hard to cross the plains building the Union Pacific. I worked like a dog for three months, until I got sick enough of it to quit. Luckily, I had learned from a telegram from dad that had been delivered to me at the railroad camp in Colorado that my parents and brother were camped, and effectively stranded, outside one of those Hell on Wheels towns called "Rattler's Junction." It had been their plan to settle in Oregon. Due to unavoidable delays like repairing a busted wagon wheel, they had strayed off from the wagon train and ended up near that rat hole. Before leaving that "den of sin," as dad referred to the settlement, he had written and dispatched the telegram asking for my help. He wired the Union Pacific's regional supervisor. I arrived four days after the telegram had caught up with me. Much of their gear was gone. Several drunken oafs had shown up one night and robbed them. They had severely beaten dad and scared my mother and brother half to death. At least they survived — until after I arrived.

"What happened, son?"

North gulped his coffee and refrained from spearing the last morsel of meat on his plate.

"I urged them to ditch their plan to go west at least until they could join another wagon train next spring. I told them I would guide them back to St. Louis, and they agreed. That morning, about ten miles away from Rattler's Junction, about eight or nine men came bearing down on us firing handguns. I made mom and dad and my brother, Harry, get inside the wagon. Dad soon came out and picked off one of the riders. I shot and killed two others, but while I was focused on that, a son-of-a bitch got behind dad and shot him in the spine with a dragoon colt. He fell to the ground dead. Mom must have seen this. She emerged from the front of the wagon screaming for my father. Instantly, the same backshooter shot mom through the heart. I turned to kill this animal, but an Indian shot me in the back.

"Wounded, I tried to get up, but couldn't. My brother looked at me and cried out my name." North choked on these words. "It was then that I saw a rancid, smirking, blonde, long-haired devil shoot my kid brother. I screamed out an oath at all of them, then the Indian was on me primed to slit my throat with a huge knife."

"Dearest Lord, what — what happened then?"

North contained a burgeoning rage. "I got a good look at all of the men. I recall them vividly. All five of them! The Indian, the long-haired devil, the scum in buckskins, and the skinny one in the suit. The one who shot mom and dad — the main details I remember about him were his bright, white teeth, and black hat with little mirrors around the band. He was dark, handsome, and remorseless. He was their unholy leader.

"I nearly passed out from the pain of my wound, but perhaps it was more from the agony of losing my family. I remained conscious long enough to hear him exclaim, "Blood Hawk, yuh dumb Injun, have yuh forgotten how tuh be a good savage already? Can't you see thet this pilgrim is gonna die anyway? By dyin' slowly, and thinkin' about how we destroyed his happy little family, he is gonna feel more torture than he might feel if yuh cut his throat. Don't knife him. Let him brood and bleed to death ovah his helplessness."

Naomi recognized the intense pain he was concealing. Tears formed in her eyes.

North continued. "The one with the filthy beard and buckskins, the one those people in the saloon called Jake Baker, stepped on my hand and said, 'What a shame, he oughtta join his deader-than-dirt family pronto. Maybe I can break his hand and....'

" 'Leave him alone, mountain skunk,' the leader ordered, 'ah think we made oah point.'

"Afterwards, I stared at the leader's face, tried to memorize it, then saw double. I passed out and figured I was dead. About three days later, I woke up and found myself in some doctor's office in that Hell on Wheels town. Apparently, someone found me, loaded me into a wagon, and took me into town for doctoring. It was a rotten little town, but I lucked out because there was a surgeon there who was waiting until an army attachment came to escort him to the railroad gang about twenty miles down the line."

"John," Naomi squeezed his arm. "The Lord must have saved you that day."

"I know. I just wish that I could have saved my family." John forcibly held back emotions ready to burst out.

John pushed back his chair, walked over to the coat rack, put on his hat, adjusted his gun belt, looked out the window, and said, "No, I couldn't save them. Now there is no chance for those killers to be saved. One is dead, and I fully intend to send the others away to burn in hell for what they did."

4

PARTNERS

The air was a little cool and crisp, but within a couple of hours, the steady beating down of the morning sun would make that a memory. John North did not mind; he was used to the change and even welcomed it. He loved the morning coolness, yet equally enjoyed the warmness of afternoon. It was all part of nature, and to criticize or complain seemed more bothersome than to simply adapt and appreciate the finer points of something inevitable. He had learned to live with the outdoors ever since the war and knew it was something to never underestimate but was always a force one must learn to survive and ultimately respect. He viewed much of the world in this fashion and reserved most of his criticism for the people who sought to violate respect for him in this world. The five, and now only four, violent men had unforgivably challenged his notion of respect.

North contemplated this as he rode up on the right hand side of the winding river. The river was nearly twelve feet wide and deeper in some spots than others. A short distance beyond some rapids and a slight waterfall, pungent smoke from a riverside campfire was detectable. Soon, he saw the campfire and a weather-beaten canvass tent a few feet away from it. Seated on a folding stool next to the campfire was Elijah Johnson. He was pouring a cup of coffee from a scorched old blue metal pot.

"You must be one of them eastern fellars who sleeps in late! Ah been up since sunup!"

"Good for you, Mr. Johnson. I haven't had a good night's sleep in ages, so I rather enjoyed catching up on some shuteye last night. Besides, I'm not breakfasting on gold this morning."

"Ha-hah-hah. Not bad. A gunfighter with a bent toward poetry. Ah kinda like that. Get yer ass off the saddle and have a cup 'a muh coffee — it'll wake you up fer a week!"

North got off the horse and said, "That's the best idea I've heard in at least the last half mile. Thanks, old timer."

Johnson turned, spit a big mouthful of tobacco into the river, and replied, "Why do all you young bucks keep callin' experienced, righteous fellers like me, 'old timer'? Ah ain't so old that ah couldn't teach you a couple things 'bout survivin' in this country."

North sat on a stump near Johnson and said, "Take no offense, Johnson; actually, I'll bet you could teach me a lot. I'm just wondering how well you're doing with this gold panning. Think it might pay off for someone like me to take up the occupation?"

"Huh! If it were an occupation, then ah'd have nuthin' to do with it. In my case, it's a little hobby. I can't say that ah want any pardners — and that definitely applied to that varmint you sent to his maker yesterday!"

North sipped the coffee. "Woah! You make a strong cup of wake-up, Elijah. If a grizzly got a gulp of it, he'd fly up to the top of the highest pine tree."

"Whatcha wanna talk to me 'bout, yankee?"

North looked into Elijah's eyes and knew that all kidding and niceties could be set aside.

"I'd like to know what you know about Jake Baker. Wasn't he panning gold with you for a week?"

Elijah poured himself another cup of the ultra-strong brew and replied, "Ah can't say ah evuh really warmed up to that cuss. He said he wanted to try some gold pannin' near my camp and offered to watch muh back if ah watched his. To be honest, ah had been gettin' a bit rattled about somethin' happenin' after that bastard Nate McAvee showed up in Fohtune Rivuh. That character, braggin', insultin', blowin', breezin' around town like some gritty dust devil, struck me as a feller ah'd have to put down sooner or later. I figured that Jake Baker was probably not the best egg in the nest ei-thuh, but maybe the least rotten of the two. After what he tried to do to you yesterday, I now figure muh logic maybe went haywire."

"After meeting Mr. McAvee, I definitely understand how you got a bad impression. Not knowing much about him, except by the words blasting out of his mouth like farts from an overfed steer, I think your instincts were right. However, you must have noted a few odd things about Baker after he came to stay."

"Well, that bedroll over there is his. Ah guess he planned to stay a while longer until you spoiled his scheme by shootin' him dead. No, he nevuh did say much, 'cept that he had been livin' on the move for lotsa years, an' that he used to ride with a bunch of men who did 'odd jobs.' I asked what kind-a odd jobs, and he laughed and said, 'the usual — runnin' cattle, hirin' out to people needin' work, and prospectin'. From what I saw this past week, I don't think he evuh did much pannin'. Hell, now that I think of it, maybe he was waitin' for the right time to jump me and steal my poke 'o gold dust — providin' I could find any!"

"Perhaps. I think I'll take a look at his stuff."

Baker's bedroll consisted of a couple of blankets and some saddle bags hidden inside. He opened the pockets and discovered they were empty.

"Let me guess, Elijah. You have already checked this out?"

"Hahahah! Just waitin' fer yuh to figure it out, yankee! Yer so dang slow, I wonder how your side won the war! Wal, there was 'bout fifty dollars stuffed inside one pocket, some chawin tobacco, a stash of beef jerky, a bottle of whiskey, and something kind of personal. A music box."

John walked up to Elijah and said, "I'd like to see that music box."

"Suit yerself." Elijah went into his tent, came back, and held up a silver plated box featuring a decoratively molded silver lid. There were two little angels on either side and a tastefully designed cross underneath a rising sun in the middle.

John North gently took the box, slowly opened the lid, and listened to the music. It played *Fur Elise* by Beethoven. North swallowed, closed his eyes, then reopened them feeling tears beginning to well up.

Elijah noticed the reaction but said nothing except, "I think yuh should have it, John."

"Thanks. It...it belonged to my mother."

"Would you care for some more of my grizzly bouncin' coffee and let me know just exactly what these five varmints did to you an' yer kin?"

John North narrated the same events he had told to Naomi Harrison. He had not spoken to hardly anyone about these terrible experiences in many months, but within a single morning he had confided in two people.

After listening to the last of the grisly details, Johnson replied, "Ah make it a point to tend to muh own business and have found it valuable advice fer extendin' muh life. But you know, these people are so damned misguided, and so damn wicked, that ah'd consider it an honor to ride with you and help send them off to where they belong."

North looked quizzically at Johnson, and said, "I appreciate the offer, but why stick out your neck? It's not your fight!"

Johnson stood up, stretched, spit toward the river, ducked after the spittle blew back toward his face, stood up again, and replied, "Ah've got muh own reasons. If yuh don't question me, then there's no problem. Yuh just need to know ah may have a stake in huntin' down these characters you've described. Do we have a deal, John North?" Johnson extended a hand.

Warily, John North took his hand, shook it, then stated, "Sure. I'll be glad to have the company. Keep in mind, friend, when the time calls for it, I still want to know what's your stake in all this."

Johnson merely nodded. Concluding this somewhat inconclusive agreement, Johnson doused out the fire and began to break camp.

5

STAGECOACH WEST

Hannah Olson was both excited and wary about boarding the stage to Copperhead. She had hardly traveled this far west before, and it was definitely the first time she had been on a long trip with her husband, Edward. Edward Olson was a lawyer who openly told her there were opportunities for someone as educated as he in an ignorant part of the country. Before accepting his hand in marriage, Hannah had seen little evidence that this man was so arrogant, but then, it was at a time when she did not know he had such a violent streak. He had physically assaulted her on a number of occasions during their six months of marriage.

Hannah stood under the shaded roof of the building's overhang on the rickety boardwalk and waited for the stage to arrive. She would be traveling for at least fifty miles and was uncertain that the journey would be safe. Yes, there was the possibility of attacks from hostile Indians or marauding bandits, but there was also the potential combustible rage from Edward Olson in her future.

Hannah was an attractive woman with reddish-brown hair, a shapely figure, and blue eyes. She stood a mere five feet four inches, but stood every inch with pride and dignity. She was twenty-eight years old, educated in classical literature, mathematics, history, and science, and therefore a likely school teacher should she decide to permanently live in the west. Her skills were in demand. Before marrying Edward, she dreamed that she would marry a professional man who would understand her desire to teach, as she would understand and support his desire to work in his own profession. Edward claimed he would but mainly wanted her to spend time assisting him and washing his dirty underwear and socks.

Edward walked through the shadows of the door behind Hannah and smiled. "Not much longer, my darling; the stage is supposed to reach this place — what did they call it? Henry Town? What a stupid name. It should reach Henry Town at about 11:30. That's fifteen minutes from now."

"We have certainly come a long way from Philadelphia, Edward. First, the train to Chicago, the boat down to St. Louis, the train to Omaha, the stagecoach here...."

"Yes, and the stagecoach is the ugliest form of travel yet. I'll be happy when they tear apart the countryside and build railroad tracks to crisscross every square mile. Perhaps that will run the savages out of the area and make room for respectable white people such as ourselves."

Hannah frowned and said, "Not everyone white is respectable, dear. My father used to say you judge a man by what is in his heart, head, and through the deeds he performs. He urged me not to judge someone by skin color."

"With all due respect, your father was naïve. Sure, you say he fought for the North in the War, and served Pennsylvania and Mr. Lincoln well, but did it make him much money? You know that he died without much money, and those blacks, Chinese, and injuns you keep worrying about did nothing to ever help him."

Hannah sat down, adjusted her skirt, sighed, and said, "As an educated man, Edward, you miss the point. He was talking about how we may all live together now, and in the future, and not about anything particular in his life. Besides, he did all right by me. He set aside enough money for me to get an education at Elizabeth Hemming College for Women."

Edwards loosened his tie, wiped sweat from his brow, and grimaced. "I don't know what's more uncomfortable, this damned heat or the boring words spewing from those gorgeous lips of yours. You are a delightful woman in numerous ways I am too much of a gentleman to enunciate in public, but your philosophy belongs to the genteel and idiotic platitudes of fiction. Grow up, woman."

Hannah bit her lower lip, clenched her fists, and repressed a volcano of invective she wished would erupt. She said nothing, however. From past experience, she realized he would simply retaliate with brute violence. She had had enough of that and was biding her time until she could be rejoined with her mother and then leave him for good.

A man, with a long, grayish-white mustache and white hair reaching the top of his collar, slowly approached the boardwalk carrying a carpetbag grip and tipped his hat to the lady.

"Couldn't help but overhear, ma'am. It sounds like yer daddy is a very wise fellow."

"Thank you sir. He certainly was a wonderful father. He was Nathaniel Fjord, a blacksmith. Unfortunately, he passed away about four years ago — just after I went away to college. My mother said pneumonia took him."

"Very sorry, ma'am. By the way, my name is Abel Foster. I am on my way back to my farm in California. I had to go to Kansas City to visit my ailin' brother a'fore he died. Good thing I did. He had no one else. In the meantime, I picked up lots of knowledge I can spin into stories to tell my missus and five kids when I get back to that vegetable farm they been workin'. You mentioned your mother? I surely hope she is in good health."

"As far as we know, Mr. uh — Foster?" Edward sharply interjected. "By the way, it is proper to introduce yourself to the husband first. I should hope even people out here possessed some semblance of manners and satisfactory breeding."

"Don't get yer plow tangled in your union suit, mister — I was just bein' neighborly to this very fine young lady. I have a daughter myself, and talkin' to her is like talkin' to my own lovely daughter."

Hannah smiled broadly and presented her hand to Mr. Foster. "Being compared to the daughter of such a wonderful gentleman is a great honor, indeed. I am Hannah Fjord Olson. My mother is well and is living in a small town about fifty miles from here. After father died she moved there to help my uncle run a boarding house."

"She must be a pretty spunky gal, your mother, livin' out in them parts. Where we're heading, Copperhead, ain't what you call a friendly town. They got a marshal there they say is more outlaw than law, and up in them mountains I ain't sure how safe it is. Injuns haven't been attackin' much in the last few years, but I heard some renegade Cheyenne might be prowlin' around these parts. Besides, there are always highway men to fret."

A tall man wearing a red and blue checkered shirt and large brown hat walked up lugging a Winchester rifle in one hand and strongbox in the other. He said, "Ah wouldn't worry the missy here much about highway men, feller, ah'm goin' on that stage too, and ah can knock a horsefly off a tree branch ten yards away."

Olson pointed to the strongbox and said, "Is that something valuable you are bringing along, sir?"

"Yuh might say that. It's none of yer business, city slicker, but since yer ridin' with me, yuh should know it's a payroll Wells Fargo asked me to get up the mountains and eventually over to Tuesday Junction, California. Ah got a long trip ahead of me, but ah've done this sort of work before. Muh name is Robert Smythe, and ah'd be proud to protect this beautiful lady as well as the gold in this box."

"Thank you, Smythe. You can, as 'yuh say,' protect her 'til we arrive at some God-forsaken place called Fortune River. Her mother lives there, and you, curious Mr. Foster, can now know her name is Naomi Harrison. The old bag is using her maiden name again until she marries some old fool of the town. She figures it safer than calling herself 'Widow Fjord.' We're heading west to meet her." He gave Hannah a cruel look and then sneered. "If takin' one's woman to a non-entity location like that isn't proof enough of true love, then I don't know what is. Right *sweetheart?*"

Instead of replying to her husband with words, or even a glance, she rose from the bench, pointed down the street, and said, "Good. It appears that our stagecoach is pulling in now."

6

BLOOD HAWK

Blood Hawk was a tall and imposing figure. Standing six feet three inches, the Cheyenne looked down at his prey as if he really were a predatory bird closing in on his kill. Behind a rock, checking to see if a cartridge was in the chamber of his rifle, another Indian, also of the Cheyenne nation, seemed unaware he was being watched. Blood Hawk smiled and stealthily closed in on the man.

The Cheyenne with the rifle was Buffalo Charges With No Fear, or, loosely translated, "Charging Buffalo," an appellation he did not particularly like, but tolerated. He had been educated by Christian missionaries but did not appreciate the non-Cheyenne life style. He was a hunter and passionately devoted to the land and ways of his people. He hated the coming of the railroad but recognized its alarmingly rapid expansion and the influx of white settlers would not be stopped. His father had fought the yellow leg cavalry, but the persistence of the leader known as General Sherman had brought him and his fellow warriors to defeat. The war against the eastern invaders was over, but the heart of the Cheyenne warrior still sought justice according to traditional methods. Those who would slay his friends and family would be made to pay at his hand.

While temporarily deep in thought, Charging Buffalo suddenly saw a shadow out of the corner of his eye and heard the whisk of wind, as if something flew by quickly. While turning, he felt the painful blow of a heavy object against the side of his head. It was the rifle butt of Blood Hawk. Charging Buffalo was unconscious, at the mercy of his enemy.

When he awoke, he felt the stinging rays of the sun on his face and in his eyes. Feeling groggy, he attempted to reach toward the throbbing pain in the side of his head but soon determined that his hands and arms were restrained. His feet and legs were also tied down. He had been staked out on the ground like a slab of bait.

"Why did you not kill me like a man, Blood Hawk? Were you afraid to fight me as a warrior?"

"I would fight you as a warrior if you acted as a man, you weak fool. You talk like a man but track like a boy. It was easy to see that you were after me, so I bided my time until I could jump and disable you like a pitiful rodent. You thought you could kill

Blood Hawk, slayer of ten U.S. soldiers, seven Pawnee scouts, eleven stupid white settlers, and eight saloon rats? You are no match for me, child."

"You forgot to mention that you killed my friend, Talking Wolf, and my brother, Arrow Builder. You murdered them like animals as they slept near a campfire."

"That's because they *were* animals. You should be grateful I only kicked you in the face. Had I known you would be tracking me, I would have gladly slit your throat as I did the other two. I let you live so you would tell others to beware the horror of Blood Hawk. I know that you got a look at me before I struck you."

"Yes, I got a look at you. I saw that you were the same man who came upon our camp hours before asking for meat to eat, imploring me and the others to welcome a fellow Cheyenne in need of hospitality. We provide that hospitality, and you thank us by returning later to kill and rob us. What did we have that was worth committing murder?"

Blood Hawk adjusted the feather in his hat, brushed dust off his dark blue, long-sleeved shirt, stared at the tied-down man, and said, "More food, and the ammunition they carried. There aren't many stores in these parts, and they had supplies I desired. That's all. You look as if you would like to drink some water."

He untied the canteen from his Appaloosa, unscrewed the lid, and poured water into his mouth. He swished out his mouth, then spit in the face of Charging Buffalo.

"Ha-ha-ha. Charging Buffalo! It amazes me that you ever got such a name. You are more like wounded squirrel. Great Eagle, your father, would not be proud now. At least he was a warrior for a long time."

"You are worse than the white soldiers. With them, it was war. With you, it is all about greed, dishonor, and treachery. You are not Cheyenne. You are lower than any of the white devils."

"Don't be so sure of that, my brother. I know some white men that are more repulsive than a skunk rotting inside a tree trunk. There is one man I have ridden with called P.J. Callender who is probably more cruel and dishonorable than I — and that's saying a lot."

"When I get out of here, I will hunt you down and kill you for sure."

"You are not leaving here, little warrior. You are going to bake in the sun like corn and supply the ants with many meals. You shall die a slow and horrible death. If I were compassionate to a Cheyenne brother, I'd slip my knife into your heart. However, I do not care about Cheyenne brothers, or any other brothers anymore. The white devils have taught me to live for myself, and I have succeeded in doing that very nicely. I must leave you now. The ants and other insects, and even the birds of the wild, are growing impatient. They wish to dine on your baking flesh."

Before passing out, Charging Buffalo observed Blood Hawk mount his horse and ride slowly away into the horizon.

Outside the boarding house John North shook the hand of Harrison. Just as he turned to say good-bye to Naomi she abruptly pushed a cloth bundle into his arms.

"I fixed you some vittles to take with. Nothin' fancy, just some fried chicken, biscuits, and a couple extra cans of beans to take with."

"That's very kind of you."

"I'm in a very kind mood, John North. In a matter of days Mr. Harrison and I will be having some important guests arrivin'. My daughter, Hannah, and her husband, Edward, are coming for a visit."

"They're both college eddicated, North," Harrison boasted, "She's a school teach, and he's a lawyer."

"Are they going to put down roots in town?"

Naomi shook her head no and added, "I wish they would. If we got a school teacher and a lawyer, then maybe more folk would settle down in Fortune River. I suspect she just got homesick and wanted to see me and show off her new husband. I don't know anything about him, but if she picked him, then he must be a decent person." Naomi then reached into her pocket and showed North a much-handled photograph. "Here she is…Hannah."

North gazed at the photo of a young woman with hair piled up on top of her head in the style of the day, who had a strikingly pretty face, innocent eyes, and delightfully smiling mouth. She was wearing a frilly blouse and appeared every inch a lady and beauty. North could not remember when he had last seen such a purely attractive woman.

"Hey there, North, ya gotta quit droolin'," laughed Harrison. "Thet purty gal, muh step daughter, is already taken."

"Excuse me! I mean no disrespect, Mrs. Harrison; it's just that a lot of the women I have seen in the west have not been what you say, ladies, except, naturally, yourself, and obviously your daughter in this picture. She is exceptionally beautiful."

Naomi smiled, then said, "If Mr. Olson, her husband, is half the gentleman that you are John, then I shall be a very happy mother indeed. By the way, where is your new traveling companion, Mr. Johnson?"

In the saloon, Elijah Johnson secured two bottles of Rye, and told one last prospecting yarn to the bartender. He threw a coin on the bar and turned to walk out of the bar, but was stopped by someone tugging on his left arm.

"Why in blazes are yuh grabbin' my arm, McAvee? If yer that lonely, yuh oughta head down to Copperhead and shack up with one of Fulton's saloon tramps!"

"Watch yer language, you nasty old badger. I want a word with yuh before yuh head out with that killer, North."

Johnson harshly snapped his arm out of McAvee's grasp and yelled, "Don't get rude with me you mangy varmint, ah don't have tuh blab with yuh if ah don't prefer."

"I'm tellin' yuh that the stranger yer ridin' with is headin' for trouble if he's headin' for Copperhead. There's a marshal down there who ain't what you'd call an understandin' cuss. First sign of trouble, he either jails, whales, or impales 'em, if'n yuh know what I mean."

"No, ah don't know, or really care what yuh mean. What is he, some kin of yoahs?"

"Let's just say that I know somethin' about him. I don't care what happens to North, but you happen to be someone with a good nose for gold, and yuh might come in handy as a prospectin' partner some day. Besides, I used to like hearin' some of yer tall tales. If I was you, I'd stay clear of Copperhead."

Elijah took a large bite out of his plug, and amidst the saliva and brown juice visible on his lips and teeth, he gurgled, "Thanks, but yer not me. Now I say farewell, Mr. Faust."

John North and Elijah Johnson had been riding for about two hours. The terrain was gradually becoming less mountainous and more semi-arid. Since leaving Fortune

River, the two had barely exchanged six or seven words. There was no impetus to talk. No one felt the need to converse until now.

"Look — on the other side of that hill. A small flock of buzzards are circling. It would appear that something has met its maker. Should we take a look, Mr. Johnson?"

Elijah nodded, and the two rode down the hill where they had stopped to look and then up the rise where the scavengers had been espied. Soon they grew closer to the vultures, and they quickly scattered. The source of their meal was soon apparent. Two men, underneath a small group of trees, lie dead and half-eaten. They were the two Indians who had been murdered by Blood Hawk.

"By the looks of them gashes in their necks I'd say these fellers were murdered."

"Astute observation, Mr. Johnson. They are lying on their blankets, so they were undoubtedly killed as they slept. I think we had better get out of here in case some other Cheyenne stops by and assumes we might be responsible. Wait! Look over to the east!"

North squinted and mock-saluted the bright sun with his right hand. "Yes, about a mile away there are some more big birds — probably more buzzards — encircling something. Want to check it out?"

"Oh, sure, Mr. North. All we need is fer them Cheyenne to find us there instead of here to make the day complete. Why not?"

North quickly mounted his horse, and began riding. "Do what you will. I'm heading over there."

North did not look behind to see if Johnson followed. Closer now, he made his mount decelerate its charge while considering a cautionary approach to be something more requisite than optional. He saw a man staked out on the earth struggling to get free.

A buzzard was pecking at his face very close to the man's left eye. Without contemplating consequences, North pulled his Winchester from the saddle sheath, aimed, and blew off the bird's head. The captured man convulsed, but did not cry out. North deliberately walked toward the man. Soon, the hoof beats of a horse were discernible. North glanced quickly to see that it was Johnson but turned again to concentrate on the bound and helpless individual.

"Do you speak English?"

"Careful, Mr. North, if yuh cut him loose, he's apt to reward yuh by breakin' yer neck."

"I don't know who did this to you, but it seems pretty damned uncivilized to treat a human being in this fashion. I'm going to take a chance and cut you loose. So help me, if you try to move against me, I shall kill you."

North cut loose the man's wrist bonds, but the man did not move suddenly. He did pull himself up and attempt to untie the leather bond on his right ankle as North cut through the one surrounding the left limb. North kept his pistol aimed at the man but slowly stepped back, giving him sufficient room to stand.

"You are fortunate, white man. I am now indebted to you for saving my life. I say you are fortunate because you are standing on Cheyenne land, and you have, at least for the time being, my protection. Otherwise, I should be required to kill you. You were not invited."

"Listen, yuh damn injun, he just saved yuh. No need to brag! And this ain't yoah land!"

"Take it easy, Johnson. All right, I am glad that you are not mind-set about killing me. In that way, I won't have to shoot you through the head. Tell me though, who did this to you? My friend and I also saw two dead Cheyenne not far from here. This looks like the work of someone awfully bad."

"First, before we converse, it is polite to at least exchange names. I am known as Buffalo Charges With No Fear, but others simply call me Charging Buffalo."

"I am John North, from Minnesota. This is Elijah Johnson. We are hunting down some evil men ourselves. By the way, where did you learn to speak English?"

"I was taught at a Methodist Mission right after the railroads forced their way onto our land. I still say its Cheyenne land! My mother wanted me to learn your tongue since it would one day prove valuable to know how you people were scheming against us."

"You learned pretty well, but don't worry, the only scheming I'm doing is against the villains who murdered my family."

Charging Buffalo drew in a deep breath and announced, "It was a despicable traitor named Blood Hawk who left me for dead, and I intend to cut out his heart and feed it to the crows." When the countenance of North immediately exhibited surprise, Charging Buffalo nodded.

"I see then that Blood Hawk has crossed your path as well. It is the will of the Creator that you would cross *my* path today, John North of Minnesota. It must be His will that you and I seek this abomination. And you, the one who chews but spits like an vile grass hopper, why are you hunting down Blood Hawk?"

"I got my own reasons. Besides, Blood Hawk isn't the only one. There are three white men that Blood Hawk likes to go robbin' and killin' with that we're aimin' to rudely encounter."

"Charging Buffalo, we are now heading for a town called Copperhead. I think that at least some of these men will be there, including, quite possibly, Blood Hawk. You are welcome to ride with us, but since we only have two mounts, you will have to double ride with one of us."

"I shall walk. You will have to ride your mounts with care, as the hot sun and downhill ride will tire them. I know where this Copperhead is located, but you shall not be welcome there. Even more so, I will be utterly unwelcome. I will go with you perhaps to one of the nearby ranches where we may pick up another horse."

"That's fine. I'll even buy one if I can — providing you give me your word to reimburse me, Charging Buffalo."

"I give my word."

Johnson grimaced, spit again like a vile grasshopper, and said, "Let's quit chawin' the fat, and git."

7

WORK ASSOCIATES AND RECENT RECOLLECTIONS

U nderneath a massive oak tree, a thin, bald, bespectacled man brandishing a pencil-thin mustache sat cross-legged playing a game of solitaire. Every few minutes, he would put down the deck and grab a flask of whiskey to slurp down
a burning mouthful or two. He was killing time until it was more fashionable perhaps
to do another sort of killing.

Blood Hawk easily spotted the man under the tree from a distance of more than
one hundred meters. He not only spotted the figure, but knew exactly who he happened to be.

"All of that harsh drink and idleness with cards will make you weak, Chapeau. Then
again, you are a Frenchman, more in love with earthly pleasures than your own desire
for personal survival."

Chapeau quickly stood up, screwed the cap onto the flask, and replied, "Blood
Hawk, you are a valuable man in a desperate fight — and for that, I am eternally grateful to ride at your side — but when it comes to enjoying the finer details of life, you
have nary a clue. I am Pierre Chapeau, an educated man, Harvard, class of 1859, and
have spent the better part of my life avoiding the military draft, working a full-time job,
getting bogged down with screeching wives and brats, and generally stealing whatever
it is that pleases me whenever I choose. If I prefer gambling, drinking, and whoring,
then it is my businesss, not yours!"

"Fine. Go ahead and whore yourself to death, Chapeau, just don't do it today. We
have a job to do."

Chapeau opened a pocket watch, glanced briefly, then snapped it shut. "I'll hold up
my end of the work the same as you, Indian. Incidentally, my watch reads two P.M. You
were supposed to be here an hour ago. Why the delay?"

"Why don't you shut up before I kill you, Frenchman?"

"Calm down, Chief. Just tell me, does your delay mean that we are going to be
joined by some people chasing you down to tell you how utterly warm and charming
you have been to them in your last meeting?"

"Not unless they can catch a vulture and ride it through the air to meet us. The man who delayed me is keeping the vultures well fed at the moment."

"Fair enough. Unless you need to make a stop, I think I am ready to ride to the main highway. The stagecoach, if on time, should be entering the canyon in about a half hour. We still have time to get there."

Instead of answering, Blood Hawk pulled the reins and rode off up the hill behind the large oak tree. Chapeau hurriedly climbed into his saddle and chased after his criminal co-conspirator.

Inside the stagecoach Hannah felt stifled by the close quarters and the inherent heat. She sat next to her stern husband and across from Abel Foster. Foster was reading a book, but he glanced up and smiled when Hannah looked at him. Hannah returned the smile.

"What are you reading, Mr. Foster?"

"I am enjoying a novel by Charles Dickens called *Our Mutual Friend*. I find its character developments and intricate plot twists rather intriguing."

"Surely, it is a shame that Mr. Dickens passed away. Was it four or five years ago? He wrote so many wonderful stories about people trying to find loving relationships and justice in a difficult and oftentimes cruel world."

"Mr. Dickens was an idiot," Edward blustered. "I say he was an idiot because he spent so much time telling stories about weak people when he could have used his wealth to acquire even more wealth for himself and his family. I even heard that the man was dishonorable and cheated on his wife. Perhaps you, Mr. Foster, might praise such a man, and my dearest Hannah, who is just a woman, might find his romantic whimsy appealing, but I have seen the real world, dealt with real people, and conclude that there is no time for whimsical imaginings or written fiction!"

Foster set his lower jaw firmly, looked directly at Edwards, and calmly responded, "I strongly disagree with you, sir, and find it peculiar that you would use the expression, 'just a woman.' In my experience, it is rude and ungentlemanly to refer to a member of the female gender in such a condescending manner."

"I truly do not care what you think, Mr. Foster. I shall refer to my wife however I please. In the meantime, I suggest you tend to your affairs, and we will tend to ours. Is that not correct, Hannah?" Upon emphasizing the name, Hannah, Edward squeezed her left arm enough to cause sharp pain.

Hannah continued to feel the constricting confines of the stagecoach cabin, the oppressive heat, and the growing contempt she was feeling for Edward. Inwardly, she entertained a desire to escape from this mobile prison. Everything about this trip was working against her. If only she would reach Fortune River soon. In Fortune River she could reunite with mother. Then perhaps — yes, perhaps she could even say farewell to Edward. Would mother accept such an event? She would have to! Once she saw the cruelty and selfishness of Edward, she would readily sympathize.

Memories of her days with Edward were not always so unpleasant. There were the courting days back in Philadelphia. Yes, Edward was a perfect gentleman then. He invited her to dances and parties and always presented himself with charm and wit. "You are the epitome of grace, dear Hannah," he used to say. The wedding was also quite wonderful. Mildred Huntington, Priscilla Masters, and Genevieve Thatch were her beloved friends, and all attended her wedding. They all looked beautiful in their pastel-colored bridesmaid gowns. How they fussed over her wedding dress! It fit her so perfectly and lovingly they said. Everyone envied her marriage except Priscilla.

At the wedding reception, right after she and Edward were done with the receiving line, Priscilla took her aside and spoke to her frankly.

"Hannah, since your dear mother is out west sick with the ague and could not attend this wedding, I feel I have to represent her as best as I can. We have been close friends for nearly ten years, attended college together, saw through the passing of your dear daddy, and maintained our close friendship even though I myself have been married to Tom for more than a year."

"What are you trying to tell me, Priscilla? I think I *know* what is going to happen on the wedding night." She smiled, and both women giggled.

"Since we are both ladies, you dreadful girl, I shall not comment on what you just said. However, I must tell you something you may not want to hear. The other day I saw your husband flirting with Sarah Kemper in Kreingold's Department Store. When she said enough was enough, I heard him call her a flirtatious slut, and then he said, 'all you women are sluts.' I am not sure what this bodes for you in this marriage, but by all means, try not to get on this man's bad side. He is probably a mostly wonderful man. My Tom treats me right most days. You must admit, Edward's overtures to that, that woman and his verbal pronouncement to her is not what I would categorize as prime, gentlemanly behavior."

"Stop it, Priscilla. He and I will be fine. Just the same, thanks for telling me, and above all, thank you for being such a devoted friend."

Hannah's thoughts returned again to the present. She grudgingly turned toward her husband, who was now slumped over in the corner fast asleep. She saw him in contrast to the way he looked after they had been living in their Philadelphia home after three weeks.

"Did I not tell you to order the servants to have our dinner ready no later than 4:30 P.M., Hannah? Must I provide all the direction in this household?"

"I am sorry, Edward. Of course, I shall be firmer."

"Hah! The only occasion when you appear to be firmer is when you join me in our bed. I feel as if I am lying with a hitching post, rather than an affectionate wife. You may be attractive on the outside, but I hardly find you successful at attaining your essential wifely duties. All those years in college must have chilled and immunized you against the attentions of a real man."

"Perhaps, Edward, if you treated me more like a real woman, those affections would not seem so problematic."

Hannah had never been hit in face, let alone stricken down flat on the floor, until that moment. She had not been knocked unconscious, but the shock of being battered so hard by the man she had considered her loving husband was unbearable. Lying on the floor she lost track of the time expiring. How many tears she shed is unknown.

It would not be the last time Edward would cause her to sob. If it was not through physical injury, then it happened through verbal assault. This continued for two solid months. When Hannah received a telegram from her mother informing her that she had recovered from influenza and was inviting her and her husband to see her in Fortune River, she jumped at the chance. This might be her ticket to escape. Divorce seemed out of the question, but going to see mama — getting her advice — she would know how to advise her.

Hannah noticed that Foster had quit reading his Charles Dickens book and had also fallen asleep. She heard Edward snore loudly. The obnoxious utterings from the man's sinuses reminded her of a growling lion she had seen and heard at the zoo. Edward was disgusting. The more she saw, heard, and smelled, the more she felt repelled by him. It was sinful to think in such a manner, but would it be all that terrible if Edward died right now? What if he drowned in his own spit and mucous? Should that be a terrible loss to the world, or to her? Wait, I can't think that, Hannah gulped, that is an utterly selfish thought, and only the Almighty determines who should live or die. It is not my decision. Hannah suddenly felt greatly ashamed and silently prayed for forgiveness.

The stagecoach continued to bounce and sway down the bumpy, dusty highway. The journey was in most ways unbearable, but particularly more tolerable as long as Edward was not awake or interacting with her or other human beings in her presence.

There were times when the coach stopped long enough for the horses and driver to rest. Most of the time, however, they continued a steady pace down the monotonous road.

On the previous night, North, Johnson, and Charging Buffalo set up a camp. The three starving travelers rapidly polished off the last of Naomi's fried chicken. After supper, North and Johnson fell asleep while the Cheyenne voluntarily stood watch. He would spend the night with these fellow travelers, but had other plans for the morning.

8

---◆---

HIGHWAY ROBBERY

In the morning, after riding through a small forest, Charging Buffalo left the company of North and Johnson. He did not advertise the fact he was departing, he simply left without giving an explanation, thank you, or goodbye. It was the same day that Blood Hawk and Chapeau sought to keep an appointment with a stagecoach.

"If yuh ask me, Mr. North, thet injun is not only ungrateful, but decidedly untrustworthy. He may try to jump us when we're unawares — like when we stop to eat vittles or lie down to sleep."

"I doubt it, Elijah. Didn't he keep his word and watch our camp last night? He also said he was indebted. My past experience with Indians is that if they give their word, they mean it — which is more than we can say about our federal government and their treaties with those people. No one loves the U.S.A. more than I do, but I am pretty ashamed of a lot of those Washington politicians. Watch out for that low branch ahead."

"Yuh don't need to caution me on safety, Mr. North. I've ridden all over this territory and plenty more that you never seen — so ah know how to look out fer — Owch! A dang bee stung me on the neck. Blasted little hellion!"

"Hahaha. Right. Anyway, I have a hunch that Charging Buffalo will show up some time when we least expect it. He has a debt to pay, and that debt may weigh heavily on him from time to time."

"Whar did you larn so much about injuns? Yuh sound like a man thet's done some scoutin'."

"I have. After a little tussle we had with the Pawnee, I happened to meet an army captain named Edgar Bristol in Omaha. He heard about my 'success' in tracking down and bringing in three Pawnee raiders, so he started talking about needing someone to help with some scouting. I was getting tired of driving stupid cattle, so after I delivered the herd to the buying party in Montana, I looked up Captain Bristol at Fort Green in Colorado and took up scouting for a while. They only paid fifteen dollars a month, but at least it was in gold."

"Yuh don't seem to know injun tongues fer someone who was a scout."

"This is true. Hey, let's water the horses at this stream." The riders dismounted and let their horses drink from the narrow stream. "I really didn't scout long enough to become much of an Indian lingo talker, but I did become pretty good friends with a Cherokee also scouting for the army named Sammy Fivetrees. That wasn't his real name, but the soldiers called him that, and he tolerated it."

"Tell me about thet feller while I dig into another bite u' muh plug."

As John North began to talk, memory swept him back to details involving Sammy Fivetrees. In particular, he recalled one excursion when the two of them were scouting ahead for flat and reliable land for the Union Pacific to add a spur to their already completed railroad.

"John North, you have the look of a man who has seen much death and suffering. Were you a fighter in that war between the American states?"

"Yes. You are very perceptive. How about you?"

"I am a Cherokee. As far as I was concerned, it was not my fight. I do accept the truth that I am now part of the American states, but during those years I did not care. I have worked with and even fought alongside blue soldiers for many seasons, but I cannot say that I have liked all of these people. Some, like Captain Bristol, seem fair, but there was a major once named Mortimer Agee who was awfully bad. He fought very hard, but did so without honor. He liked killing human beings — namely, people of my race — and did not seem to care if they were young or old, male or female, right or wrong. I was happy that he was transferred to the southwest. Otherwise, I would have ended up killing him. Deep down, I think that Captain Bristol possessed a similar desire."

"What is it about the red man that is similar to the white man, Mr. Fivetrees?"

"It is hopeful that you phrase a question in that manner. To ask, 'what is similar' instead of 'what is different' means you are trying to keep an open mind. Yes, there are similarities. We eat, breathe, laugh, cry, fall in love, protect our families, and work hard. Still, there seem to be differences. We cherish what the world offers and do not squander what we take. We are grateful to the Creator. Your people say they are grateful, and perhaps many of them are, but others take and use what they want, then take more and more and don't necessarily use it. To live that way is sinful and insulting to the Creator. As a white man, you probably do not see this, but it would be positive if you would at least think about the possibility that I speak the truth."

Upon hearing a paraphrase of the actual conversation that took place between North and Sammy Fivetrees, Elijah winced, looked toward the sky thoughtfully, and said, "Yuh know, them Cherokees used to live in Georgia — at least until President Andy Jackson forced 'em all to move out. Thet injun sounds pretty wise. Ah guess ah nevah figured injuns as interested in much 'cept getting' revenge, and tellin' all us white folk how much they hated us."

North put his left foot in a stirrup, then lifted and swung his right leg over the horse, sat in the saddle, and said, "Thanks to Sammy Fivetrees, I started to think about a lot of things differently. You know, all this business with the Indians is not really all that different than the stuff involving the Negroes."

"What? Nigrahs? Now wait a cussed minute, Mr. North. Thet is a touchy subject with me. Thanks to them people, a whole lot of muh friends, neighbors, and kinfolk got cut up, slaughtered, and ruined in that war you Yankees caused! I ain't got no sympathy fer those people."

John North suddenly realized he had opened a new volley in the Civil War, ten years following the surrender of Lee to Grant at Appomattox Courthouse.

"I disagree with you, Johnson. The whole reason for that war was because the confederates seemed to love slavery more than they did the United States of America."

"Thet's a damned Yankee lie, and you oughta know it! The rotten federals invaded sovereign states, ran rough-shod over private property, and committed murder against decent God-fearin' men."

"There were plenty of 'God-fearin'' union soldiers who were cut up, slaughtered, and ruined as well. I lost two uncles and three cousins. One uncle and one cousin were killed at Bull Run One, another uncle got it at Antietem, and two cousins died of injuries sustained at Gettysburg."

"Then yuh'd agree that them niggrahs caused yer kinfolk to die too!"

"No. I do not agree with that conclusion. I think that slavery caused the deaths of all those men. If George Washington and the other founding fathers had just abolished slavery in the beginning like Benjamin Franklin and the church folk wanted, then a lot of my friends and kinfolk, as well as yours, would still be breathing. I thought you were beyond all that Yankee and rebel crap, Johnson. What's your problem?"

"Ah say get off your nag, and we'll settle this man to man."

"You are a fool, Elijah. Let's just say we have a difference of opinion, and let it go. I don't fight for fun or arguments."

"I'm sayin' if yuh don't fight me, that yer a yellow Yankee dog."

Once that remark was voiced, John North quickly turned and slugged Johnson in the right jaw. He fell from his saddle like a sack of biscuits.

Johnson, stunned, but not unconscious, waited for North to get down from his horse, then rapidly sprung toward him with a right fist in the stomach. North doubled over but did not collapse. More surprised that hurt, North quickly blocked Johnson's attempted left swing toward the center of his face. He followed that with two quick jabs in the center of Johnson's face. Johnson, dazed, but still standing, wiped the blood from his nose and came toward North again. He succeeded in smacking North once in the right cheekbone but found his second punch to North's abdomen blocked. Soon, North slugged Johnson hard in the stomach and hit him very hard on the right jaw. Johnson collapsed with the wind knocked out of him. He gasped for breath for several seconds while North admonished, "Give it up, Johnson, or I'm going to beat you to a bloody pulp. I will not allow any man to hit me like that. I am sorry that I hit you the first time, but you should not have challenged me. When that happens, I am no longer a gentleman."

Eventually, Johnson started to rise. North came toward him as if to help, but Johnson slapped at the air advising him to keep his distance. The old prospector pulled out a soiled red bandana, wiped the blood off his eyebrow and away from his right nostril, and began to smile.

"Yer pretty dang good, Yankee. If ah were about ten years younger, it woulda been you lyin' in the dust instead of me. Still, ah gotta hand it tuh yuh, it was a fight won fair and square. Mind yuh, I ain't changin' muh position on the War Between the States. Ah'll just accept that you and I strongly disagree."

"Fine. Still, this brings up a good point, and I am going to ask you again. Why are you riding with me, Elijah Johnson?"

"The time ain't right to tell yuh, John North. Don't worry, though, I ain't got a secret plan to bushwack yuh. Ah give yuh muh word as a gentleman from Mississippi. When the time is right, I'll tell the reason fer sure."

"Johnson, I hope you are telling the truth. If I thought you were lying right now, then so help me, I should be obliged to end your life here. Don't ever make the mistake of being my enemy. It would be better to be a friend. What do you say?"

"Mr. North, I thought it might be obvious by now. I am a friend. I'll even shake your hand — even if you are still a Yankee."

The two men shook hands, got on their horses, and continued their ride to the main highway.

Yes, it was the same day that the two undesirable visitors sought to *greet* the stagecoach. From the vantage point of a hill piled high with many boulders and a few trees rooted between some of those great stones, Blood Hawk was lying on his belly looking intently through a small telescope toward the east. He espied a cloud of dust in the distance, and smiled assertively.

"Look through the glass, Frenchman. The large dust cloud indicates a large team is heading our way. It has to be the stagecoach."

"Blood Hawk, I believe you are correct. You'd think that in this day and age of railroad transportation, the bank fools would send all their gold shipments by rail instead of shipping some this way."

"Not only that, what about the ignorant people who ride as passengers? Why would they unnecessarily expose themselves to the risks of terrible people — such as Blood Hawk?"

"I know. You'd think their mommies would have taught them better. I guess they want to shave off time by taking a more direct route to some of those far away vacation spots like Copperhead and Fortune River. What a hoot!"

"Just make sure you do the job as planned, Chapeau. I'm not so civilized that I have forgotten how to scalp fools."

"Right. Let's get ready."

Both Abel Foster and Edward Olson were awake, but now Hannah was asleep. Suddenly, the stagecoach slowed down and came to a halt.

The driver bellowed, "Everybody git off and take a piss break. I ain't stoppin' again 'til we get to Copperhead."

Hannah looked to the right and saw a cluster of trees and rocks and thought this site at least held the potential of more privacy than many other sites thus far. While she sauntered back to what appeared the most concentrated group of trees, the guard, Robert Smythe, hopped down and spoke with the driver.

"So yer handle is 'Duster' Shelley?' How in blazes duh yuh git though life with a plumb sissy name like that?"

"Cause idgits favoring to have fun with muh name usually end up having me freely give them a broken nose and a couple teeth fewer than thar used to chawin with. Savvy?"

"Don't get yer chest hairs in a bunch. Anyway, I'm walkin' up the road apiece to see what we're ridin' into."

"It's what's called more road, you nincompoop. But suit yerself."

All of the riders on the stage had stepped off to stretch and comply with the demands of nature. Nonchalantly, Smythe walked ahead approximately twenty yards and looked to the northwest at an outcropping of cliff consisting of large boulders. He thought he saw a flash — like that coming from glass. He raised his hands high to stretch, then clasped both hands on the back of his neck, and half turned either way at least twice. Upon completing the ritual, he walked back to the stagecoach.

"Are you folks ready to roll?" Shelley asked.

"I better visit the necessary myself, Mr. Driver."

"Do it, but hurry up. I wanna keep on schedule."

Shelley was already sitting in the driver's seat and thinking about a hot bowl of stew he would be feasting on in Copperhead. He had been driving stagecoaches for nearly two years and definitely liked the work. Nevertheless, there were times when it was hard on the lower back, and this was one of those times. He had tried sod busting, ranching, and even soldiering, but stage driving was something he enjoyed. He liked the riding, the challenge of keeping tight schedules, and the absence of some ugly boss-man barking orders over his shoulder. As for Robert Smythe the strongbox guard, well, he could take him or leave him. He was not the sort of fellow he wanted for a friend. As for the passengers, the only one he had gotten to talk with at any length was the California farmer named Foster. He seemed like a pleasant chap.

Shelley held the reins in his left hand and began to tug on the end of his right mustache. Maybe I better let this grow even longer, he thought....

Crack! The rifle shot was the last sound Shelley heard in this world. The bullet penetrated his lungs and heart, and he slumped forward dead. Startled, the horses reared and wanted to give chase. Fortunately, Foster had been standing nearby. He quickly scurried up to the driver's seat, took hold of the reins, and gained control before the team could race forward. Suddenly, he saw two riders galloping toward him, and he considered drawing his sidearm. However, he also considered how quickly they had slain Shelley, so he merely held tightly to the reins and wondered if Smythe, the guard, would be in a position to fight these people.

"Is the driver dead?" asked Chapeau.

"Of course he is dead," retorted Blood Hawk. "I do not miss at that range. Look at his chest. The blood is dark and heavy."

"Grampa, I suggest you get down from that seat. No need for you to meet the Almighty like the unfortunate driver." Chapeau nearly sounded sympathetic, but Foster was too much of a realist to consider these people as anything but cold-blooded and deadly.

Edward and Hannah were both inside the coach. Their hearts were palpitating, and respirations grew rapid. They had no idea what the outcome of this might be but were suspecting the worst. Hannah looked over to the clump of trees and saw Smythe slowly walking out of that area.

"Edward," she whispered. "Maybe Mr. Smythe will get the drop on these thieves."

"Shut up, Hannah. Don't count on it. Let me think about all this...but keep your trap closed."

Smythe walked boldly up to Foster, who had stepped off the stage. Foster, holding up his hands, turned and looked at Smythe. Initially, he was going to speak but then examined the man's countenance and determined a grim reality was about to unfold.

"Chapeau, yuh were right about this Cheyenne renegade. He is a good shot and has the heart of a bloodthirsty mountain cat. My kinda fella! I'm glad yuh showed up on time."

Foster looked at Smythe, and facially shot him a reaction of nausea and disgust. Smythe smiled, then struck him hard with the back of his hand.

"Don't look at me like, that you cow crap shoveling' sod buster. I'm just as good, and probably better than you. Maybe I'll leave yuh dead in the same ditch as that sissy Dusty Shelley."

Blood Hawk approached the stagecoach cabin, threw open the door on Edward's side, and ordered the occupants to get out.

"Please, sir, let's not do anything rash. I am a lawyer. I might be of value to you some day. I would be happy to represent you for free if you just let me and my wife leave here unharmed."

Chapeau studied Hannah as she stepped out of the coach. "That is an adorable lady you have there, Mr. Lawyer. Tell you what, maybe we'll let you breathe, if you let us have a little party with this delicious looking woman."

Hannah drew back in horror as Chapeau reached for her sleeve.

"You has great taste, Frenchy," Smythe chuckled. "Question is — are you man enough to handle a bundle like that or not? I been lookin' over and thinkin' about this nice little dessert ever since I first saw her in Henry City. I figure that gives me first crack."

"Edward!" Hannah screamed in desperation. "Say or do something!"

"Shut up, woman! I told you to keep your trap shut!"

"I think you are all in need of shutting up, and there are several ways to shut up," expressed Blood Hawk. "First things first. Smythe, you pig, get the strongbox of gold. Chapeau, you French animal, search these prosperous people for personal wealth."

Edward readily handed over his wallet, pocket watch, and even his wedding ring. Following her husband's lead, Hannah quickly took off her ring, a broach on her blouse, and gave those plus her handbag to Chapeau.

"Hey Blood Hawk, should I do a personal body search?"

"Do what you will. I'm going to make sure that idiot Smythe helps me load up my saddle bags with my share of the gold."

As Blood Hawk turned to fetch his horse, he thought he saw something move behind the clump of trees where the travelers had relieved themselves. Quickly, he leaped onto his horse and took off at a fast gallop.

"What in thunderation — what — "

Suddenly, John North and Elijah Johnson appeared with weapons pointed at the highwaymen. "Drop those irons, or so help me, we'll burn you down."

Smythe, instinctively a fighter, turned and took aim at North. Before he could discharge a round, North shot him in the guts. He made a retching sound as if he had a bad case of the flu and lifted his arm in a final effort of retaliation. North shot him in the neck at the indentation where it becomes the chest. He fell onto his back, gurgling on his blood.

In the meantime, Chapeau tried to run toward his horse but was stopped by Elijah Johnson who shot him in the right arm and then the right leg. He fell to the dust crying like an injured child.

North soberly looked in the distance and could only perceive the remnants of a dust cloud. Blood Hawk had escaped again. He then turned his attention to the two startled passengers.

"Are you folks all right?"

"Yes! Thank you, dear sir. Thank God for your arrival. They intended great harm to me personally. I am very grateful."

"Are you going to chase after that bloodthirsty savage, mister?" Edward asked. It was more like a command than a question. "Can't you see that he might ambush us later?"

"I don't know who you are, mister, but you show a strange way of expressing gratitude to people risking their own lives to save yours. Actually, if it had not been for this young lady, I'm not sure I would have bothered."

Johnson started to cackle and spit tobacco about three inches away from Edward's boot. The kinda attitude you're showin' here, yuh dude, is gonna git yerself killed. Yer in Wyomin' Territory now, not some fancy pants city up north. Yankees. What a bunch."

North turned his attention to Chapeau, who was now begging for mercy and medical attention. He looked into the man's face and saw that it was one of the men who had attacked his family on that tragic day long ago. He burned with hatred toward this man and unconsciously pointed his revolver at the man's head. He pulled back the hammer and thought how easy it would be to end the man's life.

"Don't do it, Mr. North," warned Elijah. "Yer among civilized folks, and this is not the time or place for this kinda action. I know this is one of the fellers, but yuh gotta take him into Copperhead where he can be properly tried and strung up by the neck."

North considered ignoring the warning but glanced out the corner of his eye at the young woman who looked frightened and confused. As he looked into her eyes, there was something about her that made him hesitate. Was she reminding him of his mother? Was she emblematic of civilization? He could not be certain. He only knew that she had an effect on him strong enough to prevent the willful murder of this sniveling rodent.

Johnson had already started to tie crude bandages on the man's wounds. North looked at the man and said, "What is your name?"

"I don't think I want to tell you, stranger."

In response, North kicked him in his bleeding leg.

"Still don't want to tell me?"

"You're a barbarian! All right, my name is Cramer. Osgood Cramer."

"He's lying," Foster corrected. "His name is Chapeau. I heard the fella you killed call him that.

North looked at Foster, who was bleeding from his side. Apparently, one of the bullets that had struck Smythe had ricocheted and grazed Foster.

"Ma'am, can you help this gentleman? Sir, I am sorry I accidentally wounded you. I did not intend that, but I'm sure you understand that gunfire is always hazardous."

The man nodded and let Hannah clean and then bandage his wound. She used a strip of her petticoat for the bandage.

"As for you, Mr. Chapeau, you are fated to have a short life. Remember a wagon with a mother, father, child, and another man you bushwhacked? Remember? Tell me, you slime!"

"I remember! I remember! It wasn't my idea! It was P.J.'s idea. That sort of thing was always his idea. I just worked for him. He and Blood Hawk like to kill. I just like to get treasure whenever I can. With me, it was nothing personal! I am sorry if I offended in any way."

"Sorry? You were a part of all this. You and four others. The man in buckskins, Jake Baker, I already killed him. There was the man in the hat with mirrors making up the hat band. Was that P.J., you say? Then there was the long haired one, I don't know his name; Blood Hawk, whose name I heard; and you. Yes, I remember you and your cheap suit, pencil-thin mustache, bald head, string tie, and filthy smirk. Yes, you enjoyed the carnage on that day like the others. If I can't shoot you like a mad dog, then I will at least enjoy watching you hang."

"Easy does it, sir — Mr., uh, North, did your friend say? You must be cautious and let this man go to trial. I am sure there is a magistrate of some sort at this place, Copperhead. I suggest we take him, and the rest of us, to that town and get all this sorted out legally. You were of great service here, and we thank you. I may be of service legally in Copperhead. Judging by your tone, you appear to be an educated man, so I appeal to your sense of morality and sound thinking."

Hannah added, "Please, Mr. North, will you take us to Copperhead? As I said, I am very grateful, and if there is a way to help your case legally, then my husband should help. He is a very fine attorney. I implore you to consider our offer. I am very, very sorry this man and others brought such pain to you. I am sure that your family would have wanted you to do the right thing." Hannah instinctively reached out and touched North's hand. He felt a chill run up his arm. His face started to flush. He smiled at her, and she warmly reciprocated. Yes, there was something about this woman that was inexplicably agreeable, yet familiar. It hit him like an avalanche. The girl in the photograph! This was the picture of the daughter, Hannah, that Naomi showed him back in Fortune River.

From Hannah's perspective, John North was like an angel sent from above. She responded to his strength and self confidence and was drawn to his handsome face and green eyes. With great discipline, she deliberately tried to resist his masculine charm and avoid the appearance of being a married woman attracted to a stranger she had just met. Somehow, it felt comforting and proper to stand close to John North.

John sensed her attraction to him, but resisted, turned from her, and said, "I think we better tie the two bodies on top of the roof and tie up Chapeau good and tight in the guard's seat. Mr. Johnson, will you drive the coach?"

"Why not? Ah drove a mule train once, so this can't be much different."

With such decisions made, actions were performed, and the party, consisting of both living and dead, set out in the stage bound for Copperhead. John North thought again about the disarming beauty of Hannah, but as he rode ahead on his horse, he primarily stayed ever watchful for a potential ambush by Blood Hawk. Fortunately, the sadistic renegade was nowhere to be found.

9

CALLENDAR RULES

Inside the marshal's office, a deputy poured another cup of strong coffee. He took a sip of the bitter brew, set down the china cup, then threw open the shutters to let in the sunlight. Its brightness was inviting, he mused, but he soon realized this enjoyment would be short-lived.

The front door was abruptly thrown open by a tall man moving as slowly and quietly as death itself. Dark shadows covered his face beneath the wide brim of the black, fancy hat. In contrast to the black shirt and trousers he wore, the sunlight danced frivolously off the many mirrors comprising the hatband. He turned slowly to the deputy but said nothing. The disapproving expression seemed to roar out the command, "Close the shutters at once!" The deputy hurriedly threw them shut and indulged again in his brew.

"What's new, Marshal?" said the deputy.

"Things ah quiet — as they should be, Wesley. I wouldn't have it any othuh way in muh town."

"I'm guessing that the boys haven't come in yet."

"You ah guessin' correctly. I went to the livery as well as the Richmond Saloon. No sign of their horses or their alcohol-starved carcasses."

Hubert Wesley was a much shorter man. He also dressed differently. He wore a pale yellow shirt, calico brown vest, Levi jeans, and a Colt .45 hanging loosely at his right side. The dark brown hair, clean-shaven face, and constant baring of half-yellowed teeth made him look inferior to the marshal in every way.

"I've gotta hand it to you, P.J., getting those boys to hit the stage lines and come back and split the loot with you in exchange for us giving them legal protection is a great scheme. It sure beats these lousy lawman wages they pay us."

Without warning, P.J. sprang at Wesley, grabbed his vest, and shook him roughly causing the man's coffee cup to fall and shatter.

"Keep yoah prattling to yerself. There is an army patrol in town, and ah don't want any of our upstandin' citizens tuh accidentally hear yuh bellowin' out our plans and take that information back to the army men. Ah'm warnin' yuh to shut up or so help me ah'll plant yuh with this season's cabbage crop."

Wesley started sweating and shaking. He had seen P.J. Callendar take out his wrath on many people, so this was no idle threat. He tried to compose himself by nodding, then whispering, "Yes — I — I hear you. I'm sorry, Marshal. I won't be so careless again."

Callendar pushed him aside, smirked widely, flashing two surprisingly white rows of mocking teeth, and said, "Besides, if you're gonna be a successful membah of muh ohganization, then yuh gotta think like a team member. We talk 'bout plans in the strictest confidence, and remembah what we talk about the fuhst time. That's what ah like about Blood Hawk and Chapeau — they don't need repeat conversations."

"At least they have an able helper along on this little ride. You know, my friend— the associate."

Callendar carefully peeked through the shutters, saw that the immediate area was unoccupied, then said, "You ah referrin' to Smythe, the guard that YOU recommended to the sheriff in Henry Town. If anythin' goes wrong with Smythe workin' as the inside man, then it's on yoah head, Wesley. He is yoah cousin."

"Smythe is a good ol' boy from Kentucky. He fought for the Confederacy just like you did. Sure, Kentucky ain't Texas, but not every great confederate soldier was from Texas like you."

Callendar walked up to a wall covered with wanted posters, shot them a disinterested glance, then said, "In a backhanded way, I surmise, you ah givin' this Texan a compliment. If not, then ah'll let it ride this time. Just remembah to keep doin' yoah job, and things will go right. Me and the mayor will do all the thinking."

Wesley pulled out a file drawer and rifled through boxes of cartridges, a sandstone, and some apple cores before finding another china coffee cup. He wiped out the dust, then eagerly filled the cup with coffee. "Mayor Agee used to be an army officer, didn't he? Do you think he knows any of those army fellers who stopped off in town?"

P.J. Callendar dropped his six-feet four inch frame into the chair, crossed his ankles up on the edge of the desk, and declared, "Know them? Indeed. He used to command one of them. The officer in town is a Captain named Bristol. Agee sent him on assignments to fight and kill Indians quite a bit. This happened until Captain Bristol escalated a complaint to a general who came to inspect the situation. Bristol complained that oah beloved mayor was violatin' a treaty with the Indians and killin' them for sport. The general relieved Agee of command. You might say that oah mayor holds a smidgeon of a grudge 'gainst the dashin' cavalry captain."

"Does the mayor know that Bristol is in town?"

"I will drop by and let him know. Right now, let's see if the prisoner is behavin' today."

Callendar and Wesley unlocked a side door and walked back to the jail cells. There were actually three separate cells, each approximately five feet long by five feet wide. Only the second cell was occupied. Its denizen was a black man in ragged, blood stained clothing.

"How yuh doin' in there, boy?"

"Ah am not a boy, Mr. Marshal, I am a grown man — and I have not had any water for hours. Could I have some?"

"You all will have some when we ah ready to give yuh some, yuh ungrateful darkie. Why'd yuh have to come into muh town and cause trouble?"

"Ah came into town to buy some supplies for my ranch. I've been buyin' supplies at the General Store for years. Kirk Mason is a fine man, a good Quaker gentleman.

He knows I has a family to look aftuh, and he knows ah only comes to town when ah has to."

Wesley interrupted, "Ol' Johnny here is right. He's been pretty good about keepin' his distance from white folk, and some of them even think he's pretty sociable — for a Negro, anyway. He didn't get into any scrape until two days ago."

"Yuh understand, Johnny," P.J. lectured, "We ain't got a judge in this community. The mayor and I do all the law makin' and enforcin' in these parts, and we really don't like tuh have one of yoah kind gettin' in fights on main street. It's a bad image for the town. We want Copperhead to appear respectable."

Johnny looked down at his boots. He wanted to respond to the "respectable" comment, but knew it was pointless to do so. On too many occasions, he had either seen or experienced the wrath of bigots such as these men, and he only wanted to leave the jail and return to his wife and children.

"Ah am sorry, Mr. Marshal. I mean no disrespect to the law or the nice folks in this town. What was I to do though? I was simply loadin' up my canned goods, rope, salt, and coffee into muh wagon when those two strangers came out of the saloon and started to push me around. I was defendin' myself so I could go home to my wife and youngins. I didn't think I'd break that man's jaw when I hit him."

"He's got a point, P.J. That Rudolph Krautmueller guy was trying to pick a fight with me in the saloon after I admonished him for being so loud. The fact that he and the feller who ended up with the broken jaw — what's his name, Wendall? — ended up getting beaten to a pulp by Johnny here was a sight kind of entertaining."

"Maybe so, but ah don't like it when colored folk get the idea they can be uppity." Following this invective, Callendar turned his cold eyes into fiery windows of rage against Johnny specifically. "It's true! The fellas you beat up deserved what they got, but if ah evah have any moah trouble with you or yoah kind in my town again, you will rue that day that you evah came to Copperhead!"

Johnny felt the deep dread of those words. He had often dealt with racial prejudice both during the evil days of slavery, as well as in this post-Civil War period, but seldom had he seen it used as such a *directly* threatening tool. Instinctively, he read the soul of this man as something capable of great evil, and wanted to avoid its company completely.

Then, to the surprise of Johnny, and even Wesley, P.J. opened the jail cell and announced, "You are free to go. Take yoah wagon, and git back home to yer nigrah family. Ah don't wanna see you for a long spell."

Without saying thank you, goodbye, go to hell ya bigot, or anything else, Johnny quickly dashed out of the cell, put on his hat, and ran out of the building toward the livery stable where his wagon had been impounded. It was not long before he hitched his team in readiness for a discrete departure from town.

Callendar walked to the front door, adjusted his fancy hat, and said, "Thet boy was taught an object lesson. If yuh evah want to be marshal, Wesley, yuh have to know that killin' is not always the answer. Yes, I find killin' works very well in many different endeavors, but when yuh can assert yer power — suppress them with your authority — then that is when you know you are a strong man and leader. Ah'm on muh way ovuh to chat with Mayor Agee. Lock up her before yuh go out fer supper. Make sure yer back an hour later."

Inside the saloon, Captain Bristol poured himself another shot of rot gut. He did not particularly like whiskey, but he found it was one way to relax after a difficult ride.

His patrol consisted of one sergeant, four troopers, and a scout. The scout was a Cherokee named Sammy Fivetrees. He was tending to the horses in the stable. Everyone agreed it was asking for trouble if he went in for a drink with the others. Copperhead was known for miles away as the town that had the intolerant marshal.

Bristol turned around and noticed the sergeant and the four troopers were scattered about playing poker or blackjack at various tables. Personally, he never cared much for gambling. It took too long to save up army wages, and he was not thrilled over the concept of blowing them on some unlucky hand.

Sammy Fivetrees was a little startled to see a black man dash into the stable and quickly work to hitch up a team.

"You must be in quite a hurry, pilgrim. Is the town all that inhospitable?"

Johnny said, "You're an Indian."

"I was a few seconds ago when I last thought about it. They call me Sammy Fivetrees."

"Sorry if ah'm seemin' rude, Mr. Fivetrees. Ah'm just wantin' to get outta here before that redneck marshal changes his mind about me. He's got the smell of death on him like I once smelled in the big war."

"Yes. I know that smell. Not only was it in the great war, but it has permeated the air often in this territory as well. Before you leave, do you mind telling me your name?"

"Thank you for askin'. Muh name is Johnny Franklin. The name Franklin was taken by muh daddy 'cause he admired ol' Benjamin Franklin so much. Mr. Franklin, you know, wanted to end slavery right at the beginning — of America, I mean."

"The beginning of America started long before Mr. Franklin was alive — but I know what you mean. Pleased to meet you Johnny Franklin. I take it you have a family, or at least property to take care of?"

"Both. Right after the war and all that slavery stuff was ended, ah took muh lovely bride, Abby — Abigail — west, where we could get away from all those white folk hatin' us for wantin' to be free like them. When we got out west, it was a little better."

"Were the white people better?"

"Some were, some just as bad or worse. Best of all, I got to homestead a piece of land, and with the help of the storekeeper, Kirk Mason — a wise and fair gentleman — ah got muh land properly recorded and deeded to me fair and square. Because ah can raise crops, chickens, pigs, even breed a few horses, ah can make enough of a livin' to take care of me and my own."

"I admire you for taking control of your destiny and setting down roots, Johnny Franklin. I have not taken roots for many seasons. I keep riding with the army because that seems to be all that I have a mind to do."

"Ah'll tell you, Mr. Fivetrees, muh ranch isn't very big, but about five miles north of here it's easy to find. If'n you evah want to drop by, we'd be honored to welcome yuh as our guest."

Fivetrees smiled and was about to speak when he saw two men suddenly enter the stable. One walked in with a heavily bandaged face, while the other walked in exhibiting cuts and bruises and a broken nose. The latter one spoke in a German accent.

"Ach, the schwartz mann ist running away from town. Ist you scared of your betters? Ist dis not da truth, schwartzie?"

Johnny did not reply, he simply finished hitching up the team, jumped into the seat, and glared at the German.

"I tink you hast unfinished bizness wit Rudolph Krautmueller. Get down!"

"Go to hell, sauerkraut! Outta muh way, or I'll run yuh over."

"That will not be necessary." All heads turned and saw that Sammy Fivetrees was aiming a Henry Repeater rifle at Krautmueller's heart.

"I work for the U.S. Army, mister, and believe me, I have the power to destroy you if I choose. You better let the man pass, or I will be obliged to end your life."

Krautmueller, visibly intimidated, stepped aside. Johnny shook the reins, hollered, "Hyaaa," and raised a hand waving goodbye to Fivetrees. He wasted no time in leaving town. Meanwhile, Krautmueller and his companion considered their next move. Sammy simply looked at them unemotionally and held the rifle in its position.

"Sammy, are the — what's going on here?" It was Captain Bristol. Seeing that Sammy had his weapon raised against a man, he quickly pulled out his own sidearm and spoke.

"Explain."

"Mein Kapitan — vee mean no harm. Dis Indian of yours threatens us with his veapon, und vee have no bizness mit him. It vas the schwarz mann vee vanted to talk vit."

"I can imagine the type of conversation you would have engaged in. You must understand that if you take up arms against my scout here, you will be attacking the United States Government. Should you be foolish enough to seek revenge, or try to ambush my scout, or even me on another occasion, you will be hunted down and hanged following a brief but decidedly prejudiced military trial against you. I insist that you promise to stay away from us, or I shall order my scout to arrest you immediately."

The man with the broken jaw worriedly turned his head back and forth and cried, "Uhh — Uhhhh!" Krautmueller's sweat poured down his whiskered face onto his filthy shirt collar. "Nicht schiesse, bitte! Do not shoot, please! Vee go avay. Vee vant no troubles mit der army. First, dis marshal threaten us, den you. Vee go now! No vorries!"

The two men scurried out of the livery stable like two frightened rats. Captain Bristol started to laugh in his typically hearty manner, and Fivetrees cracked a smile and even chuckled. They walked out of the livery stable and approached the saloon.

"Mr. Fivetrees, just seeing you laugh for a change is worth the risk of angering my former commanding officer, who, as fate would have it, is the current mayor of this town. Mortimer Agee! They can like it or not, but I intend to buy you a drink!"

With this open challenge to the local authority, the two men walked into the saloon where there were no questions or comments as Sammy Fivetrees slaked his thirst with beer.

10

TRUST IN THOSE EYES

Both John North and Elijah Johnson decided that the team of horses was tired, so they stopped near a stream where the animals could get refreshed. The passengers of the coach, except for the heavily bound and wounded Pierre Chapeau, stepped off the coach to stretch.

"I think you should have kept riding toward the town," complained Edward. "You are risking our lives."

"Ah suggest yuh go take a walk, Mr. Fancy Pants Lawyer," chided Johnson. "Yuh seem tuh value hearin' yer own gas-bagging more than the welfare of those horses."

"Hrummph! I think I will at that. Will you join me, Mr. Foster?"

Foster opted not to go and offered instead to keep an eye on Chapeau. His side still ached from the bullet that had grazed his flesh, but he did not want to admit that to Edward — a man he clearly disliked.

Johnson occupied himself by caring for the team of horses. North and Hannah unofficially began to drift off into a walk together.

"I know who you are, Mrs. Olson. I have seen your mother. In fact, I saw her yesterday morning!"

"You did? Thank the Lord. I was right then. We are close to Fortune River."

"Well, not really. By riding down to Copperhead, we are traveling about twenty miles northeast out of the way. Unfortunately, the ride is necessary since that is the official stop for the stagecoach and the only nearby town that has a lawman."

"Well, we were supposed to go to Copperhead anyway. It was there that Edward was to get a wagon, or riding mounts, that the two of us would take up to Fortune River. I understand it is part way up in the mountains."

"Yes." North rolled a cigarette and tried not to look admiringly at the beautiful woman.

"You seem to be turning away from me, Mr. North. Is there anything wrong?"

"Nothing, ma'am."

Understanding John's insecurity perhaps better than he realized, she half-closed her eyes, looked up at him coyly, and smiled. John felt uneasy; he hurriedly lit his cigarette and puffed away.

"Tell me about my mother. What did you two talk about?"

John told her about his staying in the boarding house and how her wonderful mother possessed a divine gift for getting a sullen, quiet fellow such as himself to open up about family secrets and injuries.

"My mother is very good at getting to the heart of what is bothering someone because she genuinely cares about people. She must have seen a lot of good in you, John North, or she would not have gotten you to say so much."

North looked deeply into the woman's eyes and promptly concluded he could trust her more than anyone else. He could not explain why, he just knew it. She was more than the pretty face he liked to gaze upon; she was special, a woman who could be his soul mate. It seemed incredibly unfair, but he was starting to fall in love with this married woman.

Soon, John related his story about the massacre of his family and the memories of the five perpetrators of the wicked event. Hannah winced when he told about how he gunned down one of the men, Jake Baker. She now also understood his rough treatment of the hold up man they called Chapeau and how important it was for John North to take this villain to justice.

Johnson approached. "Ah see he told yuh about the five fellers that did him wrong, ma'am. We know quite a bit 'bout three of 'em, and you met two of 'em today. But notice how little he talks about the other two, especially the feller with the long hair. By the way, John, duh yuh recall anything else about that partic'ler hombre?"

"Come to think of it, I do. He had tobacco stained teeth — sort of like yours. Besides that, he was clean-shaven, and had a big mole underneath his nose. If I saw him again, I'd recognize him."

Johnson cleared his throat and said, "I believe Mr. Olson is headin' this way, ma'am."

Without warning, John North blurted out, "Why did you marry that man, Hannah? It is clear to everyone that he treats you like dirt. You don't have to put up with that. Just say the word, and I will deal with him."

Shocked, Hannah opened her mouth, inhaled as if someone had just stepped on her foot, and replied, "Mr. North! He is my husband. Your...your words are not appropriate. I beg you to sh-show respect. I mean...."

"I apologize, Mrs. Olson. Out here, we tend to get to the point. I would bet a month wages that the man you married is a horse's behind, and you are not really happy with him. Should you ever change your mind and need assistance, I will be obliged to help." Following that sincere oath, North bent down a corner of his hat and looked straight into her eyes. For all of her expressed indignity, Hannah returned the gaze as if peering deeply into the soul of someone she might one day love. It was a sinful thought, but it somehow warmed her inside to consider it.

"Why are you bothering this stranger, Hannah? You don't know him, and it looks hideously improper for you to be standing out in the open chattering with him like a grade school girl pining for her first date. I'll thank you, sir, to give leave to my wife."

North moved toward Edward somewhat aggressively. "What are you implying, Olson? Are you casting aspersions on my character?"

"If the shoe fits, then wear it, saddle tramp!"

North punched Edward in the mouth and sent him flying toward the stagecoach. He landed about one foot from the right rear wheel. He was stunned, but still conscious.

"You made a serious mistake, Mr. North. I am a man of the law and know how to prosecute someone to the full extent of the law!"

"Well, gee willickers," Johnson mocked. "Aren't we all scaredy-cat to death! Thar's only one problem, Mr. Barrister — you need witnesses. Ah didn't see anyone hit yuh. Ah think yuh tripped and fell. What about you, Mr. Foster, did you see anyone get hit?"

"No. I was keeping an eye on this bandit — who is sound asleep."

"Thet just leaves Mrs. Olson here to testify against muh friend, Mr. North. Still, ah think yuh both ought to consider that if it weren't for Mr. North, yuh'd both be dead right now. He's the one that wanted to come and help out. Ah could have cared less!"

"There will be no courtroom action except for the trial of this wounded man who planned me personal injury. Isn't that correct, Edward?" Hannah tried to sound spousal-supportive and triumphant simultaneously and visibly came across as successful.

"Forget it. Yes, we're grateful to Mr. North. Can we just get back on the stage and resume our trip to Copperhead?"

Everyone thought the time right for resumption of travel. It was beginning to get dark, but the travelers hoped to use what light was left to ride into Copperhead. Johnson, again, took the reins of the coach, and North rode alongside on his horse. This time, there was some talk exchanged between the two outlaw stalking partners.

"I am much appreciative of your support, Johnson. Thanks. It means a lot especially since we were trying to whale the tar out of each other earlier today."

"Heck, that was just exercise. Ah haven't had such a spirited argument about the War Between the States in a long time. That doesn't change anythin' between us. Ah swore ah'd be yer partner in huntin' down the four bad men, and ah intend to fulfill muh end of the bargain. Just one thing, Mr. North. Be careful of this marshal in Copperhead. Before we left Fohtune Rivuh that bad egg, McAvee, warned me that this marshal doesn't mess around. He is supposed to be a tough hombre, and a considerably mean one at that. Ah don't know who he is, and McAvee didn't tell me his name, but ah've run into that kind before. If they don't like the way yuh part yer hair, or how badly he thinks yer horse stinks, he's apt to slam yuh in the jail. If'n that happens, yoah search for the bad men could come to a halt purty quick."

North rode his horse quickly to keep up with the stage, "I see you're trying to beat the sun going down. All right. I'll be careful around the lawman. I have always tried to respect the law, so there shouldn't be any trouble. I'm likely to even ask him about the men I'm dogging. But changing the subject, why did you ask me about the long-haired man? I'm glad you did, because you helped me remember a little more about him. I'm curious about why you asked."

"Why not? After all, if yuh think yuh want to hunt down and punish the correct entities, don't yuh think it best to have someone help yuh remembuh what in blazes they look like? The two yuh always seemed to talk about the most were Blood Hawk and that feller with the crazy mirrors hat. Maybe we'll run into 'long-hair' next."

"You have a point. I just wish I knew his name."

"Ah'm sure it exudes shame to many," Johnson muttered sarcastically.

The stage driver and horseback rider continued looking at the countryside for signs of Blood Hawk or anyone else who might choose to attack them at this late hour. Except for a curious coyote peeking at them from behind a rock and a rattlesnake slithering rapidly to avoid the pressure of the horse hoofs and stagecoach wheels nothing else alive seemed aware of their journey.

It was dark. Just over the ridge, feint traces of light could be detected. It was the town. Within minutes, they would be pulling into the town of Copperhead.

11

ROAST BEEF, A GOOD TIP, AND NOSE TWISTING

A t 5:30 PM it was the custom of P.J. Callendar to stroll into Murphy's Café and order his dinner. Tonight was no exception. He dined on roast beef, mashed potatoes and gravy, peas in the pod, and hot homemade bread. He planned to wash it down with several cups of coffee, as well as a tall glass of milk. Some men preferred guzzling down whiskey, but Callendar only drank when he thought it suitable to work with men he aimed to control.

As he lifted an especially large forkload of beef into his watering mouth, he espied a familiar face walk into the café.

"Nate McAvee! You and the devil usually ride together, so what are the two of you doing in my town?"

"P.J., I got some important news for you. I'm hoping its some news you might be willing to pay for."

P.J. quit chewing the food and stared at McAvee, expressing cold recognition of the game being played. He resumed chewing with his prominent teeth and then motioned for McAvee to sit in the chair across from him at the round table.

McAvee was impressed with the café. He liked the red, checkered linen tablecloth and the overall clean look of the establishment. He rubbed the coarse whiskers on his chin, looked down at P.J.'s plate of food, and reached for a pea pod.

Instantly, P.J.'s fist slammed down hard onto McAvee's hand causing him to cry out in pain. Not only did the striking fist hurt, but the spillage of hot coffee burned acutely.

"Easy does it, P.J. I meant no harm. I just ain't seen such a good lookin' plate of grub in such a long time. They had some good grub up in Fortune River, but I couldn't always afford it. That's one of the reasons I want to talk to you about earning some coins, cousin."

"You are not my cousin, McAvee. If you were, I should be obliged to eithuh change muh name or blow yoah putrid head off. Ah'll thank you to keep yoah diseased hands off muh meal and politely ask you to eithuh buy yoah own food or go rot in the wilderness."

"If I gave you information about a plot to kill you — do you think that might be worth a few dollars?"

Not hesitating, P.J. Callendar dropped his fork and whipped out a handgun, pointed it at McAvee's chest, and cocked the hammer.

"Tell you what, 'cousin,' eithuh give me that information now, or I shall throw yuh in muh jail, hold a fair trial tomorrow accusin' you of attemptin' to murder the good marshal of Copperhead, and hang yuh conveniently before suppah. Start talkin'."

Sweat ran down McAvee's face onto the checkered tablecloth. He was quite familiar with Marshal P.J. Callendar's promises and decided the moment for bargaining had expired.

"I am sorry if I insulted you, P.J. I will tell you all — willingly. I just came from Fortune River — that little outhouse up in the mountains. I couldn't dig out any gold there, but in the saloon yesterday, I saw a man come into town who seemed to know about you and four fellas you used to ride with."

"Careful, McAvee. Just because you used to help me out on certain jobs years ago will not spare you if you are settin' me up for a bad surprise. So help me, I will blow off your flappin' lips should you be joshin'."

"I'm telling the truth! This man — a fellow in his early to mid thirties, about average height, brown hair, medium blue shirt, white bandana, dark brown hat, colt .45 tied down for a quick draw on his right leg, came in asking about a bunch of fellers — one of them being you! He mentioned the hat with the mirrors, Marshal. He then called out Jake Baker in the bar and shot him dead. The meat and taters of all this, Marshal, is that he is huntin' down the skinny gambler, Blood Hawk, some long-haired man, and you. He wants to kill all of you! He is on some mission of revenge. I happen to believe he is coming to Copperhead. He goes by the name of John North. Have you heard of him? An old prospector I knew up there in Fortune River was plannin' to come with him."

P.J. eased down the hammer of the revolver and delicately returned it to his holster. He picked up a spoon and began shoveling large portions of potatoes and gravy between his gnashing teeth. He did not speak until he had swallowed the enormous bolus.

He reached down to his side again, and McAvee nervously jerked away from the table. Instead of facing a revolver, he heard the clang of a large coin hit the table in front of him. It was a ten dollar gold piece.

"Mr. McAvee, you were absolutely correct, and ah appreciate your total candor in bringin' this to muh attention. As an old friend, ah know you really did not seek remuneration for tellin' me this news, so I thank you foah yuh friendship."

"What is the money for then?"

"McAvee, consider it a downpayment of wages. Ah want yuh start workin' as a new deputy of mine. Go ovah to the marshal's office and see muh othuh trusted deputy who will give yuh a badge and let yuh know how things are done in Copperhead. Afterwards, come back and get some dinner. You really should try the roast beef. It's succulent."

McAvee issued a revoltingly obsequious smile, then charged out of the café, nearly knocking over a stern-jawed, rough-hewn looking, silver-haired man in a gray suit. The man cursed under his breath, then made a bee-line for P.J.'s table.

"Good evenin', Mayor Agee. Isn't it a pleasant evening?"

"Just a blessed minute, Callendar. We have some unfinished coversation. You met with me this afternoon, but I don't think we finished up what needed to be said."

"Drop yoah backside into the chair, Mayor. I warn yuh though, ah don't want yuh to spoil muh supper. Indigestion makes me kinda ornery."

"Supper! As if I cared! Look, we have had a good thing going in this town for about three years. When I took over as mayor, I saw the value in hiring a man such as yourself — with your..."

"Unique talents?"

"Definitely. I do not regret hiring you for a moment, Callendar. We see eye to eye on many things — including our desire to keep the Chinese, Mexicans, blacks, and Indians out of this town. I want it to be a properly white community and appreciate all you've done to maintain its racial purity. However, I do have a bone to pick with you."

"Pick away, Agee, but it'll do yuh no good. Ah know you are goin' to bring up that stuff about that stupid colored boy, Johnny, but I already put him in his place. Ah don't think yuh should interfere with the way ah enforce the law. If you do, ah may decide to seek employment elsewhere."

"Don't be an ass, Callendar. Of course I want you to continue here. It's not that black man I'm talking about. It's that Indian scout I saw walk into the saloon for a beer. I was amazed that you allowed the army to let him go in there and dirty-up a saloon glass."

"Actually, the glasses in theah couldn't get much dirtier if yuh tried. Odie Rawlins the barkeep is one of the filthiest men ah evah saw or smelled, and he does not keep a clean bar. Thank God, ah am not partial to drinkin' liquor."

"It was a damned Indian drinking in there! What will the decent white folk think?!"

Callendar stood up, lifted his dinner plate, and tossed it across the room. It barely missed the heads of an elderly gentleman and his wife, but some of the residual food did splatter onto their clothing. Callendar did not care, and the elderly couple seemed to know better than to protest the indignity.

"Listen here, Agee. Ah know you used to be an ahmy officer. Ah know all about yoah bad feelins foah that particular captain who invited the Cherokee scout into the saloon. If you want me to come up with a plan foah getting' rid of the captain, then let me know. If yuh want to have me dream up a scheme to do away with the troublesome dahkie, I'll take care of that too. Howevah, you had bettah pay me a lot moah than the measley one hundred dollars a month you ah payin' me presently. When you move against the government, it's goin' to cost yuh a lot moah than that!"

"How dare you speak to me in that tone of voice! I am your superior, and you shall treat me with respect!"

Callendar reached up to Agee's nose and pinched it hard. He then twisted it back and forth and made Agee lose balance and fall to the floor. People throughout the café bolted from their positions and either hid in corners or fled out the door.

"You are still nuthin' but a worthless Yankee cahpetbagger! Durin' the war we killed men ten times braver and deadlier than you. Ah used to ride with Stonewall Jackson, and so help me, he was fifty times the man you will evah hope to be. Ah don't take orders from you, or any othuh man in this world now that the War is over. Ah fight muh own battles, and up until now it has pleased me to let you work on my team. If you evah rise against me again, you popcorn colonel, I will twist off your nose and pull your brains out through the gapin' hole left behind."

Sufficiently terrified, and equally humiliated, Agee pulled himself up from the floor and considered fighting the man. He knew from first person observation that such an act would be suicide. Agee had witnessed Callendar shoot to death four very rude white men and two Chinamen who had made the stubborn decision to gamble in the saloon. No, Callendar was a dark force falling under no one's command. He would like to continue harnessing this dark force but now realized his administrative skills would have to be used in another manner.

"Very well, Mr. Callendar. I put up with this because you enable me to run the town the way I prefer it to be run. At least the army people shall be pulling out tomorrow, will they not?"

"Informed sources in this town of 'yours' tell me this is true. Excuse me for muh hostility, Mr. Mayor, but ah think we understand each othuh better, do we not?"

Agee brushed off his coat and nodded.

"Now there is something we may do for one anothuh, Mr. Mayor. We are expectin' company some time this evenin'. There appears to be some madman on his way into town with an inclination to kill yoah's truly. Ah want yuh to be the official party to meet this gentleman while ah set up a very strong trap. Since you are the head cheese in this town, yuh should have no trouble meetin' danger head on, right?"

Agee grimaced but shook his head up and down.

"Also, ah would be most delighted if yuh could stop by my office and tell Mr. Wesley muh deputy, or that new deputy ah hired, McAvee, that ah'd like one of them to hire a couple moah deputies foah this visitation. Specifically, there are those two fellas that got beaten by the black man — the German and the one with the broken jaw. Ah have a feelin' that they would like to pour out some of theah bitterness in a liberatin' way. They might be useful tonight. Would you be so kind as to do that foah me, Mr. Mayor?"

"Anything else?" By now, Agee felt he had been court-martialed a second time in life.

"No, 'cept ah promise to buy you suppah tomorrow night providin' you can come up with a fifty dollar bonus foah me this month. Aftah all, if this fella, Jim North ah think he's called, is successful in killin' me, then you might find yoahself out of business too."

"Good point. Okay. It's a deal."

"Ah knew it would be. Thank you kindly."

After the mayor stormed out of the café, Callendar dropped five dollars in the hand of the proprietor, then strolled down the street and headed for the alley between the livery stable and the general store. He walked a few feet into the dark alley, stopped, pulled out a two dollar cigar from his black vest pocket, and propped one foot behind him against the wall. He took in a long drag of smoke and waited until a figure moved slowly toward him from the shadows. He was not at all surprised and seemed a bit bored.

"What took you so long, Blood Hawk? Ah expected you woulda stopped by here moah than an hour ago. That's when Wesley agreed to meet you at this location."

"The robbery did not go well. We had interference from two strangers. One of the men killed Smythe and wounded the Frenchman."

"And the gold shipment?"

"I could not get it. These people were well armed and wary of ambush, so I could not ride back and surprise them. I did track them, however. I learned that they were safeguarding the coach here. They want to turn the Frenchman over to the marshal of Copperhead! They are doing the job for us. They are delivering the gold to your door."

"That was not the plan, Blood Hawk. It would incite suspicion and might compel some of the more upstandin' citizens to wire for a federal marshal. That is the kind of complication I choose to avoid. You did a poor job, Blood Hawk. You disappoint me."

"Are you challenging me to a fight, Callendar?"

"No. That would be imprudent. You and ah have worked well together on many occasions, so ah know that these interferin' men must have been quite a problem. We will have future occasions to steal other shipments of money, but right now ah am moah concerned about dealin' with the man who interfered today. This John North is on a death hunt for us. He claims we wronged him, so he wants a bunch of us dead. The bunch includes you, me, Chapeau, Charlie, and Baker — only he already killed Baker. You know about the time the five of us all rode togethah, Blood Hawk. Remember?"

"I remember. There was a family we attacked. We killed an aging man, woman, boy, and I wanted to kill the younger man. You let him live. This must be John North."

"I believe so. As far as ah know, this man probably believes he can send Chapeau to the law for hangin', then set out to hunt down me, you, and Chahlie. Good luck with Chahlie — ah don't know where the hell that peckerhead is anymore. Last time ah saw him he was jailed in Denver for getting' drunk and slappin' around some ugly whore. He asked me to bail him out, or at least send a telegram to his family. Ah had no interest in employin' him. Ah heard about that openin' for the marshal job here in Copperhead so ah let him decay in Denver. He might be dead by now."

"I doubt it, Callendar. I actually saw him in Fortune River about six weeks ago. He was still drinking heavily, but looked quite thin and even sickly. He got run out of town by men pointing rifles. He threw a tantrum about wanting to see his parents again. He ended up admitting they were dead, so I think he is alive somewhere, but loco."

"Good riddance, then. Ah only need people ah can rely on. That's why ah hired one new deputy, sent foah two othuhs, and want you to throw in with them as well."

"Suit yourself. As long as you pay me for the duty, I will do as you ask. However, if this John North strikes against me, I shall kill him quickly. Be forewarned."

"Ah completely understand, Blood Hawk. However, it won't come to that. He will be so ovahwhelmed in seein' you standin' alongside the fine, distinguished mayor and deputy Wesley, that it will rattle him long enough foah me to meet and greet him from behind."

"You have always been good at that sort of greeting."

"Ah accept yoah compliment. By the way, you can get outta them shadows now. You are goin' to be a membuh of the marshal's team tonight. Tonight we capture John North, and tomorrow ah will make his life miserable and make sure he is quite dead befoah the suppuhtime bell rings. You can count on it, muh friend."

Blood Hawk stared at Callendar as he smirked and drew more cigar smoke deep into his lungs. He waited for a moment, then made one stinging comment.

"You people consider the red men to be savages. We primarily just torture to make a point, or kill for necessity. You, on the other hand, make those actions delicacies."

12

THE VISITOR

The fourteen-year-old young man chased an ornery hog back into a small pen occupied by three other members of its species. Harold Franklin wanted to get all those stinking pigs in one place in order that they could be properly slopped and done with for the day. How old "Fat Papa" got out of the pen to begin with was a mystery. Right after feeding these ungrateful beasts, he thought, I might at last have some time to myself. Harold felt that he earned it. He looked at the light in the cabin and noticed his pa was still talking with the visitor who had unexpectedly shown up just before dusk.

Inside the cabin, Johnny Franklin urged his guest, Kirk Mason, to be seated on the nearest log bench and partake of some of his wife's squirrel stew.

"It looks tempting, Johnny, but I already supped this evening. I came here to see how you and the family were doing. I heard you leave town rather abruptly and wondered if the law was planning to dog you down for escaping. You just told me he let you out willingly, so I am a bit surprised that such a hateful man would actually be so merciful.

"Mercy had nuthin' to do with," interrupted Abby Franklin. "Thet marshal is spawn of Satan hisself and don't likely do anythin' outta mercy. He let muh Johnny go 'cause he was puttin' him in his place. Thet doesn't mean he won't try somethin' worse tomorrow!"

"Abby, you and Johnny need to understand that there are many of us in Copperhead who do not like this official or even want him to work in our town. He was invited by a mayor that we cannot seem to vote out, and the two of them stay on and on like the British of 1775. I'm telling you not to despair. I already sent a telegram to get you a good lawyer, as well as a fair and impartial judge to come up from Laramie, but it would have taken at least two weeks before they arrived. Are you sure that Callendar didn't let you out as means of trapping you for something else?"

"No, sir. Ah think he was cogitatin' that those army boys might complicate things for him a little bit, so it was plumb easier to just run me outta town."

"You may be right, Johnny. Mind if I smoke, Abby?" Abby smiled, told him to light up, then went back to stirring the stew in the big kettle over the fire in the stone hearth.

"Johnny, I did speak with that Captain Bristol this afternoon. He apparently visited me, and couple of others in town — namely Giancarlo Muselli, the barber; and Dr. Brandt — to find out what sort of town it was that allowed hard working folks such as yourself to be pushed around by that German reject and his toady buddy. I simply told him it was the attitude of the mayor and his gun-for-hire marshal who literally called all the shots in this town. I figured it was time an authority outside the town knew about the mischief."

"An' what did this ahmy fella suggest?"

"He said we needed to take control of the situation ourselves. He suggested we stand up to these two men and kick them out. When I shook my head, he went on to suggest that we hire our own gunman to put the run on Callendar. He suggested someone like Wild Bill Hickock of Kansas."

"Hickock?"

"I knew that wasn't a good idea. I heard from the grapevine that he's pretty much retired and isn't easily found these days. Rumor has it he has some sort of eye problem and that he might be going blind."

"If we ever do get a new marshal to run out the old one, ah just hope he ain't worse."

"Amen, brother. Anyway, I have to go now, but I want to assure you that besides you folks, and me and my wife, Roberta, there's the doctor, the barber, even Sean Murphy the café owner in agreement. At one time I thought Murphy liked Callendar, but it turns out he only tolerates him because there's no way to keep him out of his café."

"Most of them folk have not been espeshly kind to me o' muh family, 'cept you and the doctor, but ah can see why they is gettin' ripe for a change as well. Speakin' o' the ahmy, that indin scout, who was it? Fourtrees? Fivetrees? He was awfully nice today. He helped me get away from that sauerkraut eater and his buddy. That fella is welcome here anytime. Ain't that right, Abby?"

Mason said, "I heard about that. I'm glad he was there to help. Anyway, I'd better ride for home. One of us will let you know if things change. Until that time, you are always welcome to shop in my store. When you do, watch out for the likes of that German."

After Kirk Mason got on his horse and rode off, Harold walked into the cabin and reached for a book on a nearby table.

"Harold, ah yuh gonna start readin' again befoah yuh even taste the suppuh? What's wrong with yuh, youngin'?"

"I wanna read this book, Pa. It's a history book about the revolution. Didja know that there were a bunch of colored folk who fought in George Washington's army 'gainst the redcoats?"

"Ah also know that Washington and his wife owned a bunch of slaves. So what?"

"It says here on page forty-one that Washington really didn't care for slavery and put it in his will to free the slaves once he died. Dat's exactly what happened."

"Ah'm tellin' you, Harold, that the history of this country is one fulla grief for our folk. Ah think it's betta to make things work out fine foah us here and now, and in the future, rather than lookin' at the past. You and yoah sistuh ought to grow up in a better world than the one me and yoah ma started out in."

Harold sat down next to the fire, leafed through the heavy volume, and said, "So do I, Pa. That's why I wanna grow up just as smart, or smarter than, the white folk. I gotta know 'bout the history too."

"Johnny, let the boy enjoy his book. It's the Christmas present we done give him, and he works hahd ev'ry day and looks fohward to doin' the readin' at night."

"Abby, how is Ruthie feelin' now?"

"She's still feelin' poorly, ah suspect. Go in and see."

Mother and father both tiptoed into one of the small rooms of the log house and saw their ten-year old daughter breathing hard and restlessly. Johnny put a palm to her forehead and withdrew it upon feeling the intense heat.

"Abby, she be burnin' up with fever. Ah suspect she got the Typhoid fevah."

"Doctor Brandt was here yestidy and said it warn't the cholera, but somethin' he suspects called Rheumatic Fever. He said there wasn't much to do but let her rest, use cold cloths to keep the fever down, and do a lot of prayin'. Ah sure wish we had a preacher in these parts."

"We has to do the work of the preacher oahselves, Abby. Let's kneel down and pray. Life is hard foah us, but no harder right now than for my beloved Ruthie. Dear Lawd, please, please help make her well."

Throughout the evening either Johnny or Abby maintained a bedside vigil with their ailing Ruthie. Harold came in from time to time to help with the cool compresses and would subsequently return to his book. It did not occur to the Franklin family on this difficult evening that events would transpire to create greater difficulties in their lives.

13

A SLIGHT DETOUR

The stagecoach was within less than a quarter of a mile from Copperhead. Instead of barreling into town, North stopped his horse and held up one hand indicating that Johnson should stop the coach. He saw a rider coming up to him directly, so he slowly removed the revolver from his holster and kept it handy, yet pointing downward.

"It appears we were destined to meet yet again, my friend," said the rider. It was Sammy Fivetrees.

"Sammy! How are you? We haven't seen each other in at least two years!"

"I am fine. I need to caution you, John, should you ride into Copperhead, you will not be doing well at all. A trap has been loaded specifically for you. The marshal intends to imprison or kill you." Sammy went on to explain how he stealthily roamed about town and overheard conversations from the likes of Blood Hawk, P.J. Callendar, and even some new chatterbox deputy named McAvee.

"McAvee," snorted Johnson. "Rats' casket! I shouldda known he was here. He warned us about the marshal bein' ornery and all, but said nuthin' about a trap fer John!"

"You should also know that this P.J. Callendar is a dangerous man."

Instantly, things began to add up quickly in North's mind. "What does he look like, Sammy?"

I could not see him well due to the darkness. However, I did see that he was a large man dressed in black clothing. He was giving orders to Blood Hawk. I know, because I recognized Blood Hawk's voice. I had a confrontation with him several years ago."

"What kind?" asked Johnson.

"He shot me in the side and killed two soldiers I was riding with. He told me he would let me live because he knew I would suffer with a gut wound. It would surprise him to learn that killing Sammy Fivetrees is not necessarily a simple task."

North exclaimed, "That certainly sounds like Blood Hawk. Not long ago Johnson and I rescued a Cheyenne kid who claimed Blood Hawk had staked him out for the buzzards."

"That must be Charging Buffalo. The army patrol found him not far from here. Captain Bristol loaned him a horse so he could return to his people. He sent along Private O'Toole as escort to make sure we got the horse back. The Captain seemed to trust the boy though. Maybe it is because he mentioned your name."

North smiled and said, "I take it that you and the Captain wanted to give me fair warning before we plowed onto Front Street. Thank you. Tell me, is there anything else about this marshal you can tell me?"

Sammy looked down momentarily, then stared directly at North and said, "Yes. He had a fancy looking hat. The band was made up of little reflecting mirrors."

In spite of the shadows of evening surrounding his face, everyone looking at John North could sense fire raging inside his eyeballs. There was a terrible anger incipiently smoldering in his stare. The full, bright moonlight upon it emphasized a terrible wrath waiting to be unleashed.

"My dear God," Johnson heard himself blurt out. "He's the one, isn't he? Thet marshal is the one who shot up you and yer folks!"

North held up his Colt .45 and turned the cylinder carefully checking for the presence of a bullet in every chamber. Without talking, he started to ride, but was quickly stopped by Sammy who grabbed onto the reins of his horse.

"What are you thinking, John North? Do you not know that this is what they wish? You must choose the time and place of the day of reckoning yourself. Tonight you would simply forfeit your life in vain."

"Ah think the injun makes sense, John. Don't do it. From everythin' yuh told me, it sounds like this P.J.Callendar deserves killin', but choose a better time. Besides, we got a couple of innocent passengers and this here wounded Frenchman to consider."

North grimaced and declared, "You were quick to have me spare the Frenchman too. Look, Chapeau, Blood Hawk, and their leader — you all call him Callendar — are all within my grasp. This IS the time to dispense justice! I'm going in."

"You should not," contradicted Sammy. "Should you go alone, I will have to follow. I do not want to carry out my orders, so do not make me follow."

"Your orders?"

"Bristol does not want you to get murdered — either through the gunman's ambush or a jailing and hanging the next day. He told me to turn you away. You see, Captain Bristol has already sent a telegram for assistance. He notified Major Jacobs at the fort, and Major Jacobs, in turn, returned a telegram saying that a U.S. Marshal will arrive soon. You see, there are other problems here. Our 'old friend,' the former Colonel Agee, is the mayor and Callendar's boss. We'd like to put them both out of business."

North took in a deep breath, shook his head, and muttered, "Damn! Damn! Damn it all!"

Sammy replied, "Well?"

"What you are saying appeals to my head, but not my heart. With all things considered, it is probably better to err on the side of reason. This goes against every fiber of my body and soul!"

Sammy let go of the reins of John's horse and said, "If it makes you feel any better, I have to say that my inclination was to kill Blood Hawk as soon as I found him. I wanted to do something I have not done in a long time: take a scalp."

Both Hannah and Edward had been listening to most of the conversation. Hannah stuck her head outside the coach window and said, "John, please listen to your friends. They make sense. You should wait for a federal lawman. I — I mean we — don't want you to do anything that might get you hurt."

Edward leaned out the window as well and added, "North, Hannah is right. In fact, if this thing comes to trial, I offer to represent you in court. In the meantime, I think that Hannah and me, this Johnson fellow, and this Frenchman prisoner ought to ride into town while you hide out somewhere."

"Good thinking," Sammy said. "I think I know just the place to hide out."

Reluctantly, North nodded his assent and said, "Johnson, take good care of these folks. Don't let this Callendar rope them into any affairs involving me. Try to get in touch with Captain Bristol as soon as you can. I used to work for him; I know, for certain, he is a fair and decent man. Mrs. Olson — Hannah — may God bless you and keep you safe. Thanks for the offer of help, Mr. Olson. I am leaving now, but so help me — I swear here tonight, one way or another, I won't rest until these evil men either swing from a rope or fall dead at my hand. Let's ride, Sammy."

North, feeling enormous reluctance, turned his horse and followed Sammy. Not confronting his enemies grated at him more strongly than he ever could have imagined, but he respected the judgments of both Sammy and Bristol. They were to be trusted.

Afterwards, Johnson urged his passengers to hang tight as he yelled, "Giddap," to the team and came directly onto the main street of the town. He turned to Chapeau who was gagged, and yet properly and humanely bandaged and tied down, and stated, "Well, Mr. Prisoner, you may be among friends again, but work kinda hard to remember thet ah ain't one of 'em. We'll make sure yuh get a doctor. It ought to be nice to get yah well enough for a federal marshal in the near future. If we're lucky, he'll bring a fresh, strong rope."

P.J. Callendar laughed heartily when he observed a deputy badge pinned to the shirt of Blood Hawk. One of the two other men also standing outside the marshal's office laughed as well. Blood Hawk did not say a word, but quickly turned to the man with the large mustache and whiskers and struck him down with his rifle.

"The unworthy do not laugh at Blood Hawk. You are sub-human."

Wesley helped the victim, Krautmueller, to his feet. He advised, "Ol' Blood Hawk here and the marshal go way back. You might say that Blood Hawk may have invited him to laugh. Notice I refrained from humorous expression."

"Ach du Himmel! Du ist ein Schweinhun! Such — how ist it du say, "Barbarians! One day people of Deutschland vill show how superior we are!"

"Ah tell you what, German-boy, go ahead and pray to Thor, or Odin, or whatevuh mythological bein' yuh like, but tonight ah would say thet ah'm the superior one. Aftah all, ah'm the one payin' foah the work. If you can't work with us, then run off and get a beer. If you do that though, ah may have to take issue with you in an uncomfortable manner." Callendar then turned his attention away to look up the street and ignored Krautmueller's muttered indignation.

"There it comes. Not far now. Hey, what's thet kid doin' in the street?" Without another remark, Callendar dashed up the street and grabbed a nine-year old boy under the arms, lifted him, and quickly set him down on the boardwalk.

"Hey thar, son, don't yuh think yuh oughta be home with yer ma and pa gettin' suppuh? C'mon, give an answer."

"Ye-yes, Mr. Marshal. I was playin' and lost track o' the time."

"What were yuh playin', kid?"

"Me and Tommy were playin' shootout. I was Wild Bill Hickock and he was Jesse James. Next time he says he wants to be Marshal Hickock."

Callendar laughed, squatted down next to the child, and said, "Don't listen to Tommy. It's better bein' the marshal. Yuh get to sleep in clean sheets, get paid regularly, and can receive moah respect. What's yoah name?"

"Randall."

"Randall, ah think yuh better scoot to home. Things ah gonna get a little reckless out here tonight, and yer ma may not like it if yuh accidentally get hurt. Go on now, skedaddle!"

"Why do you take the time to speak with a brat?" asked McAvee. "I woulda just told him to get lost or I'd whup him!"

"That's because yer a Philistine and a brute. Children ah the future — haven't yuh heard? Imbecilic adults are the problem. Just look in the mirror, yuh'll see what ah mean."

Callendar, Wesley, and even a wary Krautmueller laughed; only Blood Hawk expressed no emotion, as his eyes were riveted on the incoming stagecoach.

From the other side of town, someone else arrived. Kirk Mason came in and noticed Callendar from the distance along with the other men. He went inside the store and walked upstairs to his residence.

Most of the townspeople had either settled down for supper or simply turned in for the night. Several, including Dr. Brandt, were aware that the stagecoach had not arrived as scheduled, so he anticipated some sort of ruckus would enfold that evening. Seeing the gathering of the marshal along with a collection of dubious looking new assistants emboldened such speculation markedly.

As the stage pulled in Deputy Wesley authoritatively strode up the center of the dirt street. He waved his scattergun in the air signaling the coach driver to stop. Elijah Johnson had seen the lawman and planned to stop, and he felt prepared to deal with a litany of questions. This authority did not resemble Callendar — he did not have the mirrors hatband, and he looked below average in height. From the left, he observed a bigger, silver-haired man in a business suit step out of a café. He was accompanied by Blood Hawk! Johnson thought about reaching for his sidearm, but he noticed now that the silver-haired man, Blood Hawk, the deputy, plus two other fellows flashing badges were also brandishing weapons. Son of a wolf mutt! One of them was Nate McAvee! He wondered what possessed that rascal to throw in with this bunch?

The silver-haired man did the talking. "Are you John North?"

"He ain't here. Why yah askin'?"

"That man next to you looks injured! Why is he tied up?"

"Simple. He and that heathen standin' next tuh yah tried to rob this stagecoach today, so me and another feller put some lead in him. We woulda done the same to that scoundrel at your shoulder only he took off like a jack rabbit when he saw us comin'."

"You lie, you dirty old creature," Blood Hawk admonished. "Me and Chapeau came to assist you. We heard that the guard was actually trying to rob the stage. It appears that one of you killed Smythe and mistakenly shot poor Chapeau."

"First off, you in the city duds, are yuh some town official?"

"I should think so. I am the mayor of Copperhead, Mortimer Agee. I am here representing Marshal Callendar who is otherwise occupied. Who are you? And you had better have an explanation of what happened. The regular driver is obviously absent, and it is suspicious that one such as you is driving the stagecoach. Are there passengers?"

Wesley opened the stagecoach door and ordered Mr. and Mrs. Olson and Foster to step outside.

Instantly, Hannah spoke. "Mr. Agee, we can vouch for Mr. Johnson. He is a wonderful man to whom we are indebted. He and another gentleman saved us from the prisoner, and — Ohhh!" Upon seeing Blood Hawk, Hannah found it difficult to catch her breath, but she pointed and managed to cry out, "Him! That is the other man who tried to rob us!"

Agee turned to look at Blood Hawk, but he had sprinted and caused all eyes to follow him as he fled. Foster then spoke, "Yes. The lady is correct. That man — the Indian — was the other holdup man who stopped us. He and this Frenchman were in cahoots with Smythe. In fact, I think it was the Indian who murdered the driver, Shelley. We brought his body back."

Wesley almost mockingly ran in the vicinity where Blood Hawk had flown, but clearly, everyone observed that the effort was half-hearted. McAvee helped Johnson pull Chapeau off the stagecoach. As they untied the gag, Chapeau was about to spew invective, but the presence of someone altered the focus.

"May I be of assistance here?" It was Dr. Brandt.

Edward spoke next. "Mr. Mayor, I am so relieved to see you and the other legal officials here tonight. Suffice it to say, my dear wife and I have been through a terrible ordeal, and we would like to find a hotel bed and get some rest."

"Who are you?"

"Edward Olson, Attorney at Law. Here is my card."

"It's too dark to read, but I'll take your word for it. I used to be an Army Colonel, so I can read people fairly well. As for this Blood Hawk character, he was sent here by the marshal. I suspect he didn't know him as well as he thought. I suppose you, too, can verify that he and this wounded man were responsible for the attempted holdup?"

"Definitely. As for myself, I was not convinced that this man Johnson, or the other one, John North, needed to perpetrate violence against these men. North, I can tell you, was the one who slaughtered that Smythe person."

"Edward!"

"Be still, woman. Also, you should know that this John North was accompanying us until some Indian Scout stopped our coach and warned him not to come into town. The scout seemed to be quite frightened of your marshal, a Mr. Callendar?"

"At yoah service, sir." Callendar stepped out of the shadows holding his dragoon colt in one hand, and a colt .44 in the other. Hannah saw that the man's gaze turned to her, and it became uncomfortably evident he was sizing her up carnally. She remembered what John had said about this man, and her abdomen felt cramping.

"Good evenin', ma'am. What a delightful lookin' lady. Is this Mrs. Olson?"

"Yes, she is my wife, and you are Callendar?"

"Ah find it more neighborly if you precede muh surname with eithuh Marshal, or Mistuh. Also, I think the lady might want to speak foah herself."

"Th-that's all right. I let my husband speak for me when I'm in a strange situation."

"Ha-ha-ha! Ah have heard Copperhead, and me in particular, referred to by many colorful metaphors, but nevah as paht of a strange situation. You ah chahmin' indeed."

Urging Edward to find them a room, Hannah briskly walked away from the scene with Edward. While still within earshot, she turned and cried out, "Thank you again, Mr. Johnson — and good evening."

"Good evenin', fine lady!" Johnson looked somewhat wistfully at the beautiful lady walking toward the two-story hotel building nearly one block away. "What a waste," he mused. "Such a special woman wed to an annoying blue jay."

The marshal approached Johnson. "Judgin' by yoah accent, ah get the feelin' ah'm speakin' with a fellow southerner. Welcome to Copperhead. Ah you from Mississippi?"

"That I am. And you?"

"Originally, muh roots were in Perdition, Mississippi, but I later ended up in Abilene and many pahts of Texas. Howevah, I have been all ovah the west doin' all sorts of jobs."

Like murdering innocent folks traveling west in wagons, Johnson thought. No, this is not the time and place. I will not pick a fight with this devil tonight.

"It pains me to treat a fellow southerner so shabbily, but until we get things straightened out, ah think yoah accommodations foah the evenin' have been established."

"Yer throwin' me in the hoosegow? What'd ah do wrong?"

"Nothin', *yet*. If yuh refuse muh hospitality, then we can talk a great deal 'bout what you did wrong. One thing is evident: you, this othuh stagecoach passenger, and the lady seemed mighty reluctant to engage in talk about Mistuh North. Only the pettifoggin' lawyah seemed eager like to talk 'bout him. It came to my attention that Mr. North was intendin' to hahm me personally. Is that true?"

Elijah stood silently until McAvee struck him with the back of his hand.

"McAvee, you double crossin' polecate!"

"The two of you seem to know each othuh. Good. Maybe you can tell me moah about Mr. Johnson and Mr. North, McAvee."

As McAvee smirked and parted his lips to speak, Johnson abruptly threw a left uppercut connecting beneath the novice deputy's jaw. He literally rose from the ground and landed hard on his back. He was knocked out cold. The marshal smiled almost approvingly, then quickly struck Johnson across the face with the dragoon colt. He subsequently asked the German and the mayor to carry Johnson to the jail cell. Everyone let McAvee lie in the street until he either died or woke up.

Sammy and North approached a secluded log cabin near a narrow stream. There was a solidly built wooden fence that provided a pen for a group of pigs, chickens, and, separated from the other animals, about six horses. As the two riders dismounted, a man stepped out of the cabin holding a rifle. It was Johnny Franklin.

"Izzat you, Mr. Fivetrees? Yeah, ah believe it is. Ah see yuh didn't have trouble findin' muh spread, but how come ya out ridin' so late?"

"Johnny Franklin, this is John North. We are friends who have done hazardous work together and would shed our lives for one another. When you said you owed me for helping you, I figured you were sincere. I have come to cash in that debt. My friend needs a place to stay for a while."

"Ah don't know — that marshal wouldn't like it if ah was to give refuge to some fugitive. Ah you a fugitive?"

"No. I have done nothing illegal. That is more than I can say for your marshal. He wants me dead because I want him dead."

"We got a problem here, Fivetrees. Muh little Ruthie is awful sick, and we ah gettin' terribly worried. Her fever is so high, we fear she got Typhoid or somethin' worse."

"May I see her?" suggested North. "I fought in the war, and I saw a lot of men hurting from battle and disease. I might know what it is."

Guardedly, Johnny let North into the cabin where he was quickly introduced to Harold and a teary-eyed Abby. He looked down at little Ruthie. North observed that the breathing was labored. He listened to her chest. The heartbeat was solid, but the presence of chest fluids appeared obvious. Her forehead burned to the touch. He held the kerosene lamp close and had Abby open the girl's mouth so he could look inside and down her throat as best as he could under the circumstances. The tissues appeared inflamed, but the tonsils were not grossly swollen. The girl was wearing a nightgown and covered with a wool blanket.

"I've seen Typpoid before, and that's not her malady. Abby, did she complain about a lot of pains in elbows, knees, and muscles?" Abby and Johnny nodded.

"I'd bet a month of my old federal army salary that she has the ague, or the flu as many call it. Her problem seems to be the high fever. You need to keep the heavy blanket off her, and we should strip off the clothing for now and dunk her in a tub of cold water."

"Strip her?" Abby seemed at first horrified but then amazingly wizened. She urged Johnny to pull out the big, wooden washtub they used as a bathtub. North, Johnny, Fivetrees, and Harold all took buckets and pans, filled them with creek water, and started filling up the tub. When there was a sufficient level, Johnny and John carefully lifted the sickly, naked form of the little girl and dipped her into the ice-cold water. The shock of the chilly water awoke her and set her off into a round of screaming and coughing. The anguished mother held out a blanket as they removed Ruthie from the water so she could be dried and protected from prolonged temperature reduction.

North compelled the family to do this two more times within the next hour. Soon, Ruthie's temperature seemed to drop and stabilize. When the sun rose, she seemed alert and said, "Mommy, I'm hungry."

"Mistuh North, ah don't know you from Adam," exclaimed Johnny, "but because you helped save muh little girl I'm now beholdin' to you too."

"Please don't feel that way, Mr. Franklin. I used to have a little brother once, and…" without warning, North's eyes suddenly filled with tears, and his voice sounded choked up. He wanted to say something, but Johnny saw that this man was engaged in too much personal anguish to say anymore. Johnny had endured a lot of personal anguish in his life, and he was more receptive to unsaid pain than most of us could ever imagine.

After North composed himself, Sammy stood before him and said, "It is time for me to leave. I must return to Captain Bristol and the others. There will be tension when I return to town, but I will avoid seeing the Marshal at least until I regroup with the Captain and the other soldiers. One, or many of us, will return here in a few days. We shall let you know when the federal authorities arrive to deal with the criminal authorities. Until then, goodbye my friends."

"Let us not say goodbye, Sammy. My God go with you and let us hope that we will meet again under more pleasant circumstances."

Sammy and the Franklins also bid each other farewell. After he left, everyone thought it a great idea to get a couple hours of sleep. Of course, the chickens, pigs, horses, and cow had to be fed first. North had not fed livestock in a long time, but he volunteered to help and ended up enjoying every minute of the duty.

14

DREAMS AND REFLECTIONS

Hannah had slept surprisingly well in the hotel bed. In a sense, this was a little surprising since she had shared the bed with the husband she had steadily come to loathe. During the night, her dreams were mostly glorious. There was the dream of her beloved father carving the Thanksgiving turkey and telling his joke about the wild turkey that laughed at him during the chase. It was one of her precious childhood memories. Another dream involved being reunited with her mother in Fortune River. She did not know what Fortune River looked like, but when she arrived — oddly, without Edward — she was greeted by her mother's radiant smile, her uncle kissing her on the cheek, and both of them making her run over to the river that was loaded up with bars of gold. A fortunate river indeed.

Lastly, there was that one dream she dared not remember. It involved a forbidden desire. She dreamt she was in John North's arms. He strongly, yet tenderly drew her up against him and softly kissed her on the lips, cheeks, and eyelashes. He went on to place tiny kisses on the back of her neck and began to unbutton her dress. Soon, she was naked, and he was also undressed. He carried her over to the hotel bed, gently placed her down, and then made passionate love to her. The dream was exquisite, and it was one that she wanted to continue. Unfortunately, during their lovemaking she heard the snarling sound of a great cat. Its breathy growl grew louder and closer. John seemed to ignore it even as Hannah pictured herself becoming intensely disturbed. Finally, the growl turned into an ugly roar, and John was harshly cast aside by ripping claws! It was a horrific beast with long, sharp talons, blood-red eyes, and pointed fangs. It was filled with hateful rage, and it possessed the face of Edward!

Such a beautiful dream turned into one of her worst nightmares. When she awoke, panting and puffing, she still heard the growl. Turning to her side she realized that the growling really was occurring. It was the aggravating snoring of Edward.

Nothing had changed. She was still married to Edward and she wished she were not. She thought about John North and smiled. She could not help herself. It was adultery she was committing in her mind and heart, but she knew she was falling in love with John.

John North only slept about three hours. When he awoke, the rest of the family, except for Ruthie, was already up doing several chores. He heard the chopping of wood outside, so he sat up and decided he had better help. He observed Abby through the bedroom doorway inside the kitchen flattening bread dough with a rolling pin. He considered how lucky Johnny was to have such a devoted and loving wife. His thoughts turned to Hannah. Hannah brought him an inner peace he had not felt in ages.

In his mind's eye he pictured her soft eyes, sweet smile, and gentle motion as she walked. She appeared to be a living embodiment of artistic treasure. Such a woman was made to be adored and cherished. It angered him that her husband spoke to her so rudely and unfairly. How could a man be blind to such perfection? Was he a fool, or just an evil worm? Hannah was special. Married or not, John North decided he and Hannah would one day be together as man and wife. He felt it deep within his eternal soul.

Elijah Johnson did not have a restful night. He woke up tied to a wall post in the jail. His back was stinging severely. All through the night, Callendar or one of his henchmen deputies took turns ripping at his back with a bullwhip. They demanded to know where John North was hiding. They said they would stop if he would tell them. At first, he would not say anything. He only screamed as the pain intensified. Then Blood Hawk showed up. Right. He was the one they were going to chase after. All show from a totally corrupt bunch of town officials. He simply ran away to escape the questioning. Callendar knew he was in the marshal's office. So did the silver-haired mayor. The mayor was even there when Blood Hawk did the dirty work. He was there when that damnable sadist took the hammer and drove the nail through Johnson's left hand. Johnson could not see the hand. It was now tied with the other one behind the post. The blood had run down his backside. He felt the soaking of the liquid. It was morning, but he was not sure if he would survive the day. This was comparable to his worst days in the war.

Through his bleary eyes, he thought he made out the image of the black-shirted, tall, inappropriately grinning, self-assured P.J. Callendar walking toward him carrying a cup.

"Mistuh Johnson, you look just like buffalo dung. Ah'll bet yuh would like a cup of water right about now."

"If-if it's not...much trouble, pl-lease."

Callendar lifted the cup to Johnson's lips and allowed him to gulp down a couple of sips. He motioned for Wesley to untie the man's hands and help take him into a jail cell. Johnson felt the pressure subside from his wrists, but as Wesley made him move, he felt the throbbing pain in his hand and the unbearable stings on his back intensify.

"For the sake of God, Mr. Callendar, can't we get him a doctor?"

"Well, he did finally say that North took off for Fortune River or west of there, so we did break his spirit. Ah think we oughta show him that we are capable of exhibitin' humanity in this community and get him the proper help. Go fetch Doc Brandt."

Doctor Brandt was in the café eating breakfast with Kirk and Roberta Mason. They were not particularly relaxed, or for that matter, evidently very hungry for their pancakes and bacon. The doctor was intently listening to Kirk talk about the latest problems with their illustrious mayor and police officials.

"To be honest with you, Kirk, I am not sure what to do. That army captain and his detail rode out of here just before daybreak. I wished they would have remained. I wanted to tell them a thing or two. Do you think they know what has been going on?"

"I know they do. That Captain Bristol confided in me that a telegram had been sent asking for a federal marshal and a circuit judge to come in and deal with the likes of the Frenchman, Callendar, and even Agee. We better not speak very loudly though — these walls may have ears."

Dr. Brandt nibbled his bacon and asked, "So they know, but why did they pull out?"

"Neither the captain or the Indian scout would say. They simply said that North was in a safe place, and they and North would return in a matter of days. They said they had to return to their fort due to some sort of Cheyenne uprising."

"Great. Now we have to worry about Indian attacks again."

"We don't know that," said Roberta. "We have not had difficulties with the Cheyenne people since the late sixties. We never go to their land, and they stay away from ours. Who knows what the army has to do these days?"

"I guess you're right. Wait! Quit talking. Here comes Deputy Wesley." Dr. Brandt resumed his gnawing of the overcooked bacon and blankly stared at the cheap painting of a riverboat on the wall.

"Doc! Come on. You're needed at the jail. Someone needs yer help."

"Is it the Frenchman again? The pills I gave him should have knocked him out for a day."

"It's not him. It's that stagecoach driver. Better come now. Ask your questions there."

After the two men left the café, Roberta turned to her husband and asked, "That man they call Chapeau — how did things work out for him? Will he live?"

"Doctor Brandt pulled out the bullet from the man's leg. The wound was in the flesh, so the Doc said he got it cleaned out really well. However, there was a pretty bad arm wound. The bullet in that limb had shattered the bone. Some gangrene was starting up, so the doctor amputated the arm close to the shoulder. If that rogue gets properly tried and convicted, then he'll be the first one-armed villain I ever saw hanged."

"If he gets tried, you mean."

Kirk thought about the unfair treatment suffered by citizens like Johnny Franklin and others in his community. He shoveled another bite of hotcakes into his mouth and mumbled, "It's a wonder any of us can get sleep around here. There's always something foul in the air in Copperhead."

15

ALTERED JOURNEY

Charging Buffalo resented the escort back to his land ordered by the army captain. In his mind, it was sufficient to borrow the army horse and return it at a later time. It was more pressing to use this horse as a means of finding Blood Hawk and destroying him. This white soldier riding with him was not only an insult to his honor but also an annoying distraction to his mission.

The escort, Private O'Toole, did not seem disagreeable, but exhibited little indication of an intentional friendliness. There was an inchoate hostility or anger in the man's eyes, and in Charging Buffalo's judgment it still seemed unclear that it generated from dislike of the assignment or the company he had been commanded to keep. Finally, when they camped for the evening, O'Toole revealed some inner character.

"Listen to me, lad, there is nothin' 'bout you ah yer folk ah got a thin agin. Twas from Arland I hael, 'n many uvus could nuh ford a loaf, or sack o' grain fer that matter. I guess ye Cheyenne folk taint too prosprus these days ayther. I must tell ya lad, I feel none too safe bein' the only soljur headin' inta these parts. I wantcha unnerstan', I'm feelin' plenty rattled ridin' out this way. I only wanna get ye close tuh yer land, so I can leave with my horse an' the one we loaned ye fer ridin' here. How much further?"

Charging Buffalo realized that the soldier was probably more apprehensive than hateful, but sincerely understood the motivation. "You talk about this land, Arland — or is it Ireland, that's what the teacher used to say — was it better than this land to you?"

"Yes and no. Here I get the opportunity to earn a wage and get some meals. Back home, its darlin' lovely, mind you, but the famine made it clear to me folk we had to migrate somewhar else. We came here in fifty-three, but mooder an' dah is long daid I'm afraid, Lord bless 'em."

Charging Buffalo threw some large sticks on the fire. O'Toole insisted on maintaining the fire as unwise as it might seem. Still, since it was there, he would enjoy it too. "Soldier, you barely speak and speak almost in a way I hardly understand. I think you miss this Ireland and don't see much of anything like it the closer we get to Cheyenne country. You may relax. After about three hours ride tomorrow, you may turn around with your horse. In any event, as long as you are in my company, the Cheyenne people will not harm you. Besides, when I leave your horse, it will be outside Cheyenne territory. You need not be afraid."

O'Toole scowled. "'Taint right to say I be scared. I never run away from a scrape. I just figger you an' yer gang got me vastly outnumbered. In any event, I find it pleasin' that you boys don't plan to lift me scalp anytime soon."

Charging Buffalo saw that this fellow had some semblance of humor and in some ways also felt out of place with the powers and people trying to determine the direction of the tide in this country. He felt emboldened, so he spoke what was on his mind. "Soldier O'Toole, I offer you a different plan. Let me borrow this horse. I will pay you for it later. I give you my word as a human being."

"The Captain warned me you might change your mind the closer we came to yer folk. Can't do it, lad; I gave me word. The horse is government property. I know you have this mission to find this Bloody Pheasant — or wa-tever ye call 'im. You are young, an' like most of th' young, ya must larn to be patient."

No more was said that evening. In the morning, the two broke camp and began the three hour ride previously discussed. Charging Buffalo thought about Captain Bristol trusting him enough to ride a horse with only one army man as escort and realized that perhaps he had been somewhat rash. It was certainly better to be borrowing a horse than stealing one and end up getting hanged by these people. Back in Cheyenne country he would obtain his own horse, and the hunt for Blood Hawk would resume.

He glanced at O'Toole after the soldier abruptly stopped riding. He noticed the man looked troubled and concerned. Charging Buffalo then looked to the west where he was staring and identified the cause of his concern. There was a huge thatch of wild grass and there appeared to be something moving inside. Just as he was going to suggest they head toward cover, there was a dull "thud" sound and a small volume of red liquid spraying from O'Toole's chest. This hideous sight was accompanied by the report of a rifle. O'Toole bent forward, clutched at his wound, looked around in amazement and pain, then slipped off his mount onto the dirt. He was dead.

"Stay put, injun," cried a voice from the tall grass. "Don't move or surely ah will put yuh down as well." Charging Buffalo quickly deduced that the attacker would have killed him as well had he so desired such an outcome. Instead, the person gradually walked out of the grass and calmly and perpetually walked toward him. As the form of the man drew closer, Charging Buffalo felt he was a magnet and the figure was a magnetic inevitability of death personified.

"Ah was only aimin' tuh kill one o' you boys, an' you won the luck of the draw, injin. Besides, ah know ah'm near Cheyenne country, so ah don't want to rile up Cheyenne injins. All ah want is a horse. Too bad that soljuh's hoss run off, 'cause tha's the one you all has to find. Ah need the steed you are ridin', son."

Charging Buffalo stepped down from the horse. He looked closely at the man as he approached. He was lean, fairly dirty and unkempt, and had very long, yellowish brown hair. He wore pants with suspenders, but no shirt. He had the shirt of what those white people called union suits underneath the suspenders and it was considerably grimy and smelly. There was a mole on his upper lip. The worst feature of all was the man's teeth. He smiled as he took the reins away from Charging Buffalo and revealed horribly brown, diseased teeth damaged from years and years of tobacco chewing. Why the white man chewed that disgusting material was a mystery to the Cheyenne.

"You did not need to kill the soldier, stranger. If you wanted to use a horse as far as Copperhead, he probably would have let you ride it. He was going back to that town."

"Wall, it sure weren't his lucky day then, was it? As it works out, ah am headin' in that direction. Since yer an injin, obviously headin' to Cheyenne country, ah'm assumin' ah don't hafta worry none 'bout you tellin' the army who done this. Anyway, like ah sez, ah don't wanna rile up the Cheyenne. Ah don't care 'bout the ahmy, them's a bunch a Yankee dogs anyway. As it is, red man, ah am headin' for Copperhead. Ah'm lookin' for some folk ah know there. Let's hope we nevah meet up again, son. Should we do that, ah will natcherly blow yer head off the shoulders. Goodbye."

Without another comment or look, the long-haired murderer galloped in the direction of Copperhead. Charging Buffalo looked down at the dead soldier. Under different circumstances, he possibly would have been his enemy. He did not want to care about the death of this person, but the killing seemed so senseless. He thought again about the deaths of his own people at the hands of Blood Hawk. Their deaths were also unnecessary. Would anyone want to avenge the death of this one called O'Toole? Certainly, the army captain would be angry.

Charging Buffalo stooped and searched through O'Toole's pockets. He found a wallet containing a photograph. There was a picture showing O'Toole as a very young man standing next to an elderly man with bushy hair who was not smiling and a pleasant looking woman who was smiling. He surmised these were the parents. Since he said they were dead, O'Toole's spirit might join them. The Christian missionary always said a prayer should be said for the Christians who died. There was a cross around the neck of O'Toole. Other than the picture of the dead parents, there was no one he could tell about O'Toole's death. Would only the army men mourn for O'Toole?

Charging Buffalo had never accepted the missionary's Christian ways, but he felt he understood them. He understood now that someone should say something for O'Toole.

"Lord — You to whom the white men respect and pray to — I pray to You now for this man, O'Toole. I do not know him, but I got to know him a little. I am sorry he is dead and sorry he had to die the way he did. It was not necessary. I hope that You can accept him and help him find peace, now that he is with the spirits." Charging Buffalo swallowed, paused to think if there should be more to say, then added, "That is all I feel I must say. Thank you, Jesus, Lord of this man."

Charging Buffalo heard a noise, turned, and saw that O'Toole's horse was slowly trotting toward him. Its snout bent forward and sniffed at O'Toole briefly, raised its head and somewhat mechanically gnashed its teeth, and then walked forward a few steps and grazed. Charging Buffalo cautiously patted the horse, then slowly put a foot in the stirrup and pulled himself onto the horse. It pulled back a bit startled but did not appear overly nervous about the new rider. Charging Buffalo patted him on the neck, uttered a few soothing words, and began to ride. As he rode, he thought to himself, "This white man's God apparently listens to prayers. As soon as I spoke to Him, He sent the horse. For that, I say to Him — I am very, very grateful."

Charging Buffalo concluded it was altogether appropriate he should go to Copperhead.

The long-haired killer galloped for a while but knew enough about horses to consider that sustained heavy riding would only exhaust the beast. He located a stream and let the animal rest and drink its fill of water. He wondered if the Indian might recover the other horse and follow him, but thought it unlikely. Just to be on the safe side, he regularly looked around to see if such a thing might be possible. So far, he was a no show.

The killer strongly felt he had to go to Copperhead. He knew that his old "boss" was now the respectable marshal of that unfortunate town and based upon past experiences was a likely source for a job. He had to be — there were no more options. In Fargo, he nearly got hanged. Luckily, that guard got careless so he got overpowered, and the escape was possible. The stagecoach robbery near Rustwater gave him some hell raisin' money for about a year or so. All those other towns increasingly became more and more inhospitable, so it was time to move west. Wyoming Terrritory still had some options. Wilderness, lawless towns, some old friends — yes, this just might be the ticket.

"Ah wonder how good a sweet deal ol' Callendar is runnin' in Copperhead? Ah wonder if much othuh old buddies are workin' there or not?" He thought about the gambler, Chapeau, buckskin clad Jake Baker, and remorseless Blood Hawk. Yessir, it'd be somethin' to see the ol' gang again. Maybe some other old acquaintances might be in the neighborhood too!

Dr. Brandt attempted to cleanse and bandage the wounds on Johnson's back as best as he could. As for the mutilated hand, he treated it with some boric acid and iodine, but worried about subsequent blood poisoning. The brutality in this town was monstrous, and he was quite ill from it.

"I patched you up as best as I could, Mr. Johnson. The pill I gave you will help you sleep on this bed in the jail cell."

"Thanks, doctuh. Truth of the matter though, it don't matter much. As far as ah'm concerned, ah ain't got much kin to fret about me, and I wouldn't want any friends to get in danger on muh account. Maybe it'd be better if I just moved on."

"Don't talk so. It's the medicine making you feel despondent. You'll be better with hours of rest." Dr. Brandt hoped his homily might be valid, but he was not certain.

16

RECONSIDERATIONS

John North forcefully drove the sharp axe into the circular chunk of wood situated on the block. The piece shattered and splinters flew briskly in numerous directions. He subsequently grabbed another round and repeated the process. His host, Johnny, had begun the task, but North had insisted on assuming the labor to free him up to attend to gardening responsibilities. Already, the stack of firewood had substantially increased, and Abby noticed the growth in supply as she walked outside with a cool pitcher of apple cider.

"Mistuh North, you been doin' awful well with that axe this mornin'. I insist you stop long enough foh somma dem apple squeezins I stirred up."

"You are not only kind, but prophetic! I was just thinking about drinking something refreshing." John sat down on the chopping block as Abby poured him a glass of the liquid. He suddenly felt self-conscious about sitting in front of a lady devoid of his shirt but was quickly put at ease when Abby seemed to read his thoughts again.

"Nevah mind 'bout sittin' there half dressed in front 'a me, Mr. North. Ah seen just about everythin' there is to see on men folk, and then some. Ya gotta work with your shirt off in these parts in July. You'd faint dead away if ya didn't."

John grinned, then took a large gulp of apple cider. It was cool, sweet yet not to excess, and utterly refreshing. "This is nectar from heaven. I am much obliged."

"Who is dat girl you was talkin' 'bout last night?"

Startled, John nearly choked on the next sip of cider and replied, "T-talked about?"

"Surely, somebody musta told yuh 'bout the talkin' yuh do it your sleep? Yuh muttered half the night how much yuh cared about some gal named Hannah."

"I apologize if I kept you and your family awake. I had no idea I ever did sleep talkin'."

"Well?" she replied and playfully smiled.

"I think I am in love with the young woman we rescued aboard the stagecoach yesterday. There is only one problem: she's married to the lawyer she was riding with."

"Does it look like she loves her man?"

Feeling uncomfortable, yet somehow willingly conversant in this discussion, he said, "Oddly enough, I have generally been fairly good at reading people. I know when someone is lying, attempting to spare someone's feelings, or whether or not they are fond of someone. In Hannah's case, I think she despises this fellow. After getting to know him in less than five minutes I began to despise him!"

"That doesn't ansuh muh question," Abby asked as she refilled his glass.

"My head tells me she wants to stay true to her husband. My heart says she wants to run away and ask me to take her along. Worst of all, my heart tells me I may one day find it necessary to shoot her husband."

"You is a pack o' trouble, North!" Johnny exclaimed this judgment as he walked stooped over carrying a heavy basket of apples.

"Johnny, don't be judgin' this man too hard — you ain't properly familiar with all his history."

He put down the basket, stared into North's eyes, and said, "Ah ain't arguin' whethuh o' not he's had a rough life o' not. Lots of us has had rough lives. Bein' some bastahd's slave is 'bout as hahd as it can get! What ah'm sayin' is that we ah just poah folk tryin' to work our land, get some crops, raise some chickens and pigs so we has enough food to eat, and help our youngin's grow up an' have a better life. We don't need anyone else's troubles."

Abby was about to speak, but Johnny gave her a stern look. She nodded her head in silence, then abruptly turned and walked into the house. North put on his shirt, glanced at Abbie's departure, then fixed his attention on a patient, resolute Johnny.

"You helped me make an important decision, Mr. Franklin. I need to leave and leave right away. Thank you for the refuge and hospitality. I am indebted to you."

"'Taint necessary to leave with bad feelin's, North. Ah am keepin' my promise to Sammy. You don't has to leave right now, just soon!"

North smiled, almost authoritatively placed his right hand on Johnny's shoulder, and remarked, "Consider the debt paid. When I see Sammy again, he will understand. Besides, I do not want to endanger you and your lovely family either directly or indirectly. These wretched people after me are the spawn of Lucifer himself, and before they harm you or anyone else, I mean to deal with them."

"Deal with 'em?"

Pausing, North put on his hat, inhaled, and promulgated, "Putting it plainly, I mean to make them dead. Please give my regards to Abby and your kids. I'm delighted that your little girl's fever is gone. Tell the boy to keep reading those books. Knowledge will help him better than anything save the Almighty. Some day if I am fortunate, I might be blessed to have half of what you have, Franklin."

By the time John North's horse was saddled and he was ready to ride, dark clouds gathered in the sky. A cool wind was starting up, and all signs were pointing to heavy rainfall.

"Best you find shelter durin' the storm, John North," cried Abby. "Wish yuh'd stay here at least 'til the rain stops."

"Thanks, but I better leave. I have a poncho to help skid off the rain. Look at it this way: heavy rain will make it harder for those boys to track me."

Johnny did not say a word as North rode off. Young Harold energetically waved to North. He wished he had had the opportunity to talk with Mr. North about his schooling and especially his time in the Civil War. Did he serve under General Grant? Were all the rebels a hateful bunch? Did he go to college after the war? Harold did not get to ask any of these questions. All Pa wanted him to do was feed pigs and chickens, dig up weeds, and milk the damned cow. A rotten life this was, he concluded.

North thought about the friendly interrogation about him and Hannah. Abby had made him think about his moral dilemma. She offered no answers but forced him to introspectively search for how he must confront this situation concerning an unavailable woman he most assuredly loved and adored. He would do anything for Hannah whether it involved leaving her forever or killing Edward at the drop of a hat. Right now, it was up to her.

In the Copperhead Hotel room, Hannah looked at her image in the mirror. She knew her life was owed to the handsome man, John North. Upon meeting him, there was electricity crackling through the dry Wyoming air that bound them more strongly than any sensation she had ever experienced. Long before she met John, she had decided the marriage to Edward was a mistake. How to undo the mistake was a solution indescribably elusive.

Edward had left the room hours ago and had prohibited her from venturing out into the town. She was weary of his prohibitions, scoldings, beatings, and all other reactions to her life. Her trip west was now only a means to reunite with her mother in Fortune River, except for this sudden magic between her and John. Would John return to her? What would he do about Edward? Instinctively, she knew he was a decent man, how could he approach, let alone spirit off with, a married woman?

Hannah refused to wear her hat. She left the hotel lobby and walked down to the café and entered alone. There were a few married couples inside. It was lunchtime. Several men, unaccompanied by female companions, rudely ogled her as she stepped up to an empty table and sat down. While considering the possibility that some of these unsophisticated citizens might approach her, she saw the man introduced to her last night as Dr. Brandt get up from his own table and walk toward her.

"Mrs. Olson, may I sit?"

Hannah smiled, and the doctor sat across from her.

"I regret to say that the stage driver who brought you into Copperhead last night has been sorely treated by our marshal and the scoundrels in his employ. He was bull-whipped and severely injured."

Hannah insisted on the definition of "severely injured," and since Dr. Brandt usually was not one to mince words, he imparted the definition as the description of a man who had just suffered a spike being driven through his left hand so brutally that the possibility of permanent disability was likely.

"Barbarians!"

"I regret describing such cruelty, but from conversations I overhead, I had the impression Mr. Johnson was a good friend of this Mr. North everyone keeps looking for. Sammy Fivetrees had told me the other day that one of his best friends was a Mr. North, so I am guessing they are one and the same. Should there be any way that Mr. North might come here and take his friend out of this hell-on-earth, I would strongly advise it."

Edward suddenly walked up to the table and scowled at Dr. Brandt.

"Edward, I didn't see you in here," an alarmed Hannah cried.

"Of course you didn't. I do have some powers of stealth a female such as yourself would naturally lack."

Brandt looked uneasy, then got up to leave. "Excuse me, folks."

"Stay put, Brandt. I heard enough of your conversation. You are meddling in affairs none of your concern. This John North you seem so willing to chat about is a rake and a villain. He killed one and wounded another before our eyes. He should be caught and lynched. I intend to defend the poor maimed and maligned Mr. Chapeau in court."

Sitting with his back turned to Hannah and the two men was the other passenger who had accompanied them on the stagecoach, Abel Foster. He suddenly rose from his chair.

"You, sir, are not a lawyer, but a LI-AR! You disgust me beyond shame!"

Startled by all the commotion, one man exclaimed, "Hey! You men better not raise a commotion in this town! Our marshal doesn't tolerate fighting."

Foster ignored the man. He glared at Edward and stated, "I watched you belittle and abuse this poor woman during our stagecoach ride. I've been married for eighteen years and I never spoke one foul word in those years as often as you did in ten minutes. You do not deserve to have such a wonderful woman as a wife. In addition, if it weren't for Mr. North and Mr. Johnson, it is probable that all three of us would be dead."

Lighting in the room grew dimmer. There was a broad shadow of clouds blocking out much of the sunlight. Without warning, a loud crash of thunder was heard. A large bolt of lightning was evident in the distance followed by more thunder.

Without replying, Edward stepped forward and seemed ready to strike the man. Before acting, a harsh female voice assaulted his ears. "For the love of God in heaven, what kind of man are you? The lady is your wife, and no civilized man would dare to publicly treat his wife so shabbily in public! Stop this meanness, or so help me, I will knock you to the ground myself!" It was Roberta Mason, the store keeper's wife, and she was standing protectively in front of Hannah. Moving close to the two women was Kirk Mason. He said nary a word but looked at Edward with purposeful eyes threatening mortal retaliation should Edward touch a hair on the head of Roberta.

Then a loud voice boomed at the front door. "Don't start nuthin' you can't finish, you no-good Yankee, carpetbaggin' coward." It was a weak, barely standing, bedraggled Elijah Johnson. Deputy Wesley was helping him into the café. "As poorly as ah may look in your beady little eyes, ah can still whip three o' you any day in the week!"

"There'll be no whippin' by you, Johnson, Foster, Kirk, or the ghost of Robert E. Lee hisself. I released yuh from jail so you could eat in the café and hopefully get your ugly backside out of town before the marshal gets back." Wesley spoke as a man bestowing a magnificent favor on a marked man, and perhaps he was.

After helping Johnson to a chair, Wesley turned around and looked as Mortimer Agee thoughtfully strolled inside.

"Mr. Olson — I thought a man of your high privilege and education might prove to be an asset in this community, but from what I hear of you, I am seeing a rather unmanly specimen. Where we come from, we don't treat womenfolk like property. I think you ought to leave this community — and if your wife chooses to not accompany you, then she has the blessing of this town."

Flabbergasted, and visibly humiliated to the point of puffing his face into an unintentional replica of bloated jellyfish, Edward ranted, "This — this is an outrage! I shall seek recourse with the marshal and eventually a Circuit Court Judge! You people are barbaric hicks and interlopers! You cannot come between me and my wife!"

Hannah considered stifling a response, then did no such thing. "Edward — your behavior has been inexcusable. In front of all these people, I am declaring that I want a divorce. You wore a mask when you courted me. Ever since we married, you have been peeling off that mask and revealing the monster you truly are. You are — are — an educated, privileged embodiment of male corruption! I despise you!"

Edward lunged at Hannah with his fist, but she adeptly stepped away, thus forcing Edward to lose his balance and fall directly toward Foster. Foster caught Edward with a right cross to his jaw. Stunned, but still conscious, Edward fell back toward Hannah who smiled sweetly, then delivered her own well executed punch directly into the man's nose. Edward lost his balance again, then fell backwards and hit his head against a dinner table. He was out cold.

For a moment, the only detectable sound was the steady beating rhythm of the rain downpour outside. Huge water drops pounded against the roof, but it held up, and not a drop of rain threatened the inhabitants. More thunder and lighting crashed and blazed through the Wyoming sky. The rampaging storm outside could not match the emotions that had been unleashed in the room.

"Ha-a-haha-hahaha," cackled Johnson. "Up until now ah felt worse than a possum clamped up in a bear trap, but seein' you slug that polecat just sped up muh recovery, missy!"

Agee scratched his chin and said, "Wesley, you better toss him in the jail cell."

"Mayor, but what will Callendar think when he gets back?"

Collectively, several people exclaimed, "Back?"

"Yes," Agee confirmed. "He took Blood Hawk, McAvee, and that German beer guzzler with him out to look for your Mr. North this morning. He left Wesley in charge of the jail, but Callendar doesn't know that Wesley is more loyal to me than to him."

"Ain't that a might unhealthy for you, Mr. Wesley?"

"Maybe. But after what I saw Callendar allow the primitive, Blood Hawk, do to you old timer, I figured it was time to go over to another side. I have been wearin' down considerable for some time. I know that tough times call for tough lawmen, but this man seems to have a keen appetite for rare roast beef and suffering."

All eyes turned to the mayor, who felt obliged to add, "I — I have done some things I am not so proud of, but since this morning, I have decided we cannot keep going on the way we are. I was hoping you, Mr. Johnson, along with some folks such as you, Mr. Mason, Doc Brandt, and others, might throw in with me and Wesley so that we might run that redneck grand inquisitor out of the territory."

No one replied, but many faces manifested a doubt of his sincerity. Subsequently, a few people ran to the windows upon hearing the approach of horses being ridden.

Hannah let out a gasp, "He came anyway. It is John!"

Johnson painfully found his way to an adjacent window and said, "Ah'll be danged. He came into Copperhead along with that angry Injun buck, Charging Buffalo."

North rode bolder than life into town, but he was brandishing a rifle across his arms. The young Cheyenne was also equipped with a Winchester. John wore a long, yellow rain slicker over his shoulders. The Indian wore a heavily woven, blue and white blanket over his head and body. Huge splats of rainwater dashed off the two riders who seemed so oblivious to the storm's attack, that one might mistake them for humanoid ducks. Warily, they got off their horses and walked into the café.

"Hello, Hannah. I see that Edward finally opened his yap once too often."

Impulsively, Hannah rushed to John, threw her arms around his shoulders, and kissed him hard on the mouth. Instead of discretely pulling away, John pulled her towards him and returned the kiss with greater passion.

"It is not a proper time for love," said Charging Buffalo. "We need to fight soon!"

"Young man," Roberta chided. "We don't always know when it is the proper time for love — we just hold onto it when we're lucky enough to find it."

Most of the café denizens laughed, especially Johnson, who added, "Ah kinda think ol' Edward here now has proper grounds for divorce! Pathetic, little Yankee spittoon."

Hannah, Johnson, Agee, and the others brought North up to date on events that had precluded then led to Callendar's leaving town to search for him.

"I think he will have a difficult time tracking us in the rain," smiled Charging Buffalo.

"Elijah, your hand is bandaged and arm is in a sling. I think you took a bullet for me."

"Ah know yer speakin' figuratively, but literally, ah took a bullwhip and a very large nail for yuh instead. Sorry, but ah won't be tradin' fists with yuh anytime soon!"

North sat and shook his head. The old rage was festering inside. He desired confrontation with his enemies more than anything. Still, when he looked at Hannah and considered the risk to this precious woman, along with all of the friends and innocent town people in Copperhead, he wondered about the wisdom of flaring up. On the other hand, people like Callendar, Blood Hawk, Chapeau, the mysterious long-haired man, and others of that stripe had to be stopped.

Johnson asked, "Tell me, John, how'd you an' the chief here end up meetin' up?"

John North narrated the events prior to today's entrance in Copperhead.

17

Unspeakable Storm Damage

Shortly following his departure from the Franklin property, John North considered how he would arrive in Copperhead. Merely riding in there bolder than life seemed foolhardy, not to mention potentially fatal. He would wait until the storm came and hopefully come into town through a back or side entrance and attempt to literally skulk his way around town until he either reunited with his friends or met Callendar face to face. Either way, it was his intention to put the man down like he would a predatory beast.

The first drops of rain began to fall, and there were crackles of thunder occurring. The storm was still somewhat in the distance but was rolling in fast. Moreover, on the horizon he saw something else rolling in quickly. It was a rider on a horse.

North finished putting the yellow rain slicker over his head, then pulled a pair of field binoculars out of his saddlebag. He had kept them from his army scouting days, and today it was obvious they had come in handy. He stared intently at the rider and nearly dropped the glasses as he began to recognize the facial and physical features. He could be wrong. Was it possible? He had better be right about this. Right now, the flash of lighting and booming thunder did little except put him further on edge. He peered even more intently through the glasses. A flash of lightning struck a tree not more than five yards from the galloping rider. Clearly, the identity of the man was revealed. It was the long-haired man who had ridden with Callendar, Blood Hawk, Chapeau, and Baker and helped destroy his beloved family. A smell of scorching ozone permeated the damp air.

Coldly, methodically, and resolutely, North put the binoculars back in the saddlebag, pulled up the secured Winchester, and set the man in his sights. He drew a bead on the man. Allowing for speed and distance, it might be difficult to shoot the man at such a range, but the time had come to exact retribution. Retribution? Perhaps murder. Cold blooded murder. Surprising himself, North considered the action about to be executed. Cutting him down in this manner was assassination. Not so long ago an assassin killed the president. Was this what he really wanted to do?

No, this is war, he reasoned. All kinds of atrocities occur in war, and this man participated in a personal, dirty war against the family. He had to die now!

Again, North steadied his aim, placed his finger near the trigger, and slowly began to squeeze — Blamm! A bolt of lightning struck a low hanging tree branch near him. His horse spooked, reared up, and tried to throw him. John started to slide off on the left side. He caught his balance but accidentally dropped his rifle. He promptly tried to calm the horse, regain control, and subsequently swooped down to collect the weapon. Fearing the longhair had spotted him and already had a rifle bead on him, he turned the horse to ride toward a protective clump of trees. Turning as soon as he considered it feasible and anticipating a duel on horse back of some sort, he instead was provided the sight of the longhair galloping away and anxiously looking in back of him several times. Why did he not look in my direction, pondered North? Soon, he saw another rider galloping down the hill. By now, longhair was gone and the other rider came closer. It was Charging Buffalo!

North rode forward and called out the man's name. The young Cheyenne stopped, looked at John, shook his head, then slowly trotted his mount toward him.

"I nearly caught up with a murderer until you arrived, John North. Your timing was more intrusive than the storm."

Charging Buffalo explained what had happened to Private O'Toole, and John declared that the man was one of Blood Hawk's companions.

"I think the spirits intended that we should rejoin forces, then find and kill this long-haired devil at another time."

The rain began to fall more heavily. "You have an interesting way of looking at things, son. While you are consulting with the spirits, do you think you might ask them to turn off some of this rain?"

Waiting for Charging Buffalo to don his heavy blanket to ward off some of the heavy rain, North declared, "I remember the hill the man just went down. It descends toward either Copperhead or branches off to the home of some friends of mine. Let's check out his tracks before the rain washes them away."

The Franklin family still had many chores to complete. Harold wanted to get back to his book, but he was told to take the horse and plow some more furrows. Pa said he wanted to plant more potatoes. Abby was tending to Ruthie who felt good enough to sit up and talk a little. Johnny planned to finish helping Harold get the plow started before returning to the fruit trees with another basket. Raindrops were starting to fall, and the rumblings of thunder presented storm conditions increasingly closer.

"We better wait on th' plowin', son; it's best to secure the stock and get inside 'til we see how big this storm gonna be."

As father and son were heading for the cabin, a group of riders came nearer. The splashing mud propelled by the horse hooves encroached. The black and white horse of the lead rider looked ominously familiar. It was the horse of the marshal. Here he was riding on his property accompanied by three other men.

"Get in the cabin, son. Big trouble has found us. Let me do all the talkin'."

Callendar wore a yellow slicker similar to the one owned by North. The other men, including Blood Hawk, also wore similar rain slickers.

"Lookee here, boys. This is what yuh call a fahm of a man who was probably the property of one o' muh friends in the cherished South a few ye'rs back. Ah wanna talk with yuh, dahkie."

"Marshal, ah want no trouble. Ah'll ansuh yuh questions, but ah gots tuh get inside and tend tuh muh family."

"Ah suppose yuh do. Just remembah we ah yoah bettahs, so no lip from yuh."

"No suh." Inwardly, Johnny relished the idea of knocking this offensive dog flat on his back, but he knew that the man was dangerous and the other men probably were as well.

"This is official po-leece biznuss, niggrah. We ah lookin' foah a dangerous man. This man is about average height, has brown hair, broad shoulders, and accordin' to the scalawag friend of his, is wearin' a shirt with blue stripes, a red bandana, dark brown hat, and rides a brown steed. Ah will ask you once, Johnny: have you seen this man?"

Harold looked nervous upon hearing the description, and his reaction was immediately noticed by Blood Hawk.

"The boy's eyes do not lie. He has seen John North. Let us persuade him to talk."

Both Krautmueller and McAvee started to smirk. They had both witnessed Blood Hawk's methods of persuasion, and since they considered all black people inferior, the possible torturing of this boy actually held appeal.

"Ah think it's wrong to pick on a child foah any reason," Callendar said. "Wipe those smiles off yoah faces deputies, o' ah might have to considuh doin' it muhself."

Sensing, and even hoping, for some semblance of humanity, Johnny turned to Callendar and said, "Thank you, suh. He is just a boy."

Callendar viciously struck Johnny to the ground, then kicked him in the ribs.

"He is just a boy, but you ah nuthin' but a li-uh. We can tell that North has been here. Tell us when and fer how long."

"Don't hurt my pa," Harold cried.

Blood Hawk responded by throwing a knife into the boy's thigh. He screamed and fell to the ground, bleeding profusely.

"Really, Blood Hawk. That's too savage even foah you. Ah thought you injuns didn't believe it hurtin' kids."

"Yes, but I am no longer Cheyenne. I am not one of you either. I just act and do as I please. I am damned no matter what, so who cares?"

Abby rushed out screaming for mercy. She tore off part of her dress and tried to slow down the bleeding. Blood Hawk sauntered up to the prostrate boy and clinging mother and pushed Abby aside. He cruelly yanked the knife out of Harold's leg.

"Your whelp is fortunate, black woman. I did not hit the artery. If you can avoid the gangrene, he probably will live. Now tell us about John North."

Abby confessed that John North had been brought to them by an army scout. She said they never wanted him there but were forced to take him in because of the army scout's insistence.

Satisfied that she was probably telling the truth, Callendar mounted his horse, wished Abby good day, looked down at Johnny, and chuckled. He then stated, "Take good care of that boy — he's gonna be the only man yoah gonna have around foah some time."

Instantly comprehending the hideous intent of that statement Abby cried, "No! God! No! Don't!"

Callendar pulled out his dragoon colt and shot Johnny in the right wrist. Groaning with pain and straining in anger, he cursed, then cried, "Ab-by, Ab — ." Callendar then shot him in the bicep of the same arm. He fell back unconscious into a bloody mud puddle.

The German laughed, McAvee spit near the fallen man, Blood Hawk said nothing, and Callendar promulgated, "Ah warned him not to evah cross me — no uppity niggrah will evah get the bettah of me, especially when he collaborates with muh enemies. Woman, look aftuh yoah youngins, but if you o' them evah come lookin' foah me, so help me God, I shall put all of yuh to death like I would scavengin' dogs."

The coldness of Callendar's words even chilled Krautmueller and McAvee. Slaughtering women and children didn't seem natural — even if they were black, they now reasoned. Only Blood Hawk seemed to appreciate the declaration. He actually looked at his leader with understanding and pride. Both of the men excelled in the craft of terrorism.

As John North rode toward Copperhead he felt a growing dread. He regretted his stay at the Franklin property. He was torn between going back to protect them or confronting Callendar directly in town. No, Callendar would be in town. They would not track him in the storm. Even he would not be that insane. Or would he? What goes on in the mind of a cold-blooded killer? Still, his own mind commanded that Callendar be found promptly and then put to death.

18

DELIBERATE DECISIONS

Now that the rudimentary facts covering the recent events concerning North and Charging Buffalo had been communicated, there was a strong sense of uneasiness permeating the café. North, especially, was feeling restless in this environment of more talk than action.

"Look," he opined. "We did not ride into town expecting an easy-going afternoon of conversation. I told you how and why my Cheyenne friend and I met up, but we were more prepared to ride in here and settle some serious issues with your marshal. I aim to make sure that happens."

Mortimer Agee slyly interrupted and suggested a whole new strategy. "North, you served under my command back in your army days. You know I am a man who does what he says he will do. Hiring Callendar was a big mistake. I freely admit I made that mistake. I refuse to endorse his barbarism any longer — not that I really ever did in the first place. To help make amends, I hereby declare P.J. Callendar officially sacked and appoint you his replacement as marshal of Copperhead."

Wesley stared at the beaming face of Agee in surprise, then looked at North for a reaction. North was poker-faced. Before anyone else could speak, Wesley declared, "Great idea. I second the motion. I mean, yeah, I know I got no authority in this, but I am all in favor of a new marshal, and I pledge my service as the first deputy of the new marshal."

North now spoke. "Are you serious, Agee? You were one of the reasons the local Indian tribes kept going on the warpath. You would not respect their points of view, let alone look at them as human beings. I couldn't wait to end my scouting service for you. Putting it mildly, you lack credibility."

Kirk Mason spoke. "I hope you might consider that some of us citizens in Copperhead might possess a little more credibility than Agee. As far as he is concerned, I agree with you. I would not trust him to give me a drink of water if he rode up to me in the desert driving a cart loaded up with two hundred pound barrels of spring water. He's trying to save his own skin and reputation. Right?" At this moment, Mason was looking for responses from his fellow townsmen. Most of them eagerly replied, "Right!"

"We wouldn't blame you for ignoring this rascal who brought the villain here in the first place. We have a good mind to impeach the son-of-a bitch today! The idea of you being the new marshal is about the only good idea I've heard from him in a year of Sundays. Don't be the marshal because he suggested it, man; be the marshal because we all want and need you to assume the office."

The group of citizens practically said "Amen" in their support of Mason's declaration. Still unsure, he looked at Johnson and Charging Buffalo, who nodded in assent. Finally, he turned to Hannah, who gently touched his shoulder and said, "It is up to you, John, but these people need your help. It is the right thing to do, but only you should make the decision."

Pausing, shutting out the others, and looking through the rain steadily drizzling down onto the muddy street, he said, "I accept the offer, however, I will only do the job until this mess is cleaned up. Furthermore, I will not take orders from Agee or any of you folks. This is something that has to be done my way."

"What about the federal marshal and the circuit court judge we're expectin' in a couple of weeks?" intoned Dr. Brandt.

"That is another reason I'm doing this on a temporary basis. Once they show up, I intend to move on."

"Fair enough," Dr. Brandt concluded.

"To start with, I choose my own deputies. Charging Buffalo and Elijah — I'd like to make the two of you my deputies. Mr. Foster, I know you are anxious to get to the nearest train depot, so I would not hold you to any promise, but if you felt inclined to help us out, I would be honored to have you as a deputy."

Foster smiled and said, "I thought you would never ask."

North turned his attention to Wesley. "As for you — you're fired!"

A collective gasp could be heard until North added, "Your dedication to law enforcement only seemed to appear when it became evident that Callendar's ability to wield all the power was in question. I can't rely on a man like that. You either have character or you don't. I don't think you have much character, mister."

Insulted, Wesley yanked the badge of his shirt, threw it at a wall, and missed Hannah's face by six inches. As he turned and started for the door, Johnson extended his foot and tripped him. Wesley fell face down, displacing a half-full spittoon.

"You probably shouldn't humiliate a man like that in public, Mr. North," cautioned Agee.

"I believe you are right." Suddenly, North pulled out his pistol and stuck it in Agee's ribcage. "In fact, it is very dangerous to publicly humiliate anyone with questionable character. This is why I will not turn my back on them. Charging Buffalo, help me escort Mayor Agee and former deputy Wesley to the city jail."

"Hell," roared Johnson. "All these changes are makin' me feel better by the minute. Ah'll give yuh boys a hand lockin' up these varmints!"

"Let's not forget dear Edward," North stated.

"Me? What law have I broken? I am a man of the law! You can't do it!"

"This pistol and the badge I now have say I can do it, so it will happen. If you want a charge, then here it is: assault and battery. You have used your wife as a punching bag for the last time, you dandified maggot."

Following a few rumblings from the exasperated, dethroned personalities in current disrepute, the new marshal and deputies marched off the prisoners and locked them up in jail cells.

The longhaired rider waited out the downpour fairly well protected inside a cave he had located. There had been a cougar inside, but once it had been flushed out, it was killed by two of his rifle shots. Yes, the particular army carbine he stole from the slain soldier was more accurate than one might have thought.

The man considered his next move. Should the Cheyenne Indian or the other man catch up with him, there would be a desperate battle. So far, they had not reconnected. The rain appeared to be easing up. Perhaps it was time to go hunting for them. Should they be waiting out the storm somewhere, it might be relatively simple to sneak up and shoot them through the spines. In that way, even if they didn't die, they would at least be too crippled to follow. Still, it seemed more likely he could merely slaughter them outright.

It was time to head out for Copperhead! Wait, maybe it wasn't! There was no reason to leave this nice dry cave. The cougar certainly didn't need it anymore. The man also considered the appearance of scavenging birds. Such a presence might draw just about anyone to the location. The man then set out to dispose of the cougar's corpse. He used a large tree branch to dig a pit not far from the cave.

After loading the corpse into the pit, he covered it with the mucky dirt and loose stones nearby. Over the top of the cat's grave he rolled some fairly large stones. It would be fairly difficult for the critters to find this thing as their next meal, he reasoned.

The man stretched out on some moss and leaves he had spread down on the cave floor and wrapped up in the warm, woolen army blanket. Yes, thank you Mr. Army Man, he chuckled, I appreciate your dyin' for a fellow American!

P.J. Callendar and his posse drank more coffee inside the farmhouse where they had waited out the duration of the downpour. The farmhouse belonged to Bobby McGill who had never been a problem. However, McGill had seemed annoyed today that his home had been staked for quartering by a group of lawmen.

"Beggin' the pardon o' the marshal," Bobby said as he threw another log into the kitchen wood stove. "I wonderin' how much longer ye thinkin' o' stayin' in muh home today?"

"Just as long as we want to, McGill. We ah engaged in a majuh pahsuit of a desperate killuh. Ah told yuh that when we fust came here, you ignorant scotchman!"

"We cull erslves, 'scots,' not 'scotch."

"I'll tell yuh, McGill," cackled McAvee, "My folks were Scottish too, but I ain't found anything Scottish that's as pleasing as a good bottle of scotch whiskey. At least you ain't some Negro — be grateful for that. The last one we saw probably wished he was scotch by the time we left him."

"McAvee, you gotta untrained mouth." Callendar then took his coffee and tossed it into McAvee's face.

Krautmueller grunted, "Ja! Dis schwein cries as Kinder — he ist vat you call a big baby! Ha-hah!"

McGill looked at these men and suppressed the disgust he was feeling. He had never approved of those black people moving in and buying a farm. After all, it was at least two miles southwest of his own property. Nevertheless, the potential cruelty of this so-called lawman and his immoral deputies seemed to outweigh any revulsion he generally felt for the black family. He could only imagine what this bunch of people did to the Franklins. These magistrates seemed as bad as the British in his judgment.

Ignoring the gaze of the disapproving, yet silent Scotsman, Callendar said, "We have a bit of a problem if those ahmy people evah take a notion to join up with North, or even feel indignant about how we left those niggrah folks. Ah'm thinkin' it may be time to move on."

Blood Hawk scraped his long knife against a flint and said, "Our time in Copperhead is over. Agee will turn against you if we go back. You will have to kill him and possibly that other one, Wesley. It is only a matter of time until the army seeks us. It would be better if we sought the army as it seeks us."

McAvee, now recovering from the slight scalding of his face, and Krautmueller, sitting with cheeks puffed out due to overstuffing his gut with McGill's bread, nervously looked at one another and wondered what they had gotten themselves into.

"Mein, freund, bitte, vee need to — to have con-fersation — ve did not plan to go against ahmy men."

"Listen to me you ovuhstuffed sausage, you pledged to join up with us, an' ah hold yuh to yoah word. The consequences of not keepin' yoah pledge means death at the hands of muh Cheyenne renegade associate. Savvy?"

McAvee replied for both of them, "Yes — P.J. We savvy."

"Besides," Callendar smirked. "By finishin' oah business in these parts and then movin' on, we definitely will find bettuh pickins elsewhere. This means a lot moah cash and advenchuh foah you boys. Right? McAvee, ah am awful sorry about tossin' thet coffee your way. Here's somethin' to help yuh fohgive ol' P.J." Callendar tossed him a ten dollar gold piece.

"Thanks, P.J. I'm feelin' better already."

"Maybe we'll head down to New Mexico territory. Maybe we'll go up to that northwest territory instead — you know, Oregon. Ah nevah been there, have any of you?"

Blood Hawk stared at the Scotsman. Without warning, he lunged toward the man and shoved the long knife into his solar plexus and cut upward. A terrible scream resounded in the kitchen and the sixty-year-old McGill blacked out and gradually passed away.

McAvee cried, "Yuh crazy redskin, why didja kill the old feller? He was helpin' us out!"

Callendar coldly pulled out the dead man's wallet, removed about three hundred dollars, then said to McAvee, "It is poah policy to question Blood Hawk in these matters. The old man heard too much of oah plannin', so his days had to end. If we ah goin' to ambush an ahmy patrol and murder Mistuh North, then we can't have some righteous ol' man dashin' off to wahn othuh folk!"

"Ja! If dat ist the case, marshal, den vee should go back and finish off those schwarzes — dose blacks!"

Callendar thought about the possibility then said, "Maybe — before we leave the territory. Ah think it best to tend to any ahmy patrol headed oah way first, then North second. Besides, that Johnny and his black youngin' ah moah then likely gonna bleed to death. Ah you 'fraid of the man's wife and little girl, Krautmueller?"

"Nein."

After the three white men heartily laughed, and Blood Hawk expressed no emotion, the four men drank more coffee, then hauled McGill's body out the barn where they had earlier and quietly murdered and hidden the scotsman's two hired hands.

Abby Franklin fought back the tears as she worked diligently to stem the hemorrhaging limbs of her son and husband. Young Harold faired the best. He was lying still, resting as comfortably as a traumatized person might under the savage circumstances. Abby had seen violence and cruelty perpetrated against others in her experience, so she knew that covering her son with a blanket would help stabilize him once the bleeding had diminished.

Johnny, on the other hand, was in bad shape. The man's right arm had been badly shattered from the lead balls fired from Callendar's dragoon colt. She had no choice but to install a tourniquet above the upper arm wound. Somewhat miraculously, Johnny woke up long enough to tell her, "You got no choice, Abby. The ahm has gotta come off. If yuh don't cut it off, ah gonna eithuh bleed to death, oh get gangrene. Eithuh way, ah would die. Ah ain't givin' up, but if yuh do nuthin', it's all ovah."

Assured that Abby would carry out his request, and further convinced that poor Harold would be all right, Johnny passed out. Abby wiped his brow, kissed him on the lips, and prayed silently to the Lord that she would have the strength to do what he asked.

"You are a brave woman," a voice said. Abby jumped — momentarily wondering if it was an angel. She looked behind her and saw it was that Indian Scout, Sammy Fivetrees. He was there along with four other soldiers, and one of them appeared to be an officer.

"Ma'am," said the officer as he got off the horse. "Can you tell us the direction these criminals went? I promise they will meet justice for perpetrating this crime!"

"Jus' help muh husband an' boy. Nuthin' else matters!"

Captain Bristol ordered two of his men to start searching the area for signs of the assailants. The third man and Sammy were asked to help carry Harold and Johnny into the cabin. It was still raining, and the Captain was concerned about the two wounded people contracting pneumonia.

Abby wiped away her tears and declared, "Ah prayed foah help, and yuh came. God bless you, Mistuh Fivetrees. God bless all of you!"

"Mrs. Franklin, I am deeply sorry that I brought such sorrow to your home. I swear to you as a Cherokee, and as a man who has never broken his word, I will avenge you and your family."

"First things, first, Sammy," Captain Bristol announced. "We had to check out the recent uprising of the Cheyenne. As soon as they found out it was one of their own, that evil Blood Hawk character, they settled down. We made a promise to them as well as our own Major that we had to find and turn Blood Hawk over to the Cheyenne. Remember, Sammy, that's why we came back."

"I am aware of that, Captain. However, there might be circumstances preventing us from bringing in Blood Hawk alive. I would be more than pleased to return him to the Cheyenne as a corpse."

"We'll discuss this later, Sammy. Meanwhile, we have the sad duty of dealing with this unfortunate man's arm. It must be removed. Mrs. Franklin, this would be a good time to look after your children in the other room."

Abby resigned herself to leaving Johnny for the time being. However, she did remember what Sammy Fivetrees said and believed this man might move heaven and earth to find the one known as Blood Hawk. Would they also look for and deal with the man who actually mutilated her husband — this wicked marshal? Perhaps John North held the answer to that question.

Inside the marshal's office John North spoke frankly to his two deputies. "Elijah, someone needs to keep an eye on these prisoners. Since we need to keep these scoundrels locked up until that judge finally arrives, I am directing you to be the jailer. You need some time for those wounds to heal, and I trust you implicitly."

"Ah don't want yuh tuh do anythin' rash, Mistuh North. That Callendar and his wolf pack are pretty rancid, and they mean to kill yuh. Besides, there is that fifth fella — the longhaired one — that is unaccounted for."

"Why all the interest in that one? I noticed your ears perking up when I told about the meeting Charging Buffalo and I had with that no-good killer."

Johnson reclined in his chair, took a large bite from his tobacco plug, and said, "Ah told yuh when the time was right ah'd explain muh motivation foah helpin' yuh track down those men that wronged yuh."

"Go on."

Johnson sat still, then nearly shouted, "That long-haired man is someone ah cannot permit yuh to kill!"

"Are you insane, old man?" Charging Buffalo began to raise his voice. "I witnessed the senseless killing of that army man O'Toole. The longhair slaughtered him as he would a head of livestock. He has no regard for human life."

"Ah know, son. Ah know. In fact, ah know all about the longhaired man. His name is Chahlie."

"Charlie?"

"Yesuh, Chahlie Johnson. Regrettably, the man is muh younguh brothuh."

19

---◆---

OVERDUE EXPLANATIONS

Following the announcement that the much talked about longhaired criminal was Elijah Johnson's brother, the marshal's office stood as silent as the interior of a grave. North stared at Elijah, who tried to look away but ultimately returned the stare with an equal determination. Who knows how long this silent duel would have lasted except for the appearance of Foster.

"Gentlemen, I will stay as a temporary deputy for about a week or so. I figure everything will be pretty much resolved by then. I do ask that I be released from my commitment if I receive a telegram citing any sort of baleful developments at home. I sent my own telegram to California briefly saying I got delayed on account of a need to help friends."

Initially, John North appeared oblivious to Foster's interruption, but he continued staring at Elijah and said, "Thanks for being square about it, Foster. Any help you might give, for however long it might be will be appreciated. Some of us are more willing to be straight forward than others."

Elijah Johnson spat on the floor and growled, "You ain't got any call tuh make innuendo 'bout me not bein' honest. After all, ah always said ah would tell you muh motives when the time was right, and the timin' was not opportune until now."

"Why, Johnson? Why now? What if we had run into your brother on the way to Copperhead? What if he had participated in the attempted stagecoach robbery? What then? Would you have turned on us?"

Johnson rubbed his sore hand and leaned his head against the boarded wall in back of the chair. He squirmed a little as the tender tissues of his back flexed painfully. He calmly said, "Tuh be honest, ah am not sure what ah would have done. Ah only know I wouldn't let yuh kill Chahlie. Ah'd probably help yuh knock him down, hogtie, and cart him off to the hoosegow, but ah won't let you o' anyone else make him dead."

Charging Buffalo set his blanket on the floor and began to stretch out for a night of sleep. "Did you merely ride with John North to stop him from killing your brother, or did you ride with him to join up with your brother and kill North?"

Elijah tossed a lawbook at the Cheyenne and would have hit him in the face had the younger man lacked protective reflexes.

"Take action against me again, old white man, and I promise you will die before your murderous brother does!" Charging Buffalo was now on his feet gripping a long knife.

"Stop it — both of you," North admonished. "Keep this up and I'll throw you both in jail with those other model citizens. Johnson, he does ask a direct question — well?"

Elijah shook his head and said, "Ah'm surprised you would even consider treachery from me. Didn't I shoot the Frenchman? Didn't I take the coach into town while you rode away with that Fivetrees character? While we're at it, didn't I take the lash and get muh hand mutilated outta loyalty tuh you, North? How do you answer those questions, man?"

North relaxed, walked over to Johnson, and extended his hand. "Please accept my apology, Elijah. I never should have doubted you. You are absolutely right — you have been more loyal than most men I have seen. You practically sacrificed yourself for my actions, and I owe you a debt."

Johnson took his hand, grimly looked up at him, and replied, "Then repay the debt by not killin' muh brother. Ah know he's no damn good, but he's still kin. You have been badly wronged by him and those othuh four. You already killed Baker, we've put Chapeau with a sawed-off arm into a jail cell, and you'll have to be quick tuh shoot Blood Hawk and Callendar afore ah do. Ah just ask thet yuh don't kill one of them five. He's the only brother ah got."

"Elijah, I also used to have a brother. No one at the time was concerned about sparing him. I will promise you this much though. If it is within reason, I will try my best to bring him in alive. If he resists, and I have to choose between his life and the lives of the innocent, then what happens happens. That's the best I can offer, and I am giving you my solemn oath on it. If you can't live with that promise, then you better get out of here now. I like you a lot, Elijah, but if you work with him in causing any more hardship or death for anyone else, then you will change from friend to enemy. That's the way it has to be." Again, North offered his hand, and Elijah took it unhesitatingly.

"Ah suppose there will be a trial."

"It will probably be out of my hands in the long run. Charging Buffalo witnessed your brother murdering a United States soldier. I know Captain Bristol. He'll want to try and convict your brother. I strongly advise you to avoid going against Bristol."

"Ah understand. It was bad enough that Grant sent Sherman and his ahmy through the south to burn it down, but now Grant is the President of the United States. No, I'm through fightin' the blue bellies — if you'll excuse the expression."

"I think we had better get some sleep," Foster said. "Who knows what the level of acrimony might be tomorrow."

"Ah think yuh read too many o' them store-bought books, Foster. Try talkin' American!"

"You mean speak Cheyenne," quipped Charging Buffalo.

Everyone laughed a bit nervously and realized that sleep was a great idea. Johnson agreed to keep watch that evening while the others got some shuteye. On the way to the hotel, North decided to pay a visit to Kirk Mason. The light in Mason's room above the store was still burning, so he knocked on the door.

Kirk Mason was already dressed in a long nightshirt and looked ready to snore at any moment. Still, he did recognize North, and realized that if the new marshal had felt it important to disturb him, then he had better listen.

The two men sat in the wood chairs on either side of a table in the corner of the general store. North was offered a bottle of beer, but he declined and said he just wanted to talk for a short while.

"Mr. Mason — Kirk, if you don't mind a first name basis — I need to know if there are any other allies or other hoary friends of Callendar around here I should know about. I just learned that the fifth member of that group of killers I have been searching for is a man by the name of Charlie Johnson. Yes, he is related to Elijah. They are brothers."

"Brothers, you say? This is a complication. I had hoped we might be able to trust Elijah Johnson, but you have to admit, he got through a terrible ordeal at the hands of Callendar, so I don't think him likely to stand in your way in getting to Callendar or Blood Hawk. Let's just hope we will not have added Elijah Johnson to the list of villains if this brother of his is killed."

"It is my hope too, but I need as many deputies as possible. I only have him, Charging Buffalo, and Mr. Foster. Because things are likely to get stirred up pretty gravely, I'd like to temporarily swear in you and some other citizens as deputies as well."

"Certainly. I don't want to become a full-time lawman, but this is my town, and I want to do what I can to help keep the likes of an Agee or a Callendar from ever gaining the upper hand again. I think you can count on Doc Brandt. I'm not sure about any of the others. I think that Johnny Franklin might like to help, but because he is a Negro, I am not sure that he would feel accepted by some of the folks. There are plenty of folks in town with some backward ideas about anyone not white."

"That's the kind of thinking that's going to make all of us weak in the long run. As you know, I have met and gotten to know Johnny and his family a little, and I think they are wonderful folks. I am very worried about them though. If Callendar is riding all over the countryside looking for me, there is no telling how he might try to extract information from innocent, peace loving folks on their ranches."

"I've known Johnny for a spell, and he is peace loving, but he is also getting mighty sick and tired of people judging him to be less than white folk. He would have good reason to stand up against a bigot like Callendar."

"That's what concerns me. Callendar is exceptionally dangerous. I'm thinking about riding to his ranch tomorrow to help him and his family come into town where better protection is available. Callendar will return, but I'm afraid that he might show up while I am out gathering the Franklins and their gear."

"Say no more, Marshal North. I'll be glad to ride out and bring 'em to town. Johnny and Abby trust me, and my own Roberta is fond of Abby and the children. If you're making me a deputy, you understand that if we are fired at, I will fire back and shoot to kill?"

"I wouldn't expect you to do otherwise. If that does happen, be careful. You'd be better off just riding with those folks as rapidly as possible to town. I will station someone at the edge of town to meet you and help you get inside without the outlaws picking you off."

Mason was about to rise and walk upstairs, but North abruptly stopped him with, "There is one more thing, Kirk. I need to know if Callendar has any other friends, allies, or other assorted sidewinders in this town whom we need to be concerned about."

"Ha-hah-hah. I knew you would be good. I have a talent for matching up a man's character and talents with the appropriate job. It goes back to the days when I ran a barrel making factory in New England. You pretty well nailed the worst of 'em when you jailed Agee and Wesley. However, there's a nasty bunch I wouldn't trust that works in the Saloon. You can't miss it. It's the only establishment called, "Saloon." How unimaginative! The proprietor is a slimy snake known as Bradley Fulton. Plenty of mischief goes on in that place including card cheating, whoring, and other blasphemies you might imagine. It is well-known that Fulton paid Callendar and Agee protection money, in order that all manner of vice might continue. Worst of all, there's a young woman working there named Sally — er, I can't remember her last name. A shame such a pretty gal ended up with a pack of sinners. Fulton's other employees are some bartenders and another whore called Laura. They're bad eggs too."

"With that information, Mr. Mason, I think it prudent to pay Mr. Fulton a visit tomorrow. Remember what I said: if I accepted this job, it had to be done my way."

"That's fine by me. On behalf of me, Doc Brandt, and every other decent citizen, you can shut down that nest of vermin in the blink of a moth's eyelash. A word of advice, don't expect to find any future deputies in "the Saloon.""

"I won't. Good night, and thanks."

North considered a brief visit with Hannah before turning in. He chose not to disturb her, then simply went into his hotel room, crashed onto the bed, and effortlessly fell asleep.

20

MORE RATS EXPOSED

The new marshal's decision to round up and jail basically all of the town's remaining authority figures surprised many in Copperhead. Few protested the action, and even fewer seemed willing to register complaint to the face of Marshal John North. One person who felt prepared to complain outright was Brad Fulton, the saloon owner. It was a new day in Copperhead, and Fulton felt he had to speak his mind to this intruder, North.

It was 9 AM, but Fulton decided to open the bar an hour earlier than usual. All this excitement about jailing the mayor and Deputy Wesley made some of his regular alcoholic customers uneasy, and it was unclear if they would patronize his establishment at all. Apparently, he did not understand the compulsiveness of alcoholism.

Fulton generally wore a gray suit, black and white striped shirt, and string tie. The tie really did not mean much in such a primitive territory, but it somehow made Fulton feel prominent. The heavily waxed handlebar mustache supposedly communicated his dignified qualities even though he made no effort to conceal the revolting truth that he slept with the two saloon hookers in his employ; in fact, one of them he often raped.

Fulton ran a tight ship. He employed two bartenders: Arnie Mitchell and Odie Rawlins. Arnie, a tall, beefy, curly-haired, heavily bearded lout, showed up for work on time even though he usually slept in until 9 AM most mornings. Where in blazes Odie was at this hour, he did not care. He took the late afternoon and evening shift. The two saloon employees, "hostesses," as he preferred to name them, were Sally Redmond and Laura Roscoe. As he strolled into the saloon he was not surprised that Sally and Laura had already preceded his arrival at work. Such promptness was required!

"Awfully early to be opening up, Brad! I kind of like to have some breakfast before I start entertaining your delightful patrons."

"Don't wag that tongue, Laura. We've got problems. We had a great thing going here when Marshal Callendar was running things. Now that the respectable folk in town have ousted him and hired this stranger, North, it is only a matter of time until they start looking around to force me out of business or into jail with the others."

"What's the matter, sweetheart?" Laura sassed. "Are we breakin' some laws in the eyes of these decent folks? Decent folks like that barber who was all over my body two nights ago?"

"Did he give your body a haircut, yuh naughty gal?" interrupted Arnie Mitchell.

"Shut up, the both of you. Here comes that new marshal — that John North!"

North slowly walked through the swinging saloon doors and said, "Good morning. I guess folks in this town start drinking early?"

Laura quickly sauntered over to North, put her arm around him, rubbed her body against him suggestively, and said, "Some of us open up for more than just whiskey, handsome. My name is Laura."

North had seen this type of woman many times in the past. If there was a western saloon, it was likely that there would be a whore or two inside ready to solicit and serve. Much to her credit, he mused, this woman is at least fairly attractive: chestnut colored hair, full lips, nice figure, and remarkably large breasts. He also glanced at the other saloon hostess. She was also attractive: red hair, young face, good figure, but very quiet, and undeniably melancholy.

"Uh, thanks, but I am here on official business, Laura." He discretely disengaged from Laura's clutches and turned to the man in the suit. "Are you, Fulton, the proprietor?"

"Yes. But remember, mister, I have been in business for years — much longer than most of the straight arrows living here. You might say I am one of the pioneers — both me and my wonderful Laura here. Before you start leaning on me, keep in mind that I pay city taxes and don't allow fights or discord in my establishment."

"I am sure that you don't. However, I want to ask you about former Marshal Callendar and some of his associates. I assume that they might be what you might refer to as 'regular customers.' Right?"

"Yes. In fact, Marshal Callendar was good for my business! He kept rowdy cowboys and all disgusting non-white people out of here. People would just come in to drink, maybe play some poker, and seek some friendship from the girls here. In fact, the marshal got to be good friends with Sally over there!"

The placid, quiet, red-headed Sally suddenly jumped out of chair and exploded, "You're lying, Fulton! The man was an animal — treating me like some sort of sexual slave. He slapped me several times when I said I did not want to sleep with him. I was sick, and he did not care, and — and — forced me."

Laura burst out laughing. Oddly, her laugh emerged more like the wailing of mirthful apparition of some kind. It was irritatingly disruptive and excessively unattractive. "What in hell were ya thinkin' when you got into this line of business, you little tramp? He's a man, you're a saloon hostess, and you ain't gettin' paid just to roll yur eyes for him. Yur supposed to roll around in the sheets for him!"

Sally picked up a deck of cards and threw it at Laura. It struck her on the right breast and compelled her to fly over to Sally and start yanking her red hair fiercely.

"Break it up you two," commanded North. "The jail is already full, and I really don't want to make you share bunks with Agee, Wesley, and Edward Olson. Even for you ladies, that would be an injury to personal pride."

Arnie the bartender aggressively walked over to North and declared, "You have no business in here — get out! When Callendar returns, he'll kill you!"

"Step back, mister," North warned.

When the bartender apparently did not heed the warning, North quickly pulled out his revolver and struck the man sharply between the neck and shoulder. He abruptly collapsed and cried out in pain. He tried to rise again as if to strike North in retaliation, but North struck him across the face.

Expressing controlled anger, North yelled, "Get one thing straight. Should any man raise a hand against me I will cut him down. So help me, as long as I am marshal, I will not condone any disrespect. I can shut down your business and run you out of town today. Make up your mind on how to behave, or you will be out of here before sunset, Fulton!"

Fulton nearly panicked and cried out, "What in blazes are you asking of me? Sure! Yes! I recognize that you are the new marshal! What else must I do? I'm just a businessman!"

"Running a business for profit is fine, but getting people liquored up enough to start fights and shooting is not so fine. I have seen a lot of trouble come from people running death holes like this one. People in this town have told me how thick you were with Callendar and Blood Hawk. You should have picked better friends. These men are murderers and their time is coming to a end. If you want to meet the prosperity of the future, then you had better run a legitimate place."

"You have a talent for making friends, don't you, Mr. North?"

"Not at all. I have a talent for flushing out rats. They either run away or get shot. Are you a rat, Mr. Fulton? Keep in mind, you do not have to be vermin."

"Anything else?"

"As a matter of fact, yes. Miss — Sally, did I hear correctly? Sally, you do not have to work here any more if you choose not to. It isn't too late to change your line of work."

"Thank you, Marshal. But I have no other place to go, and I don't have much money."

"Get your things. I intend to introduce you to someone who might be able to help you out temporarily."

Fulton shook his head in disgust. Now he knew he really hated the loss of Callendar. He wanted the outlaw to come back, kill this upstart, North, and return to the sweet deal he had before. As long as he was giving Callendar and Agee 40 percent of the profits and let them bed both Laura and Sally whenever they chose, the authorities left him alone. The prostitution, crooked roulette wheel, marked decks of cards, and watered-down liquor being sold were just fine with these men. The only law that mattered was their law. Real law could be damned to hell as far as they were concerned.

"You can't take Sally away from me! She signed a contract!"

North stood in front of Fulton, scowled, and stated in a threatening voice, "A contract requiring a girl to sell herself is not legal and binding in civilized society. Most of the people in this town happen to want such a society. That so-called contract is hereby null and void. Furthermore, Mr. Fulton, your saloon is hereby closed for the rest of the day. If you ignore what I said and try to reopen, then I will close you down permanently and torch the place."

Stunned, Fulton only nodded and began to perspire profusely. He looked down at Arnie, who regained consciousness and groaned pitifully.

Hannah had decided to give up on the gingham dresses and frilly feminine attitude as long as she remained in this town. She managed to purchase some riding clothes which included Levis, a light blue plaid blouse, and a hat. She thought of simply wearing a riding skirt, but this town did not have any. She looked in the mirror and thought she or any other woman dressing in this manner did not look bad at all. This was rough country, and it seemed appropriate to dress for the environment.

She left the hotel room and restrained herself from racing down the stairs. She was anxious to see John North this morning but did not want to come across as some sort of man hungry floozy. She wanted to divorce Edward as soon as possible, but it would be difficult in any event to remain separated from John.

As she entered the hotel lobby, she saw John standing next to a young woman obviously heavily painted in makeup. She reasoned that it would not require a detective to tell her that this woman was a hooker. Why was John with such a woman?

"Good morning, Hannah. I'd like you to meet Sally Redmond. Sally can tell you her own story in good time, but she was unfortunately in the employ of one of the few remaining undesirables in town, a Mr. Brad Fulton. She desperately wanted to remove herself from a terrible situation, and I thought you might be able to help her out at least until she gets settled somewhere else."

Hannah understandably looked startled at John's sudden interest in this girl but thought again at how little time had passed since she herself had met John. Hannah suddenly felt compassion and smiled at the uneasy girl.

"Of course. I would be happy to help. Sally, my name is Hannah Olson."

"I am very, very sorry to be imposing upon you, Miss Olson. Mr. North here was very kind and considerate to help me. He happened to reach me when I was at wit's end. I have done some awful things, miss — I won't deny any of it — but I was desperate! My husband brought me here about a year ago, then got into an argument with some drunken cowboy and got killed. Fulton said he felt sorry for me and offered me a job! Next thing I know, he started turning me into a wh... well, I think you can figure it out. The rest of the town just assumed I was no damn good and never would talk to me."

Sally started to sob, and Hannah quickly took her into her arms and gave comfort. "My dear girl, you aren't the only woman around here who has made a bad decision or two. I did not exactly make the same kind of decision, but mine was pretty awful too. Come on. You can stay with me as long as I'm in Copperhead."

John smiled, thanked Hannah, then started to leave.

"John," Hannah cried. "Where are you going? I wanted to... to see... I mean talk with you."

"Hannah, I am more than a little worried about Callendar and his bunch coming back. There is no telling what they'll attempt to do to this town. I sent a telegram to Fort Green early this morning and asked for the assistance of federal troops in case I don't survive the encounter with these boys."

Horrified, Hannah pulled away from a semi-bewildered Sally and embraced John. "Don't say that! You must survive! John, I need to believe that you will survive!"

"I'll do my best, Hannah, but you should know by now that we can't write every page in the book ourselves. A bad snowstorm, getting tossed off a spooked horse, getting outnumbered and overwhelmed in a surprise Indian attack, or just being unlucky in a shootout with villains like Callendar can change things for the worse. On the other hand, if we try to be courageous, keep cool heads, make sound decisions, choose our friends carefully, and look after one another, the tide may get turned in our favor. We live, work, plan, try to live honorably, and even love when we have the chance. Sometimes these virtues give us the needed edge."

"I love YOU, John."

"Just hearing you say that gives me more incentive to survive than you might ever imagine. I love you, Hannah."

Following these pronouncements, Hannah and John kissed tenderly and said not another word. Hannah took Sally shopping for something less brazen to wear, and John went into the marshal's office. It was time for some additional conversations with deputies and prisoners.

Fulton complied with Marshal North's edict that the saloon be closed for the rest of the day. However, this was an incident he swore would be avenged. He directed Arnie to saddle a horse and ride out and try to locate the Callendar posse. It was important that P.J. Callendar receive advance warning that North had mucked up things in his town.

"Listen to me, Arnie. You have to find Callendar. He told me that while he was out looking for this jackass he wanted to kill that he planned to pay a little call on the army patrol he figured would be coming back here. How he'll wipe 'em out, and cast no suspicion on himself, is something too clever for me to cogitate. I'm still thinking he plans to come back and pick up where he left off. He has to! Copperhead can't continue with bible thumpin' bullies like this North runnin' things. And Agee! He shouldn't be in jail! He protected us all! Yes, Arnie, you have to find him and warn him. North is waiting for him to return. Tell him the rest of the town seems to cotton to this North, so they ain't going to want him to leave. Tell him that he needs to come back and bushwhack the bastard and any deputies he might hire!"

"Are you sure ya wanna say all that in front of that whore, Laura?"

"That whore, Laura, is loyal to me, and she knows her livelihood ends if this place ever gets shut down. Do what I say, and let me do the thinking."

"Bradley, dear," Laura whispered closely behind. "What if our wonderful Mr. Callendar is killed by Mr. North? Where does that leave us then? Have you thought that far ahead?"

Brad chugged a half-glass of whiskey, slammed the glass onto the bar, and said, "If that's the case, then we better think seriously about moving to a new town. Personally, I think that is a lot of trouble. Let's keep an eye on this Mr. North and find out if he has any weaknesses."

"You mean — like a lady friend?"

"Yes. We can always get back at him through such a friend. In the meantime, I need to dream up a reasonable excuse for getting over to the jail and visiting with Mayor Agee. He needs to know some of my thoughts, and he may have a trick or two up his sleeve for helping us get back on top."

Laura snaked her arm from Fulton's chest down below the man's waist. "You are such a vile man, Bradley. I like dirty, scheming, vile men like you. You are almost as horrid as I am. Since the bar has to be closed, let's go upstairs for a while."

"Just a while, heh-heh. We have some work to do in town today. And you, Arnie, quit grinning like a fox in a henhouse, and go look for the real marshal!"

21

COLD CALLENDAR CALCULATIONS

McAvee and Krautmueller were amazed at how swiftly Blood Hawk had jumped and murdered the two soldiers currently lying still on the ground. Given the chance, they would have dutifully dispatched these two men themselves, but Blood Hawk genuinely relished the art of murder. Expecting the renegade to scalp these soldiers, they instead watched Blood Hawk rifle through their belongings and steal the few coins, food supplies, and canteens of water they had possessed.

"If you stupid dogs were not so slow, you would have shared in the spoils. Instead, you only earn my ridicule. You pretend to be outlaw men, but you behave more like homeless women. If it were not for Callendar, I could leave you here with these soldiers."

"Vait! Vait! Dis insolence ist not acceptable," Krautmueller protested. "Ve do not have to endure such treatment. Ja?"

"Ja? Listen, Krautmueller, ah'd advise yuh tuh remembuh the last protest yuh saw puhformed on the Scotchman. Blood Hawk may not take kindly tuh yer attitude." Callendar then watched the three men as if he were about to witness some sort of lopsided gladiatorial event unfold.

"Shut up, you crazy Kraut," MvAvee squealed. "Don't cross the Injun. Can't you see how much he *loves* his fellow human beings?"

"At least I am more honest than you two. I hate nearly everyone and trust no one. I do not trust you two. Should Callendar give the word, I will kill you instantly. If it pleases him to let you work for him, then I will not necessarily kill you today."

Callendar suddenly guffawed and said, "Get on yer horses, men, we need to find the rest of the patrol. These were only a couple of the soldiers scoutin' the perimeter. Ah'd expect thet the entire party was made up of six or seven boys. We need tuh deal with the othuhs as soon as possible. Blood Hawk, ah appreciate yoah providin' the blue bellies an iron lullaby."

On the surface, it appeared there was no end to the fearless villainy perpetrated by Callendar and his henchman. Deep down in his soul, Callendar was worried. He knew someone like North was potentially dangerous. Letting North link up with the army patrol was even more hazardous. Between the soldiers' federal jurisdiction, and North's unrelenting hatred for him and the others, it was looking more and more like a great idea to leave the United States all together. After picking off the surviving patrol members and returning to town long enough to pick up some more weapons, ammunition, food, canteens of water, and other supplies, it would be better to move steadily down to the Rio Grande and cross over into Mexico. Hopefully, Blood Hawk would agree to journey that far; he could use his skills.

Callendar quickly explained his intended change in plans. While dodging McAvee's question about what there was to look forward to in old Mexico, a familiar rider approached and looked quite eager to speak with them.

"Since we recognized you, Arnie, you remain alive. These hya' soldier boys met with an accident. A sort of Cheyenne uprising occurred!"

Satisfied with his own dreadful joke, Callendar nearly ignored Arnie the bartender as he practically belched out a big warning. "You has to watch out marshal. They threw Agee and Wesley in jail and made this John North the new marshal. You are now a wanted man! They mean to cut you down if you head into town."

"Another rider approaches, Callendar. Fresh from the devil — it's Charlie."

Charlie Johnson had seen the bartender riding fast on his mule and had followed him. Remaining out of sight, he crept up until he was close enough to see that there was a parley taking place between the mule rider and his old business partners, P.J. and Blood Hawk.

"Looks like a family reunion. There's Blood Hawk and muh ol' pal, P.J. How the hell are you varmints? I hear yuh had a cozy job in Copperhead."

"Not anymore," cautioned the bartender. "Some guy named North has taken over and he's out for our blood — actually, not my blood, but P.J.'s, — and well, I think you might have heard of this John North."

"North?"

"Yuh longhaired numbskull, remembuh the family in the wagon a few years back? We bushwhacked 'em and let the wounded one live. It was muh happy little joke of the day."

"Oh yeah, ah remembuh now. There was this kid screamin' and bawlin' for his pappy and mammy, and ah shot him in the chest. Ah nevah could stand the wailin' of brats. Elijah always liked kids, but every time ah got in contact with 'em, they made muh head hurt. Ah didn't like bein' a kid either. The old man used to beat me and Elijah, so to hell with childhood, I always say."

"Elijah? What? Elijah Johnson?" McAvee was visibly astonished that the stranger was probably referring to the aging prospector he had known in Fortune River.

"Elijah is muh bruthuh! What of it? How do you know about Elijah?"

"Your brother is in Copperhead right now and sidin' with North. Callendar here had to teach him some manners."

Without hesitation, Callendar whipped out his dragoon colt and smashed it across McAvee's upper arm. The man fell down from the saddle writhing in pain next to the body of one of the cavalry soldiers.

"You taught muh brother respect? P.J., you ought not better have killed him." Charlie reached for his own gun, but P.J. shot off the horn of his mount's saddle.

"Cool down, Chahlie. Ah don't wanna kill you. Rest assured that yoah bruthuh was not killed. Blood Hawk and I roughed him up a little. We had no idea the man was related to you. When we rode togethuh, you used to talk about 'big brother;' we nevah heard anythin' resemblin' a name."

"This is true," confirmed Blood Hawk.

"What you need to know," Callendar added, "is that he's gotten thick with this John North who we shoulda killed with the rest of his family. Leavin' him to die wounded was the biggest damn mistake I evuh made. Chance played out in his favor, and some Good Samaritan rescued him. You gotta know somethin' else, Chahlie. This North has locked up some othuh membahs of muh gang in jail, and we need to get 'em out. If yuh keep a cool head, ah think ah have a plan that will reunite you with Elijah and help us all solve the John North problem."

Charlie listened skeptically to Callendar at first, but he warmed up to the scheme as more feasible elements unfolded. Yes, he thought, this just might work — and provide a whole lot of entertainment to boot.

Sammy Fivetrees now had the Franklin family loaded into the buckboard. He tied his horse behind the wagon and hopped up into the driver's seat and took the reins. Captain Bristol asked him to have another word with him before he set out for town.

"Sammy, I wish you weren't so headstrong about resigning from the army. Since you're only a scout, I can't in all good conscience discipline you to do exactly as I would order a regular recruit. I know you want to help these folks by taking them into town, and I think that's agreeable. However, the army could still use you as a scout."

"Captain Bristol, you know that my written agreement to serve as a scout expired last month. I have stayed on only because of the hint of a possible Cheyenne uprising. There is not going to be an uprising — at least not this summer. If that General Miles has his way, there might be all kinds of blood spilled — especially up in Montana. No, I am just tired of living on dusty trails and getting shot at all the time. Four times I have been wounded — either shot or pierced with arrows. The greater good right now is helping these people. Thanks for your help in keeping Johnny alive. After losing an arm though, he is in no shape to provide for his family. After I see that they are safe in town, I want to come back and look after their place. Abby has promised me a job."

"Yes. Johnny is sleeping now, but before he dozed off, he sez we'd like Sammy to stay an' work wit us. We want him."

"Good luck to you then. Me and the other men are worried about Harris and Applesford. They should have reported back by now. We aim to look for them before heading into Copperhead ourselves."

"I suggest you go straight to Copperhead, pick up some people to help, then go out and look for those two men. There are only three of you, and you might fall into an ambush."

"I know. The telegram that North sent to the fort seemed rather grim. We're going to have to help put down a vicious gang. Looking back, I should have taken action against Agee and his hired gun, Callendar, the last time we were in town. Orders are orders. We had to return to the fort."

"Captain, after I take my friends to town, I will help you go out and find Harris and Applesford."

Bristol thought about it and replied, "I accept your offer, but Ewell, Warshinski, and I had better take a look alone first. The missing men might be hurt out there. It doesn't look like it will rain today, so tracking might be easier. Bring back the wagon, Sammy."

"It's a deal. See you soon."

As they rode away in the wagon, Harold asked Sammy, "Do you think this pain in my leg will ever go away?"

"Yes. We do not know how long that will be, but until it happens, you must be brave and prove how strong you can really be. I once was pierced in the stomach with an arrow and left to die in a cornfield. I lay there for half a day. Although the pain was tremendous, I refused to give in and die. My anger and pride told me to survive and recover. I prayed every hour to the Great Spirit for courage and strength. Then, when I least expected it, another scout came and rescued me."

"I'll bet you felt like he was going to be a friend for life," Abby remarked.

Sammy turned, smiled, and said, "Exactly. It was John North who found and saved me."

"Look," Harold cried. "There is a man ridin' toward us. It looks like Mr. Mason the storekeeper."

It was indeed Kirk Mason, who was visibly shocked, angered, and depressed about the violence perpetrated against the Franklins. He then related to all of the conscious riders in the buckboard, namely everyone except Johnny and Ruthie who were napping, the recent developments in Copperhead. A new marshal had been chosen, and the acting mayor was none other than himself.

"Let us hope that the Captain and his men may rejoin us in Copperhead. We shall need their assistance."

Captain Bristol found the farm of the tragic McGill. Soon, they found the bodies of McGill and his two hired hands in the barn heavily covered with hay. The abundance of buzzing flies had easily revealed their precise locations. Bristol told his men they would have to come back and bury these unfortunate victims later, due to the necessity keeping up the search for their own troopers. He was pretty sure that McGill and the others had been slaughtered by Blood Hawk and Callendar. The knife wound in McGill's midsection looked like the type caused by a Bowie knife. Blood Hawk was well known for using that particular weapon.

Inside the house, Bristol looked for other clues to confirm the identity of the killers. There were several coffee cups scattered inside the kitchen. Several chairs had been pulled out and not set back under the table thus indicating three or four people had been in the kitchen. There was a streak of blood on the wooden floor between the wood stove and the back door. Someone obviously dragged McGill or one of the others out of the kitchen. Next to one of the chairs Bristol found something peculiar. It looked like a small mirror. It was half-shattered. Where had he seen such a mirror before? He picked it up and put it in his shirt pocket. Details such as these were Bristol's specialty. Some day when he finally retired from the army, he thought about becoming a railroad detective. He loved the business of looking for evidence and solving cases. Keep thinking about it, Bristol, he reflected, this little mirror is something you shall recall.

Riding toward Copperhead from a direction parallel to, yet still a half mile away from, the buckboard party, P.J. Callendar took off his hat long enough to wipe the sweat building on his brow. He looked at his beloved hatband and privately gasped in horror as he discovered a glaring defect. One of the delightful mirrors constituting his hatband was missing. This was outrageous! Forget being pursued by North, the U.S. Army, and consideration of any level of guilt concerning multiple murders committed through the years — a precious possession was missing! How could God be so cruel, he snorted.

Callendar continued to ride toward town with his three deputies, Arnie the bartender, and Charlie Johnson. Soon, Charlie and Arnie pulled ahead of the others and raced toward town. Callendar and the others found a patch of forest, got off their horses, and made a temporary camp in a dense area. Callendar tried not to think about his beloved mirror as he directed his thoughts to a clever plan he had hatched. Its execution was underway.

22

CONSCIENCES OR MANIPULATIONS
IN THE OFFING

Some walls work effectively in muting sounds reverberating from the room on one side to the room on the other. This was scarcely the case of the wall separating the marshal's office and the room of jail cells.

Mortimer Agee had extended his beefy ear into available space between steel bars in the hope that detailed eavesdropping might be maximized. He ascertained that there was a wedge driven between John North and his loyal friend, Elijah Johnson. The wedge was an outlaw brother who had willingly committed crimes with P.J. Callendar.

"Deputy Wesley, did you overhear the birth of our opportunity in that other room?"

"Some, Mr. Mayor," he shrugged, "but I've mainly been payin' attention to that Frenchman in the next cell. He seems to be fevered and ailing. I'm thinkin' his getting well ain't working out much."

"The man probably has an infection," reasoned Edward Olson. "If this were not such a backward village he might entertain a chance of surviving."

Mortimer, the retired army officer opined, "This is not unusual. I saw it in the Civil War and in some of the Indian Campaigns. Men with shattered limbs who have to get them amputated quite often take on infection and die. This fellow may or may not have gangrene, but I don't hold out much hope. One thing is certain, he is not going to perform mayhem with Blood Hawk anymore."

"I could have defended him in a trial and used him to help put away North. I think we better yell for that Dr. Brandt and see if it's still possible to get the man to pull through."

"Fine, fine," Mortimer Agee uttered somewhat irritatingly, "but we have bigger fish to fry. I only wish we might get word out to Fulton at the Saloon that this Charlie Johnson is the key to helping Elijah Johnson letting us out of here. If Callendar were made aware that these two men are long lost, beloved brothers, then he would agree with me that the relationship could be used to maximum advantage. Fulton or one of his cronies could ride and get the word out to Callendar."

Almost as soon as this was stated, the door of the jail cell room opened, and two men stepped into the hall facing the cells.

John North stepped up to the cells accompanied by Arnie the bartender.

"Arnie claims he is Wesley's cousin and wants to check up on him. I have no objection, but I'm leaving a deputy nearby to listen in on your conversation," North declared.

Soon, Foster walked in and North prepared to step out. Suddenly, there was a troubled groan from Chapeau, and North investigated. He opened the cell, checked the man's forehead for temperature, listened to his struggle for breath, and observed the man's reckless thrashing about on the bunk.

"Foster, keep an eye on things. I'm going to fetch Dr. Brandt."

"Can't you send Elijah?" Edward asked.

"Not that it's any of your business, but Elijah is not here right now. He is taking a short, well-earned break."

North ran out the office and down the street.

Foster walked up to Chapeau's cell and watched the troubling form of an seriously ailing Pierre Chapeau.

"Psst! Arnie!" Mortimer Agee felt he had to communicate his message to Fulton quickly.

"Mr. Agee," Arnie whispered. "I run into Mr. Callendar and the others — they know you're in jail, and they got a new friend with them. It's Johnson's brother."

Mortimer Agee and Edward Olson looked at each other and nodded. Agee smirked and said, "Then all we need to do is wait for a move?"

"Yes," Arnie replied.

"What are you fellers whispering about over there?" Foster demanded. "Don't try anything funny. I may be a farmer, but I've shot more than my share of skunks, coyotes, and weasels. I heard you babble something about Fulton?"

"Mr. Foster, I — uh — ahem! I w-was inquiring about those two gorgeous ladies in the employ of Mr. Fulton. I really miss them and wondered if Arnie could arrange one of them gals to at least come up and visit me some time soon!"

"As long as I'm deputy I'm not makin' it easy for a character like you to frequent with strumpets. What you do with fallen ladies is your business, but I'll not be your pimp!"

"Forget it," Agee snapped with feigned indignity. "I'll just have to find my pleasure with these delightful females after I am rightfully set free by that circuit judge. Of course, a bible thumping sod-buster like you would not know what it would be like to lie in the arms with a woman of exquisite passion."

Do not let him bait you," Charging Buffalo interrupted. "They are wanting to anger and catch you off guard. You, the one with the face covered with black sagebrush, get out of here. Visiting time is ended."

"No damn Injun is gonna t — Ufff!" Arnie doubled over, gasped for breath, and struggled to stand straight after the Cheyenne poked him in the ribs with the barrel of a Winchester rifle.

"Leave — now!" Foster reiterated the demand.

Arnie left just as North came in with Dr. Brandt. The doctor examined Chapeau carefully. After listening with a stethoscope, he rose, turned to North, and declared, "This fellow needs some extensive medical care. You and one of your deputies ought to help me carry him over to my office. I may need to perform a surgery just to help the man drain out some poison that's starting to collect in his body. I want to avoid infection spreading."

Much to his own surprise, North looked down at the pain-ridden form of Chapeau and felt a glimmer of pity. Perhaps the sight was triggering memories from such places as Gettysburg or the mere fact that it was not deep in his nature to enjoy great suffering in human beings — even of one who participated in the destruction of his family. No, this was never the concept of the fitting revenge he had envisaged. He reached down to help lift Chapeau onto a blanket that Dr. Brandt, Charging Buffalo, and North planned to place him on, then use it as a makeshift carrying stretcher. Chapeau abruptly opened his eyes, grabbed North's shirtsleeve, and, under great labor, began to speak.

"North — J-John N-North. Listen...I do not want to die this way. May God forgive me for what I did. I never wanted to shoot those people on the wagon. I only wanted money. I-I'm a gambler. I just wanted to help sell some of those things in that wagon. I steal — I don't favor killin'! I didn't shoot you or your family! That crazy one, Johnson — he shot the boy. A Visigoth! Callendar — he and Blood Hawk were also killers. Me and Baker just liked easy money. Honest! I don't wanna be remembered as a child killer! You g-gotta believe me!"

"John...." It was Hannah standing in back of him. She had heard everything Chapeau had said. She gazed sympathetically at John and put her hand on his cheek.

"John, I want to help. Counting me, there are four of us to help carry this man."

Edward observed Hannah's tenderness but said nothing. He clinched his teeth tightly and burned hatefully in the corner of his cell. He would make Hannah pay for this public adultery. It was humiliating enough to be in jail, but her brazenness? Unforgivable!

Outside the saloon, a hobbling yet recuperating Elijah Johnson leaned against a hitching post and rolled a cigarette. Out of the corner of his left eye, he saw a figure move and heard, "SSStttt! It's me!"

Elijah instantly recognized the identity of the presence. He knew the familiar voice, general physical form, and sneaky nature of his brother. Upon walking around the corner of the Saloon building, inside the alley between that building and that of the stable, he saw his brother Charlie.

"Chahlie," he blasted in a loud whisper. "Why on earth are yuh here? How did yuh know ah was in this town? Did yuh follow North or that Injun here? Is that it?"

"Yes — er — yes! Ah followed them. It's great tuh see yuh again, Elijah! Who in hell hurt yer hand?"

"Yoah old gang boss, P.J., and his demonic Injun pal, Blood Hawk, both did some ugly work on me. Some friends yuh keep, baby bruthuh. Ah don't approve of 'em, ah'll have yuh know." Elijah stifled a desire to just read him a vociferous riot act and instead continued the whisper-to-low level voiced conversation. "Are yuh well, Chahlie? Ah yuh gettin' any second thoughts 'bout this sinful life yoah livin'? Ah keep tellin' yuh, the Lord can't keep makin' excuses foah yuh, Chahlie. Didn't Pa always tell yuh that too?"

"Yeah, yeah — poah Pa. He didn't deserve gettin' shot by them cahpetbaggers. The war ended in sixty-five, and in less than a year he gets shot just 'cause them Yankees thought he was paht of that mob tryin' to string up that uppity nigrah claimin' he was a new legislator. Imagine! One of them dahkies thinkin' he could work in government!"

"Look, ah didn't like them cahpetbaggers anymoah than you did, but Pa was always talkin' 'bout lynchin' people, and he was in the wrong place at the wrong time. A seventy-year-old man ought not be fussin' 'round with the hangin' type. But Pa's gone, and you and me are still here. When ah you gonna quit this outlaw life and be a normal fella?"

Charlie looked at his brother as if he were talking about a funny actor he had long ago seen in a stage play. Once he overcame that amusement, he said, "Elijah, we gotta break those fellers out of jail. The mayor, and that lawyer espeshly, they gonna help me get a fair trial. It ain't gonna happen in Copperhead though. That fella you rode with, John North — he's a crazy son-of-a bitch. All he wants to do is kill me and the othuhs. Ah hear that Chapeau is badly wounded and dyin', and North still wants tuh kill him. Worst of all, he won't talk to me to hear muh side. He's gonna listen to that lyin' Injun boy, instead of a superior wat man lak me, and jus shoot me. Ah don't 'spect yuh to throw lead at North, ah just want yuh to help get those fellers out so them and me can get ovah to some place like Laramie where we can get a fair hearin'."

Elijah listened to this plea, but remained skeptical. "Those men in the jail ahh not good men. The lawyer you want beats his wife, and the Mayor is at heart just anuthuh cahpetbagger."

"Elijah, they is the only chance ah got. You gotta do this foah me. Ah'm yoah only livin' kin. Please, Elijah. Muh life depends on it."

"How about if I take yuh in muhself, Chahlie. Ah can protect yuh. That's why ah rode with North to begin with. Besides, he promised he would not move to kill you unless you slapped leather yoahself. What duh yuh say?" Elijah seemed almost desperate in this entreaty. Deep down, he knew that his wild, unprincipled brother would reject his suggestion. Charlie had always looked for a fast, easy, selfishly convenient solution. For the most part, Elijah did not think Charlie was worth it. However, there was a driving fraternal responsibility in Elijah's soul that trumped all other considerations.

"Chahlie, before our mama died of diphtheria back in fifty-seven, she called me close on her deathbed and made me promise to look aftuh you — do all ah could to keep yuh safe, and not let yuh die young like Uncle Micah did. Uncle Micah was so much like you. He ran wild, played cards, chased loose women, slept with married women, and ended up gettin' shot in the face by an irate husband. Ma didn't want you tuh meet a violent end. Ah gave her muh word — and you made it hahd foah me to keep close on yoah tail all these years, 'cause you just had to run off and be a damnable sinner. Ah wish ah nevah had made that promise to Mama! Damn it, man — did yuh have to kill that little boy? Why did yuh have to kill that little brother of John North?"

Seeing an opening on his behalf, Charlie shrewdly replied, "This is one of the mis-understandings, bruthuh." Charlie instinctively grabbed Elijah's injured hand, then apologetically pulled away. "Ah didn't kill that boy. It wasn't me, Elijah. North is plumb crazy with revenge. It was Hector Long thet killed the boy. He was shot by North, but wasn't killed right away. He fell close to the screamin' boy. Before he died, he shot the child. See? Ah didn't do it! North is so full of hate, he's bat-blind to the truth."

"What about that Yankee yuh killed the othuh day? Charging Buffalo said yuh killed him just to get his horse."

"Damn right I shot him! He was haulin' out his rifle to pick me off! He saw me there and said, "Ah recognize you! Ah saw you on a wanted poster! Prepare to die, boy!" Wouldn't you shoot first, too? It was a lousy Yankee!"

Elijah thought it over, closed his eyes, rubbed his aching hand, and looked up to the heavens. "God forgive me — but ah have to save muh bruthuh!"

Charlie instantly fell to his knees and folded his hands in prayer, "Yes, Lawd, give muh bruthuh strength. Ah know ah been bad — very bad in muh time! But give us both the strength to prevail, so we can take these folks with us to a new town and help get me a fair trial — then ah'll go straight, so help me God!"

Impressed, Elijah looked at his brother and remarked, "You really did swear an oath to the Lord that you would try to go straight. Yuh did swear to Him?" Charlie nodded.

"All right, then let's do it. Listen up, though — we're goin' to do it in under a couple of conditions. First, no one gets hurt, and ah'll be the one to deal with North."

"Fair enough."

As the two men slowly walked down a side street, Charlie remembered those actors he had seen in that funny stage play in Kansas City a few years ago. He remembered how great it was that those city folk performers pretended to be someone other than who they really were. Charlie felt he should have been one of those fancy-pants actors. After all, he just gave a convincing performance of a man delivering an oath to the Lord. Heck! Charlie did not believe in the Lord! He always thought that Sunday school stuff was for ridiculous cripples and sissies. Charlie only believed in Charlie!

Since North and the litter bearers were at the opposite end of town, and quite preoccupied with the ailing Chapeau, it never occurred to any that Charlie and Elijah Johnson were meeting at that exact moment. Instead, John North wondered about the wisdom of his long-time quest for revenge.

Hannah said, "I know what you're thinking, John. I was feeling pretty hateful toward Edward until recently. Very recently. There has been so much ill feeling and cruelty that it's hard not to feel huge resentment. We have to keep telling ourselves there is a lot more to life than merely hating those inflicting harm."

John roughly stroked the stubble on his chin and said, "Hannah, seeing this man suffer and die doesn't make me happy. I don't really feel sorry for him, and I can't bring myself to forgive him, but I'm wondering if I'm just turning into a creature like these lowlifes. I don't want to be sub-human. I want justice and peace in my life."

"John, can't we just leave? Why can't we just saddle up and ride to Fortune River?"

"Hannah, that's not going to work. Callender, Blood Hawk, and those others are relentless killers. They cannot be allowed to roam free any longer. They must be stopped. If I can bring them in — lock them up like Agee — then justice will be served. I'm not certain it will play out that way. In my stomach I feel a violent resolution is inevitable."

Hannah looked at him sadly, brushed away tears beginning to form in her eyes, and then affectionately embraced John. Reluctantly, Hannah then eased away from the embrace.

"John, I promised to buy a decent dress for Sally. She is meeting me outside the General Store. Will you join me for dinner tonight?"

"You can count on me." John winked as she flashed him a flirtatious grin.

John watched as she dashed out the door. Inexplicably, he felt uneasy about her departure.

23

TREACHERY, VIOLENCE, AND ESCAPE

Sammy Fivetrees at last reached Copperhead with his passengers. Both of the children had fallen asleep. Johnny, seated between them in the back of the buckboard, had awaken. He caused Abby in the front to turn with a start when he first spoke.

"Why we goin' into town? Who's lookin' aftuh muh spread? Abby, tell me who's drivin' this wagon?"

"It's Sammy Fivetrees, Johnny, and he had tuh get us into town. Thet bad lawman and his thugs problee would be comin' back had we stayed. They say he's in the killin' mood."

"Den he ain't alone. Foah what that redneck polecat done to me an' muh boy, ah aim to kill him. Jus' as soon as ah'm strong again, ah'm knockin' him down. He's gonna die!"

"Johnny, we are outside the office of the town doctor. I will ask him to come out." Sammy looked inside, did not find the doctor, and returned to the wagon.

"There is no one inside. I will have to ask around and find the doctor. You and your son need help right away."

Walking up the street, Hannah and the now liberated saloon hostess, Sally, saw the traumatized family and ran up to the side of the wagon. "You must be the Franklins! Oh, dear God, this is what John was afraid of — you have been hurt! What can we do to help?"

"Ladies," Abby replied. "Thet terrible lawman came and shot muh Johnny — he lost his arm on account of thet evil lawman. They call him law — he uses the badge to jus' carry out the devil's will."

"He is not the law anymore, ma'am. Pardon, but I am Hannah Olson, a friend of John North. John North has locked up the mayor and — and some other bad people — and the folks in town made him the new marshal. John is now the law."

"Wish he had been the law befoah he came to visit," Johnny replied with sarcasm. "Them men came lookin' foah yoah 'friend,' and gave us hell 'cause we helped him out. We nevah harm anyone, and look what it gets us!"

Hannah felt strong empathy for these wronged people and felt particular pain for the child who was bandaged with the leg wound. Abby, noticing the direction of Hannah's concerned eyes, said, "It was that renegade injun. Blood Hawk — he hurt muh little boy like he was stoppin' a deer. These men ain't human!"

Sammy interrupted, "Mrs. Olson, where is the doctor?"

Hannah explained that they had been in the doctor's office but that John had a tip from one of the townspeople that Elijah Johnson had been seen talking with a long-haired stranger, so he left to find them. The doctor had to leave and help the Mulrooney boy who fell off a barn and broke his leg. The only person in the doctor's office was Mrs. Mason — who was watching over Pierre Chapeau.

"The wounded Frenchman who rode with Blood Hawk?" Sammy asked.

"Who is now dying," Hannah corrected. "Look, I am certain that the doctor would expect you to take your husband and son directly into the office, Mrs. Franklin. Sally and I can help you get them inside. Sammy, maybe you could find someone in town who could locate Dr. Brandt and get him back here as soon as he can?"

"Yes. I'll take care of that." It was not Sammy who spoke, but Kirk Mason. He had accompanied the buckboard into town but had chosen to check out something else at the end of town.

Upon learning the physician was at the Mulrooney residence, he said he knew where it was, so he was the ideal choice to find the doctor the quickest. Prior to leaving, however, he took Sammy aside and said, "There is trouble down in front of the saloon. I saw Fulton, the owner, talking with a longhaired stranger who kind of matches the description of the fella John North told me about recently. What worried me though was the two of them talking with Elijah Johnson as if they were hatchin' up some sort of plan. I think you better find North and warn him about some foul play. I'm not so sure we can trust that Elijah Johnson."

"I will find him," Sammy replied, then quickly left.

Sammy ran around a corner building. Nate McAvee suddenly emerged and struck Sammy over the head with a rifle. He remained unconscious more than fifteen minutes.

John North had already located Elijah. He was standing outside the saloon talking with Fulton. Charlie was not with them.

"Elijah, I got a tip that you were seen speaking with Charlie not more than ten minutes ago. If you know where he is, then you know I have to arrest him."

Elijah did not reply but turned and looked at Fulton as if he were the proper individual to provide the answer.

Fulton blustered, "Marshal North, I don't know what you two are talking about. This man wearing a badge — your deputy, I presume, asked me if he could go inside and buy a drink, and I told him that you ordered me to shut down the business today. Now he argues that when a deputy needs a drink, then the 'barkeep had better provide it or else.'"

"You sound like a man stretching the truth tighter than a catfish gut in the beaks of two contrary crows. Is the longhaired man inside the bar?"

Almost immediately, the blood-curdling scream of a woman was heard. They heard it through a front window of The Saloon. John turned and ran toward the building's entrance but lost his balance when someone tripped him. Elijah had extended his foot in front of John and caused him to lose balance and plunge headfirst into the boardwalk. Surprised, and obviously angry, John attempted to rise quickly but was kicked in the ribs by Fulton. Next, he heard the hammer of a revolver pulled back. Catching his breath after the painful fall and kick, he looked up and saw that Elijah was aiming a pistol at him.

"John, if yuh make a move toward that saloon, or me, so help me, ah will kill yuh. Ah can't let you harm muh bruthuh!"

The saloon doors swung open and Charlie Johnson strutted out like the chief rooster in the chicken coop. With her arm around Charlie's waist, Laura the hostess looked every inch the hen of his conquest. Her smirk was both irritating and defiant.

Charlie chuckled to himself, then kicked North brutally in the face. North flew back, and Fulton once again kicked him in the side. John North struggled for air — this time the wind had been knocked out of him.

"How'd I do, boys? Did I sound like a damsel in distress? Hahahaha! What's the matter mister big-strong-marshal? Cat got your tongue? Maybe that lawyer's woman, or Sally, wrapped you around their fingers and let you get your guard down? You don't look like such a strong man now. You missed out badly rejecting a real woman like me!"

"Enough with the beatins'," Elijah roared. "Ah didn't say yuh could treat 'im like a cur. Ah did what ah said I was gonna do. Now get busy."

Fulton quickly got a rope he had hidden under the front porch and with Laura's assistance tied John to the hitching post. They made the knots extra tight. As soon as they felt John was secure, Fulton kicked dust into his face.

"Stop it, yuh damn saloon trash — ah said nuthin' 'bout not killin' gahbage like you. Hurt muh friend again and ah'll blast out yoah livuh."

North repressed a steaming rage and said, "You're no friend of mine. You showed your true colors. I suppose you were an admirer of Benedict Arnold. Better yet, I'll wager you played ring around the rosie with John Wilkes Booth."

"Shet up, John. Don't rile me."

"Why not? You've thrown in with scum and vermin."

Fulton took John's red bandana, stuffed it between his teeth, and gagged him. Convinced the gag was not going to slip loose, he turned to Charlie and said, "All right. We got him subdued. Are you ready to carry out the jail break?"

John's eyes expressed extreme anger and frustration, and his cry of protest emerged only as an effectively contained muffled utterance.

"You ain't springin' no one from jail, Saloon boss. Me an' thet barkeep, Ahnie, are handlin' it. You stay here an' help out muh bruthuh. We need someone with the will to shoot this lawman dead if he's lucky enough to escape. Sorry, Elijah, ah won't kill 'im if he's tied, but ah make no promises should he evah get loose."

Charlie sprinted away but turned and yelled, "Come on, dahlin', we need you foah owa little drama. Actin' is equally as fun than robbin' banks!"

Laura giggled, pulled up her long skirts, then ran behind the immature Charlie Johnson.

North felt powerless, betrayed, injured, and, above all, helpless. The last time he had felt this inert and useless, he had been cut down by Callendar and his gang. Once again, Callendar and his gang had bested him. How many innocent people would be injured or destroyed this time? This was wrong — all wrong — and it was his fault. His gravest mistake was in trusting a man he had believed to be his friend — Elijah Johnson.

McAvee had witnessed the capture of John North. Believing himself undetected by anyone of consequence, he swiftly rode back to Callendar and his henchmen to tell them it was time to move in for the kill.

Laura sashayed into the marshal's office and found Foster seated at the desk. She took note of his startled reaction and turned on the charm.

"Hello, Mr. Deputy. My, you are a handsome fellow, aren't you? I'll bet you have charmed more than your share of the pretty ladies in your time!"

Embarrassed, Foster nervously replied, "Er — uh — I dunno. I'm not such a big deal. I managed to court muh sweetheart back in California and convince her to marry me. Shucks, there's nothin' special about me."

Laura walked close to the deputy then slowly sat on the edge of the desk. "You have a wife? My, oh my. Does she know that you like to undress other women with your eyes? Maybe she likes that." Laura wet her lips, then began to run her gloved hand up and down Foster's arm. "Some women like hearing about their men having fun with strange women. It gets them excited. Does that get you excited, Mr. Deputy?"

Absolutely stunned and disoriented, Foster could only say, "W-wait a second. This is all appealing and all, but what are you doing in here, young lady? Do you know I am old enough to be your father?"

"That's why you ah such a sinner, and should be put outta yoah misery, old timer!"

It was Charlie. Laura quickly slid off the desk and dashed toward the corner. Attempting to regain composure, Foster reached for the sidearm in his holster, but Charlie was too fast. He reacted not by reaching for a pistol, but by throwing a knife he was already holding in his hand. The knife struck Foster in the chest. He fell to the desk, crying out in pain. Laura quickly took a coffee pot and struck the injured man over the head several times until he became unconscious.

"You ah such a capable whore, Laura. Thank yuh kindly," Charlie complimented.

Charlie then took the keys from the wall and quickly unlocked the jail cells containing the dethroned mayor, disgraced lawyer, and rejected deputy. Agee smiled, extended a hand and said, "You must be the long-lost, longhaired wonderboy, Charlie. I am much obliged to you."

"You're durn tootin' yuh're obliged. You ah like me now — ridin' in the Callendar gang. If yuh don't like it, we'll happily kill yuh."

Wesley looked relieved and almost pleased that he apparently had returned to the good graces of Callendar and company. He joyously strapped on his gun and holster and charged out to fetch some horses.

Edward, alone, did not appear particularly jubilant. He looked at the critically injured Foster slumped over the blood-stained desk and realized he could now be cited as a co-conspirator in an attempted murder or manslaughter. He desperately sweated and tried to think up a way out of this predicament.

"Hey, mister! Thanks for letting me out! I really appreciate it. I'm on my way now, so my best to you always...."

"Not so fast, city boy...P.J. Callendar made it quite clear you are to ride with us. When we get outta this territory, somewhere south, he means to have a good lawyer with 'im. You ah a good lawyer? If not, it's easy jus' tuh finish yuh here."

Agee and Olson looked at each other worriedly, and Agee spoke for both when he declared, "He's just overwhelmed, sir. He wants to ride with us. Of course he does!"

Wesley burst through the door and said, "I've got 'em here. I got three horses. I figured the army mount in front was yours, Charlie. So we got enough for each of us."

Laura protested, "Only four? What about me, sweetheart?"

Charlie deliberately walked up to her, kissed her on the lips, and stood behind her as he encircled her waist with one arm. Laura sighed, "Charlie, you have a forceful way about you. After we leave this outhouse town, we must spend some really good time in bed."

"Maybe in anuthuh life, dahlin'." Not hesitating, Charlie took his hunting knife, still partially covered with Foster's blood, and plunged it deeply into the woman's lower back. The blade entered the left kidney, and she failed to scream when she badly wanted to cry out. She slumped to the floor dead.

"Can't have excess baggage, can we, men?"

Agee looked at the crumpled form of the hooker he had enjoyed on many, many occasions and stifled a strong desire to reach out and strangle Charlie. Wesley looked stunned and saddened. Olson felt his stomach churn and stifled the urge to vomit.

With no more delays or visible regrets, the four men mounted the horses and began to ride across town to the area in front of the saloon. It was at this location that Callendar and the others would meet them.

Drawing closer, Olson saw what appeared to be light reflecting off glass and realized it was sunlight bouncing off the funny mirrored hatband of Callendar. He could be seen with at least four other riders facing him and his own party. They were near the doctor's office. Olson saw the form of a woman step outside the door and ponder the wisdom of crossing the street. She apparently thought it prudent to wait until the riders from either end of the street passed. Olson then realized that the woman was Hannah. He suddenly broke away from the group and headed toward her.

Hannah saw her husband angrily bear down on her. Frightened, she turned and tried to go back into the doctor's office, but Edward knocked her down with the horse. Luckily, she was not trampled. Instead, she was knocked backwards and fell against a bench. Her head struck the armrest, and she was made unconscious.

Callendar outdistanced the others in his group, and galloped up to the scene. Blood Hawk had already drawn his knife and was ready to toss it into Edward's spine, but Callendar directed, "Don't kill 'im, chief. I might need 'im." Turning attention to Olson, he sneered, "You shoah is a piece of work, barrister. Ah kill whoevah gets in muh way, but ah don't go out of the way to harm ladies or children. This is yoah wife, yuh Yankee cowpile. Maybe she's jus' too much woman foah the likes o' you. Put her on yoah horse. We're takin' her with as a hostage. If yuh try to harm her again, Mr. Lawyer, I will personally enjoy putting bullets in yoah eyes."

Resuming the urge again to vomit, Olson picked up his unconscious wife and made her straddle his horse. He hopped up behind and balanced her while controlling the beast.

"Fellas, let's get ovah tuh the Saloon so we may reunite North with his long, lost family."

24

BRAVE RESISTANCE AND MORTALITY

Edward Olson and Mortimer Agee were astute enough to recognize that no matter what Callendar and his henchmen said or promised, they were still hostages. Sure, the only proclaimed hostage was Hannah, but Callendar was in command, and they both knew their survival was insured only if they provided the man enticing benefits for allowing them to live. Instantly conjuring what he believed to be one of his frequent flashes of genius, Mortimer Agee quickly stepped out of the right stirrup and swung down the left side of his horse. Before hearing any vulgar admonishments, he said, "I better check inside that doctor's office. It might pay to get some bandages, iodine, or other items that might help in case any of us get wounded during the chase out of here!"

Callendar bellowed, "All right, but hurry up. I wanna finish off North before any Yankee soldiers ride in here. I'm gonna kill them too, but pluggin' North without distractions will really give me a day to fondly remembuh."

Agee chortled as he considered the genius of his diversion. Along with the bandages, he hoped to steal any cash, extra weapons including sharp surgical devices, or anything else of value to be purloined from Dr. Brandt's office.

As Agee walked in he sensed the presence of someone behind him. It was Edward Olson.

"What are you doing in here, Olson?"

"This is our chance, Agee! We can escape out the back door. Those men will murder us once they think we're no longer useful. Come on, let's run!"

Thump! A noise came from the other room.

"Wait! Someone is back there. Doc Brandt! Hey! It's only me, Mortimer Agee. North has, er — released me and Olson from jail due to insufficient evidence. Come on out!"

Slowly, someone came out, but it was not Dr. Brandt. It was Sally Redmond. She looked at the two men meekly, looked down shyly, and advised, "The doctor is not here. He will come back soon."

"He left Chapeau alone, I take it? Let's check on him."

Abruptly, Charlie Johnson stepped in the room. "You — dude — get outside on your horse. Move, or ah'll put a crease in yoah head to match the crease in them trousers."

Olson practically leaped to the door and bounded onto his designated horse. He feared Charlie — and was correct in doing so.

"I wanna see muh ol' pal, the Frenchman. Hey, Chapeau! It's me, Chahlie Johnson! How in the name of molasses at Manassas are yuh?"

Overly mesmerized by his own imagined War Between the States wit, he gleefully threw open the door and saw a makeshift hospital room. There were three beds, and they were all occupied. In the first, there were two black children, both sleeping. In the second, a black man who had most recently lost an arm. He was being attended to by an attractive black female. In the third, he espied Pierre Chapeau. He ignored the black people and went directly to Chapeau.

"Pierre, yuh crazy damn gambler — how'd yuh get all messed up like this? What happened, did you an' thet niggrah ovuh there cut each other's ahms off? Somebody cut off yer — Hey, Chapeau!"

Charlie looked closer and noticed that Chapeau was staring straight up at the ceiling. His eyes were glassy, and his facial muscles were taught. The skin was warm, but it was indisputably obvious that Pierre Chapeau was dead.

"Why ah'll be hanged — he finally bought it. Ah always figured he'd get shot cheatin' in a card game. Hey, blackbird, did you kill him?"

"Do ah look like ah wuz in any condition tuh kill anyone, white trash? Thet new marshal, John North, and his deputy, Elijah Johnson done shot this man when he held up a stagecoach."

Charlie walked up to Johnny, scowled, then backhanded him sharply.

"Mind yoah mannahs, slave boy. Ah don't take no sass from cotton pickers like you-all. If ah had the time, I'd cut yoah…"

Before he could finish his sentence, Abby took an iron bedpan and struck him over the head with all the strength she could muster.

Meanwhile, in the other room, Sally started to cry for help, "You leave me alone! I'm not going with you! I hate you!"

"You'll go with me and like it, you little bitch! I used to pay top dollar for beddin' privileges with you, and that entitles me to own you! You're going with, and you're gonna keep on bein' my bed warmer!"

The door from the other room flew open, and a very weak, yet determined Johnny Franklin wobbled through the doorway. He rested his body against the door frame and pointed a revolver — Charlie Johnson's revolver — directly at Mortimer Agee. "Let her go, you slimy, crap-belly heathen. You people think it's fine to whip muh people, hurt women and chil'ren, and still got the nerve to call yerselves superior. Raht now the only one superior is me, Agee, and this gun says so. Leave the girl alone!"

Agee sneered at Johnny defiantly and retorted, "There ain't no way some uppity ex-slave is going tell me what to do. I used to command men in battle! A lot of my men fought to free animals like you. Personally, I wished Jeff Davis had hanged the lot of you. Now gimme that gun, you ungrateful snail…"

Johnny fired the pistol. Agee clutched at his heart and tried to talk, but death came to him rapidly. He released Sally, then fell to the floor like an irrelevant pile of dirty linen.

Terrified, Abby came out and tried to catch Johnny as he began to pass out. Both Sally and Abby helped him to a chair, and he managed to say, "Abby...Ah've always loved you and the chil'ren...."

Abby looked compassionately into the eyes of her husband and wanted to speak out her own love for him, but a man stepped inside and shot Johnny through the neck. The shot was instantly fatal.

Abby fell with Johnny to the floor. She could not lose him now — not after all that had happened. She sobbed uncontrollably.

A horrified Sally looked to the doorway and saw Nate McAvee pointing a smoking revolver at her and Abby. He cocked the hammer back and aimed at Abby, but he was stopped by another man — it was Callendar.

"Yuh damn fool. Now that the shootin' has started, the whole town will be on to us. We've got no time to shoot these women. Besides, ah don't approve o' killin' women or kids — 'specially kids, even if they're dahkies. Let's see how good yuh are fightin' men, Mr. McAvee." Callendar and McAvee quickly revived the half-unconscious Charlie Johnson, helped him mount his horse, and began riding toward the saloon.

Arnie Mitchell, the bartender, rode down the street and yelled, "Let's turn them horse hooves into fire — we gotta leave! The cavalry is ridin' in, and they got their guns drawn."

"Let us fight them — that was the plan," insisted Blood Hawk.

Callendar, always trying to stay two to three steps ahead of his adversaries said, "No. Let's ride. We can always ambush them later. In town, they have the advantage. In the mountains, we will have it. Move!"

The gang rode quickly away just as Captain Bristol bore down on them firing pistols and rifles. One of the soldiers saw a young Indian step out of an alley carrying a rifle. He aimed, fired, and struck Charging Buffalo.

From a side window, someone fired down on the cavalrymen. It was Brad Fulton. He dropped the soldier who had shot Charging Buffalo. Captain Bristol heard the shot, turned, and aimed at the sniper in the window. He put two slugs into Fulton who crashed through the window and fell onto the street. The fall broke his neck.

Bristol ordered his command to halt. He wanted to check on his fallen soldier, Trooper Warshinski. Warshinski had been shot in the buttocks but had fallen onto his head on the street. He was breathing all right, but he was obviously wounded and unconscious. To continue chasing the outlaws with the rest of his command seemed futile. After all, Bristol was down to Trooper Ewell and himself.

"We better get this man into the doctor's office."

"I'm the doctor, Captain. I can help him. What's all the shootin' about?"

Sally stepped out of Brandt's office and sadly said, "Doctor, there's a lot of death in your home. Too much death...."

At the other end of town, Elijah Johnson waited until he heard no more gunshots, then approached John North. "John, I'm dreadful sorry I helped out those scoundrels, but ah had tuh help get muh bruthuh Chahlie outta here. Ah couldn't trust yuh tuh spare him."

Kirk Mason came up behind Johnson and ordered him to release John North. "Make a bad move, Johnson, and so help me, I swear on the Good Book, I will shoot you."

"You'll get no resistance from me." Johnson then cut North lose and helped him to his feet. "They promised me no killin', and ah had to take 'em at their word. Chahlie gave me his word — that's what counted."

Kirk Mason let out a huge, "Huh! Some word! Copperhead's streets are drenched in blood, you lumbering-ox-of-a fool! There are killings at Doc Brandt's and in the marshal's office too! On top of that, those fiends abducted Mrs. Olson."

Feeling stunned, angered, and utterly powerless simultaneously, North looked to the heavens and issued a primal yell that made both Johnson and Mason literally jump.

"They took Hannah? You were in on that too?"

Before Johnson could sincerely deny such a horrible charge, John North threw a right punch into Elijah's jaw. The man was picked up off his feet and sent flying into the dust. North picked him up again, slugged him in the stomach, and then backhanded twice across the face. Blood ran from Johnson's nose as he gurgled out, "They dou — double crossed me too, John. I care for Hannah, too. I'd nevah hurt the dear girl."

North caught hold of his emotions, released his hold on Johnson, and said, "You've done a lot of damage. This is what happens when you turn into a Judah. I'm locking you up, Elijah, and if Hannah dies, so help me, I'll see you dancing at the end of a rope."

The three men went to the marshal's office and observed the carnage within. Laura, the hooker, was dead, but Mr. Foster, the proud family-man farmer of California, clung to life.

North gently lifted Foster up from the bloody desk in order that the man might be better able to say his final words, if such an act were possible. North softly said, "I am so very, very sorry for you and your family, Mr. Foster. I regret asking you to get involved."

Foster tried to smile, but grimaced and said, "No — need. I was…involved be-before we… Just tell Beatrice I love her. Please get her word that I tried to help good folks. She and the children will un…" Abel Foster exhaled loudly, then passed away.

"I'm awful sorry about this, John. It ain't right. It weren't supposed to happen like this."

"Get your sorry ass in the jail cell. Listening to you talk makes me sick."

Captain Bristol walked in and spoke. "Omigod, more killing in here too."

"Captain Bristol — what do you mean by, 'here too?'"

Bristol described the horrible events that had occurred inside Doctor Brandt's office. Three men lay dead inside: Pierre Chapeau of old wounds and complications; Mortimer Agee, killed at the hand of Johnny Franklin courageously attempting to save Sally Redmond; and Johnny himself, slain by McAvee.

"McAvee?" cried, Johnson. "I used to pan gold with that turd! If I'd knowed then what I know now, I woulda drowned him in Fohtune Rivuh!"

"Shut up in there! Talk is cheap, Johnson."

Briefly, North and Bristol considered the next move. John spoke, "With or without your help, I intend to track down and kill Callendar. If he or any of his gang surrender, I will bring them in alive. Knowing Callendar and Blood Hawk, however, I know they will not give up. Will you ride with me and put an end to this plague?"

"I certainly shall. These men have not only committed extreme local crimes, but they have killed soldiers of the U.S. Army and brought general chaos to the territory. They must be terminated. Unfortunately, I only have Private Ewell to accompany us."

"I shall ride with you — and the boy will as well."

The speaker was Sammy Fivetrees, and the boy referred to was Charging Buffalo.

"Thank you, Sammy. You are the truest of friends. Your head is bleeding. What..."

"Ambushed. I'll live. Now I want to avenge my friends. Johnny is dead, and it is the way of me and my people to seek justice in this manner."

"Charging Buffalo, you are also hurt."

"It is nothing. Just a bullet that grazed my collarbone. It knocked me down, and I was stunned, but got up and the outlaws were already gone. I feel ashamed that I did not get here sooner to help Mr. Foster. It looks like he is dead."

"Why weren't you here, Charging Buffalo? Where were you during the jail break?"

"It was my time for what you call, 'a break,' so I walked outside the town — into the area where there are no roads — and I prayed to the spirits for guidance. I have been struggling with wanting to go back to my people, the Cheyenne, or to stay in this world that you people live in. I do not feel like I belong in either place — that is why I prayed for an answer."

"What did the spirits advise you?" inquired Sammy Fivetrees.

"They said nothing except 'find Blood Hawk — you must find Blood Hawk and stop him forever.' I felt that the spirits told me Blood Hawk is ordered by evil spirits to do their bidding! They also told me in my mind that they are guiding the longhaired white man as well. They both must be silenced, and I am destined to accomplish that."

"Son, you don't have to do this. The four of us will deal with these men."

"I made up my mind. I will hunt down Blood Hawk with or without you."

"You better go with us then," advised Sammy. "Alone, you will die for certain. In joining us, we will vanquish Blood Hawk, Callendar, Charlie Johnson, and all of their toads. This must be remembered."

"Good advice," North concurred. "Let's quit blabbing, gather some more cartridges, and start riding. We still have some daylight left."

After making their preparations, North felt he must first pay his respects to Abby and the children. Doctor Brandt, Kirk Mason, the barber, and others had already removed the dead body of Agee from the doctor's office, but Johnny was still stretched out on a cot with a blanket over his face. John North walked up to the cot, took off his hat, slid down the blanket, and looked at the still countenance of Johnny Franklin.

"Mrs. Franklin, I do not have the words to describe just how deeply I regret this. You were happy with your loving family, and I brought misfortune to you and them. I will forever grieve for you."

Abby heard this pronouncement, and said "Mistuh North, this weren't yoah fault. You nevah done us any harm. Deep down, Johnny knew this too. He tried and tried to get along with these folks, but they was bad — bad as the devil hisself at times. You can make amends by stoppin' these devils from hurtin' othuh people again. Johnny stopped one of 'em, but I pray you will stop the othuhs. It's yoah destiny."

John felt a tear forming in his eye, wiped it away, then bent over and gently kissed Abby on the cheek. "You are a wise and wonderful woman, Abby. Johnny was very lucky to have found and married you. I am sure you made his life special every day. May I speak to your children?"

Abby granted permission, and John North found them both sitting up in the bed. Their eyes were red following much crying. Harold seemed pleased to see John and held out his arms. Little Ruthie did as well. Sally, fighting back her own tears, helped Ruthie sit up. John hugged both the boy and the girl.

"Will you stay with us a while, Marshal North?"

"I wish I could, son, but I have to find the criminals who brought all this suffering to your family. I know what it is like to lose a father."

"Did these men kill your daddy too?"

"Yes, they did. They also killed my mother and kid brother. They have committed great wickedness and must be stopped forever. This is why I cannot stay. I just wanted to assure you that you must never feel alone. You have your mother, and she will take care of you."

"But we want our daddy back!"

"I know you do. But your daddy will always be with you in here and here." He pointed to both their heads and hearts.

"Mr. Fivetrees says he wants to come back and help us with our ranch," Ruthie says. "He is a nice man."

"Not only that," North cheerfully added, "he will definitely do it. I have known him a long, long time, and he always keeps his word. He is a Cherokee."

Sally smiled, caressed Ruthie's hair, and said, "I will help Abby look after the children until Mr. Fivetrees and you return. You must return — and please, please, come back with that lovely Hannah Olson. She is a sweet lady and a loving person. The world needs her."

"So do I. I will bring her back — I intend to marry her. I shall marry her."

Following a pronouncement John North could not guarantee but believed he must guarantee — for if he did not, then all purpose for living would seem meaningless — he joined the rest of his posse and rode away in hot pursuit.

Several miles outside of town, it became clear to Edward Olson that riding double with his wife was becoming a burden.

"Look, we are starting to go up into the mountains. I am not a skilled horseback rider, and I am finding it difficult to ride double with Hannah. I am afraid we both may fall off as we get to the higher elevations."

Most of the outlaws laughed loudly. Charlie, in particular, found this amusing. He said, "You ain't much of a man, are you, circus britches? Muh bruthuh — who I woulda taken along if'n ah hadn't been so groggy from that black woman bouncin' that pan ovuh muh head — why didn't we go back for Elijah, P.J.?"

"Because there wasn't time, Chahlie! Besides, Elijah and North are still friends. North won't kill him. Yuh can go back for Elijah later after we pick off North and his companions. Yuh has to know that they *will* be catchin' up with us sooner or later."

Hannah was now awake. She felt sickened that Edward found her physical presence to be such an ordeal. Accompanying any of these men was cruelty beyond measure, but being derided so publicly by Edward seemed almost the epitome of devaluation. In listening to the conversation, however, she felt a glimmer of hope. It was mentioned that "North...*will* be catchin' up...." John was still alive, and if living, he would not rest until he rescued her. She knew he would do this, because she also knew she would do the same for him. They were more than lovers now — their souls were spiritually united.

Callendar once again laughed at the whining Edward Olson, then told him to let Hannah get off his horse. Callendar swung by, scooped up the auburn-haired beauty, and seated her on the front area of his saddle. He squeezed her waist and said, "Not to worry, purty lady, I wouldn't let yuh fall and get spoilt in a million years."

John North and his determined group rode hard and fast. Sammy had quickly ascertained that the outlaws were riding up the trail to Fortune River. All of the men were unified in their intent to stop the villainous gang before they ever reached that town. At the last minute, John North had agreed to take along one additional rider. This one, however, was handcuffed. Elijah Johnson was taken along as potential bait. In spite of this, Elijah shared most of the same negative feelings toward the desperate men being pursued.

25

THE ACCIDENT

"I do not fear Blood Hawk and the others. I have seen, and even experienced, the evil of such men as Blood Hawk, Callendar, and this prospector's brother. Why do you continue to caution me, Cherokee?"

Sammy Fivetrees noticed the intensity in Charging Buffalo's question and felt it was best answered with calmness and verisimilitude. "It is not a question of bravery but of prudence. We are men who willingly resist and fight actions that are unjust up to the point of taking human life. Yet, we are unwilling to cause destruction that is pointless and unwarranted. On the other hand, the men we are tracking have shown little regard for life unless it profits them personally. Going against such people is extremely dangerous. They will not hesitate to ruin or remove life. One must carefully plan any attack on them. Fearing them is wise because it breeds valuable caution. Underestimating the extent of their hostility and disregard for what is precious is foolhardy."

"You are a wise man, Fivetrees. I respect your opinion, but one can be overly cautious and reveal a weakness that they will readily use to their advantage. Bold courage will not show them that weakness."

For a moment, Sammy said nothing. He sipped a small mouthful of water from his canteen then said, "Substituting passion for reason has often ended the lives of good men. Imparting this is the last, and best, advice I may offer."

John North heard the full conversation but did not interfere. If anyone could reach Charging Buffalo, it was Sammy. Still, he recognized the anger expressed by the young Cheyenne. In some ways, it was similar to the anger that had gnawed inside ever since the family massacre. The men they were after were terrible, ruthless, savage monsters who always left misery and death in their wake — yet they always seemed to get away. Reason, passion: who cared at this point? One way or the other, there would be no escape for them now.

North looked at the saddened face of Elijah Johnson. Had he been too harsh in his condemnation of Elijah? Was the man just a fool who loved a brother so much that he became blind to the extreme evil of that brother's life? North thought about his own brother — would he have loved him that much had he grown up to be evil? It was a question deemed unanswerable. One thing was certain: Charlie Johnson had crossed one line too many.

Two down, three remaining. Baker died instantly at North's hand. Chapeau died of injuries inflicted by Elijah and North. Yes, Elijah, the same man he had compared to John Wilkes Booth. Then there was the Indian loved by no one, Blood Hawk; Johnson's hellhound brother; and the slayer of his parents, P.J. Callendar.

Captain Bristol interrupted John's self-reflection. "Did I tell you we found a farmer and his hired hands dead in their barn just before we rode into town?" asked Captain Bristol. "By the look on your face, I guess I didn't. These men were all butchered to death by a large knife — a Bowie knife, I wager. In all my years of soldiering, I have been in many battles, used a lot of force, ordered men to their deaths, and caused the deaths of enemies. Some people who dislike the army accuse soldiers of committing horrible atrocities in the name of 'fighting for America.' To me murdering men in their own home, tending to their own affairs — now that's something worthy of the definition *atrocity*."

Trooper Ewell added, "When we started out there were six of us, counting Sammy Fivetrees. If we count Sammy again, who's saying he quit the army, then we are three. I buried two of my friends — they were murdered just like those farmers. Warshinski's the lucky one. He just got shot in the ass. Who knows about us? That Blood Hawk savage must be the biggest demon of them all."

Charging Buffalo said, "There is the one called O'Toole you must not forget. I make no excuses for Blood Hawk, whom I plan to kill, but it was this prospector's longhaired brother who shot O'Toole down like a robin being used for target practice. The white man is just as demonic."

Elijah Johnson said nothing and only hung down his head in shame.

Finally, North said, "Who is the worst — the men who carry out the atrocities or the leader who plans or condones them? Callendar may be the most vile of all. Do not forget that these three are not alone. There are four others accompanying them, and the full measure of their dishonor and wickedness is yet to be fully revealed. Approaching them means approaching with extreme caution and prudence. We want to survive these 'encounters.' Most of all, they are holding two hostages, and we must save their lives."

One of the two hostages relentlessly complained as the journey over the narrow mountain trail continued. Edward Olson was not in control of this journey, and he did not like the absence of control one iota.

"This is the way to Fortune River? What kind of an animal nest did your mother and uncle move into, Hannah? Were they raving mad? Are you just as insane as they are? Is that why you absolutely had to come visit them? I was delusional to consider possibly thriving in this Purgatory. Well, we're heading their way, so are you blissful?"

Hannah turned quickly, resisting Callendar's grip that was more designed to prevent her falling, than inflicting pain. "Shut up, Edward! I don't care what you think anymore. You were a terrible husband and a discredit to the entire male gender. A real man does not use fists on a woman. If you were manly, you'd respect me and grant a divorce."

McAvee cackled and sneered, "That's right, Ed-WARD, you oughta be more of a man, Ed-WARD. I bet you never knew how tuh satisfy a woman. Was this gal too much work fer you, Ed-WARD?"

Edward was livid and shouted, "Shut up, you prairie dung pile. You're pretty tough when you gun down an ex-slave, but I notice you didn't stick around to face the army!"

McAvee raised his arm to strike Edward, but Blood Hawk blocked it with his rifle barrel. "All of you talk too much. The marshal and the posse will hear you if you keep howling like coyotes. Besides, the trail is narrow, and we are high above a deep gorge. Make a mistake, and falling to your death would be easy."

Edward glared at McAvee, then looked at a dark cloud move over the sun. "Hey, is that a storm coming in? We never had to put up with this sort of thing back east."

Suddenly, a flash of lightning struck a tree parallel to Edward Olson. His horse panicked and reared up. Edward, admittedly an unskilled equestrian, desperately tried to gain control but only made matters worse as he angrily kicked the horse in the right side. The action spooked the horse even more, and it started to buck. Edward lost his balance.

"I-I...am...fal..falling — God in Heav — AieeYeAHHHHH!" Edward's cry was heard for only a second on the trail and progressively faded as he fell further down the deep gorge. The horse went down as well. The faint sound of Edward's body crunching against the jagged rocks was heard by all the witnesses. Then the awesome sight of Edward's horse falling onto Edward's mortally wounded body produced an indescribably sickening, yet distinctive crunching sound. Both rider and horse were mortally damaged.

Hannah cried, "Edward! Oh, God, no! Not this way! Edward!" She was in shock.

Callendar drolly remarked, "Ah don't take much stock in all thet talk 'bout God and religion, Mrs. Olson, but yuh gotta admit, that lightning sure saved you a heap o' trouble in gettin' a divorce from thet man. Oh, well, ah guess ah wasn't destined to have an eastern lawyer after all."

Blood Hawk tied his own horse to the lightning stricken tree, then deliberately walked close to the edge of the cliff, pointed his rifle, and shot the horse.

"The animal was still alive. It was not fair that it suffer due to the inferior man who rode him. On the other hand, if he lives, he may suffer. I won't put him out of *his* misery."

"Ach du lieber! Er ist tot! Dis mann — he does not move. No problem."

Down on the jagged rocks Edward gasped for air. The weight of the horse's body had forced his own body to be further pinioned painfully onto the sharp stones. With his dying breath, Edward wondered why such a terrible fate should be his.

26

STEADY PURSUIT

"**D**id you men hear it?" asked Captain Bristol.

"Yes. It was a Winchester shot. Before that, I think there was the cry of an animal," answered North.

"And the scream of a man," added Sammy.

"You fellers have got better hearing than I have! I only heard a gunshot, and it weren't all that loud," Trooper Ewell declared. "Wonder what it means, besides workin' harder for my pay this month?"

"It means someone or something — perhaps both — were sidelined in their trip up to the pass. With these fiends, it's hard to tell if someone got murdered or had an accident."

North thought for a moment, then replied, "Elijah and I once came down from that pass. It is fairly hazardous even if you are proceeding at a careful pace. The likelihood of taking a spill is pretty good."

Elijah looked up, encouraged that someone might utter his name devoid of adjectives of burning contempt, and spoke. "Remembuh what ah told yuh, John — walkin' ahead of the horses, and guidin' them, 'stead of ridin' 'em down — that was the safest. I'll wager those fellers are so full of fugitive ambition and a side order of their own pride, thet they ain't travelin' too carefully."

North looked intently at Elijah and asked, "We've been pretty judgmental about you, Johnson — and with good reason. Thanks to your throwing in with your brother, some very good people ended up dead. How can you explain your actions to the widows and children of Foster and Franklin?"

Elijah's jaw tightened. He stiffened his still sore, lacerated back in a demonstrable effort to sit up proudly and said, "Ah got no excuse for the wreckage brought to them folks. Ah shall regret those deaths to muh dyin' day. I only say thet ah can make amends — providin' you all give me the opportunity."

"We'll see," cautioned North.

"I am grateful that you and North spared me from the red ants that one day, but it is difficult to reward you with trust." Charging Buffalo spoke as if Elijah were a mile away.

"We better keep our eyes open. It's feasible, to say the least, that they will set up an ambush," Bristol said.

The seven desperados and Hannah stopped as a mild rain storm commenced. Blood Hawk had pointed to a large, natural outcropping of rocks that produced a fairly decent shelter. Since the wind was blowing down the mountain instead of to the side of the outcroppings, the amount of rain sifting under the rocky ceilings was minimal. Callendar lifted Hannah off the horse and guided her to the "shelter."

"No point in y'all gettin' wetter than necessary, purty lady. Yuh can wear my rain slicker if yuh want."

"Thank you, but no thanks. You are at least thoughtful in that regard, sir."

"Ma'am, ah am many things, but ah was raised to be nice tuh ladies. Now whores, that's 'nother matter. They ain't got self respect, so ah don't respect them. You, on the othuh hand, are a lady. Ah won't bring any harm to you unless it's the way it must be."

"What does that mean?"

Callendar took a can of beans out of his saddle bags, then chopped off its top with a small hatchet. "There yuh go. Ah'll let yuh eat with muh knife. Jus' don't take a notion to cut me. If yuh did, then it'd be one o' them examples of 'the way it must be.'"

Hannah, in spite of feeling the desperation attributed to being forcefully abducted, witnessing the tragic death of her husband, and hoping that no harm would come to her almost-certain rescuer, John, dug into the beans and ate them. Much to her surprise, the food was satisfying. She felt no shame in surviving.

Callendar put a hand behind his head, leaned against the rock, stretched out his legs and crossed them at the ankle, and began to laugh softly. "It's amazin' how much the body will enjoy nourishment in times of peril. Ah seen it durin' the War, out on the prairie, and in this territory. In the end, we all jus' wanta cling onto the vine and keep on breathin'."

Hannah observed the other men, stopping to water and feed their horses. None of them made an effort to join her and Callendar underneath the rocky outcropping, and her suspicions regarding the intent of this foul man began to increase.

"If yer thinkin' ah'm gonna compromise yer honor, Mrs. Olson — well, ah'm tempted, but ah jus' plain ain't got the time. However, maybe down the road...."

Hannah interrupted what she considered the birth of an unwelcome lewd conversation, so she changed the subject.

"You seem like a man of manners and some culture, Mr. Callendar. I-I don't understand why you have resorted to outlawry. What compelled you?"

"Feed muh horse, too, Krautmueller! Ah'm payin' yuh to assist me, you blockheaded hun! Huh? Oh, 'xcuse me. You wonder what changed me? How'd you like yer home burned down along with every neighbor's home in sight? Thet General Sherman march destroyed muh home, muh family's livlihood, and oah way of life. Did you know that muh fahther was at one time a soldier under the command of Robert E. Lee in the Mexican War? He fought foah Lee, but didn't really believe in the cause. He figured we should've left the Mexicans alone."

"He was against gaining the new territory?" She observed him flash his teeth vainly.

"Damn right, he was. He figured we'd end up ownin' Mexico and with all them new brown Mexicans down there comin' into the nation as free men, it'd rile up the nig-grahs back on the plantations and produce a bloody revolution. Well, thet nevuh happened, but all them colored people caused that big War, so we fought and lost."

"Mr. Callendar, those colored people you mentioned were slaves — all they wanted was freedom in this country like you and me."

"Ah know, ah know. In a mattuh of time they woulda got their freedom anyway, but thet no-good Lincoln had to pick a fight and look what it lead to. Killin' and more killin.' Ah ended up killin' so many people, and saw a lot of good people killed beside me, than ah could count in a week." Unleashing this memory seemed to produce a boil-over in Callendar's emotions. His face turned red, and he crumpled up a cigarette he had rolled.

Hannah, the college intellectual, was now intrigued by the mind of this terrible, yet complex man. She asked, "To an extent, I understand your anger — people I knew were ruined by that war as well. But what happened after the war?"

Callendar leaned closer to Hannah, took her hand, grasped it a little harder when she flinched, then said, "Thet is prob'ly the first time anyone asked me that! Well, God Bless yuh foah askin', although ah ain't got no use foah God anymore. Ah couldn't stand stayin' in the south with them Yankee troops occupyin' oah land, so ah went west. Wesley an' othus think I originally haled from Texas. I didn't. Ah moved theah. Ended up in Texas punchin' cattle. It was a blisterin', dirty, low payin' job. Ah got bored and figured it wouldn't do much harm to rob a bank to get bettah money. Thet worked out really well! Yuh might say ah had a real talent foah that vocation."

"Great leader, too," cited Charlie who had overheard the discussion. " He and I robbed that first bank down in Texas. Where was it, near San Antonio? He planned it well, and we got away with five thousand dollars."

Hannah remembered there were five men involved in the attack on John and his family. She asked, "Were there others in that robbery?"

"This lady is like one o' them newspaper reporters, ain't she? Askin' questions."

"Be nice, Chahlie. Ma'am, to answer directly, there were three other boys in that robbery — and you met one of them — Mr. Chapeau. The others were Baker, yuh heard thet North killed him up in Fohtune Rivuh, and Magnuson the Swede. Ol' Maggie nevah made it out of San Antonio. He caught a slug in the back. Thet's when I figured it was better to shoot the bankers and lawdogs first. We always remembered Maggie."

"Little lady, me and P.J. was playin' poker with Baker and Chapeau in a saloon, and that Frenchman told 'bout all that cash thet had been stuck in the bank vault. Naturally, this gave P.J. the notion to rob them suckers."

The rain began to ease up. Hannah figured they would soon remount the horses and ride off. However, that was not what Callendar had in mind.

"We're gonna hole up here for a spell. Ah want the horses to rest up befoah we start the hardest part of the ride up the mountain. Besides, it'll be sundown in couple of hours, and we ain't goin' up in the dahk."

Hannah never got to find out how the renegade, Blood Hawk, joined up with Callendar. She only knew this man reminded her more of a zookeeper than merely a bad man. He watched her constantly as if she were a turkey or rabbit trying to leave a pen.

Callendar issued orders. "Blood Hawk, Chahlie and ah are gonna remain here with the horses. Ah want you, Wesley, to lead McAvee, the German, and Ahnie the barkeep back to that cluster of trees and heavy rocks just up from where the trail rises steeply. At that point yuh need to set up an ambush. If yuh men know what yer doin', yuh should be able to pick off the entire throng. Ah don't need to personally gun down that Captain, or even North. Just make sure yuh kill whoeveh yuh plug. Some of these men ah mad enough to track a runaway buzzsaw. Savvy?"

McAvee protested, "Now wait a minute, P.J. Can't one of you three come with us? Blood Hawk and Charlie are both pretty quick and deadly, and they'd be a great help."

"More 'n likely, yuh saddle bum. Yer forgettin' one thing — ah give the orders, and you are questionin' muh authority. How'd yuh like to take a little dive and join thet lady's wuthless husband, McAvee?"

"Didn't I do right by you and shoot that darkie back in Copperhead, P.J.?"

Without saying another word, Callendar stomped on McAvee's foot, then drove the heal of his hand between the bridge of the man's nose and forehead. McAvee stumbled backwards and was kicked in the buttocks by Wesley.

"Don't worry, P.J. I'll lead this bunch. We should all come back victorious."

"Jus' make sure McAvee doesn't shoot yuh in the back. On second thought, don't take him with yuh. Ah'll keep muh eye on him here. You were four, now three — Go!"

As the three underlings briskly, yet cautiously, sprinted down a slightly muddy trail, McAvee sat up glaring at Callendar. He hoped the time would come soon when he could exact revenge. On the other hand, he feared him so completely that such a vengeance might not come in this life — or even the next.

As suggested by Elijah Johnson, and heartily endorsed by the two Indians in the party, the pursuers all stepped off their mounts, guided them by the reins, and carefully walked up the more narrow and challenging portions of the ascending trail. Suddenly, Charging Buffalo pointed down into a gorge and announced, "There! I see the body of a horse and some man."

Captain Bristol pulled out his compact telescope, looked at the sight, then passed the telescope to North for an inspection.

"That's Edward Olson underneath the horse. Edward was killed." In the general sense, the loss of Edward from Hannah's life did not register as negative. Witnessing the death of the man she lived with? Parting with him under violent circumstances? Perhaps losing him without benefit of final words that needed to be spoken? Such questions made John's heart ache for Hannah. Her dealing with this would be quite difficult. Still, the more immediate concern remained her survival. Finding and liberating her obviously superseded any residual mental turmoil regarding Edward's untimely demise.

Captain Bristol surmised, "There isn't much point in investigating that tragedy right now. It will need to be dealt with eventually, but we need to keep up with the pursuit."

"Interpret no disrespect from this, Captain, but that was my intent whether you agreed or not. From my perspective, as marshal, this is a civil crime we're attempting to stop. From yours, it is reaction to federal murders. I will go on with or without you, but it is gratifying to hear that you will be with me."

"Ah nevah did like that slimy toad lawyer," Elijah opined. "It's jus' a shame a good hoss got lost."

"You're a real mushy, sensitive cuss, ain't you, prospector?" No one smirked at Trooper Ewell's self-congratulated sarcastic witticism. He had hoped to incite some sort of humorous repartee during this grim mission but soon realized that Elijah Johnson, at the moment, was universally perceived as an unacceptable comedic *ying* to his comedic *yang*.

Sammy recognized the effort to keep up spirits. "Trooper, do you know what the Cherokee liked best about the white man settling in America?"

"Huh?"

"It took thousands of years before he figured out how to sail over here!"

Everyone felt like chuckling at that one. "Sammy, maybe you better join up in one of those circuses. Here's a new idea — just stand up and tell jokes to an audience." North kidded him some more and said, "Either that, or open your own saloon and have live entertainment. Have some dance hall girls, run a legitimate gambling room, and get up and tell jokes after people have had a few drinks. It'd be a whole new industry."

"An entertainment club," Bristol pondered. "Naaa! It'd never work. Of course, if they were not allowed to bring in guns, it might have a chance."

"No thanks," Sammy replied. "Sounds too noisy for me. Maybe Charging Buffalo might like that."

The young Cheyenne scowled.

Wesley, Arnie, and Krautmueller tried their best to walk down the slope without skidding on their backsides. Krautmueller was not so lucky and fell down and slid about five feet.

"I told you to be careful, you dang nitwit. If you go skidding off the edge like that lawyer, no one's gonna fetch you!" Arnie, for some reason, considered himself superior to Germans. After years of being berated by the now late Mr. Fulton, it gave him pleasure to dump on someone else in the same manner. After all, in Arnie's mind, "this Hessian didn't speak Amurican like normal folk."

Wesley spoke sternly. "You two idjits better shut up. We're far enough down that those men comin' up might hear us. Look, about three yards away there's the bunch of big rocks and trees. Let's grab some cover."

Wesley and Krautmueller both positioned themselves onto the higher rocks. Arnie, armed with a twelve-gauge shotgun, preferred to find cover closer to the trail itself. In either case, all three men appeared well protected.

The rain had been reduced to a light drizzle. Wesley knew there were pros and cons to this development. If the rain had continued heavily, then their targets might be more distracted and disoriented. On the other hand, with a slight clearing, it would enhance visibility for him and the others and make the job of sniping easier.

Sniping, bushwhacking — it's all the same, Wesley thought. How did it all come to this? Sure, being Callendar's deputy in Copperhead had been a sweet deal for a long time. Plenty of free money, liquor, girls, respect, and personal power. Then this John North had to show up wanting revenge. Why did Callendar have to make an enemy like that? Sure, Wesley reflected, robbing a few banks and railroad payrolls were jobs he had somewhat enjoyed prior to becoming deputy, but wearing a badge to get exactly what you wanted was a lot easier! And North! Damn him! I was willing to switch to his side!

Rudolph Krautmueller, on the other hand, had not started out as someone relishing crime. He had left Bavaria because he did not want to participate in the battles occurring in the early 1870s. In fact, he had deserted the Kaiser's army and succeeded in escaping to Austria, Holland, and eventually, through the miracle of bribery, getting passage on a ship bound for England. From there, it was only a matter of time before he secured a ticket to sail from the British Isles to America. He and his friend, Kurt Schuster, had heard there were opportunities in the United States. Opportunities to fight in a civil war? No way! Once again, he had to evade a war he did not want. Kurt was not so lucky. He got drafted in New York and probably died on some stinking battlefield.

No, Krautmueller did not like America very much. There were too many non-Germans. First, there were the Irish, the French, and the Scotch. To make things worse, there were Chinese, Africans, and especially the Indians. What was wrong with this country? Why were there so many impure races, he wondered? Yes, when those people coming up the trail came into his sights he would first aim for the Indians. McAvee was the lucky one — he got to kill the black man that he and his fair-weather friend, Wendall, wanted to beat up in that barn back in town. Wendall was so frightened of the army he left town that day. He feared that Indian scout who pointed the weapon. Now, the Indian scout will die!

Arnie the bartender was without a job. Fulton was not an ideal employer, he reckoned, but he was at least the founder of the feast, so to speak. In the west, finding work was often difficult. Bartending was good work. No horse manure to shovel, no backbreaking farming to tire you out, no long hours out in the rain herding cattle or sheep. This John North came and ruined everything. Now the army was after him and the others. Arnie figured he was forced to be an outlaw once again. So be it. Kill them off. That's all.

About a half mile up the road Callendar drank a swig of water as Blood Hawk intently looked at him as if awaiting an important reply of some sort.

"Why yuh starin', Blood Hawk? Somethin' on yer mind?"

"It is what is on your mind that's of interest. You know that those men you sent down are the least able to fight North and the others. Why did you not send me or Charlie?"

His teeth flashed widely. "Ah will. Befoah this is ovuh, we'll all get a chance to do some shootin' or cuttin'. Ah figure that throwin' those three clods at the posse first will possibly chop them up a little. Ah don't expect Wesley and the othuhs to finish the job. If they get lucky, then Hallelujah! But if this plays the way I suspect, then you, me, and Chahlie will get oah chance, but by then, ah hope there are fewer of them then before."

Blood Hawk said nothing, then started gnawing on a slice of jerky.

27

---•---

AMBUSH

Once again the trail offered a sharp incline. Johnson noticed a distinctive array of huge rocks and trees at the summit of this particular cliff. "Ah believe we better not be in the wide open, men."

North, Bristol, and the other men knew immediately what this meant. Here was an ideal location for an ambush. Quickly, Sammy and Charging Buffalo bolted from their horses and got behind their own nearby rocks. It would be risky, because if sharpshooters were at that summit, they could literally fire downward and easily pick them off. While the others deliberately scattered for cover, the first shot rang out! The sniper's aim was true, and Bristol fell to the ground. North returned rifle fire but hit no one. With Ewell's help, he pulled Bristol into the brush behind some thick logs.

At least three more rifle shots came at the party. No one was hit. Someone grew bold enough to expose the top of his head and rifle barrel. This was what Sammy was counting on. He quickly fired two successive shots at the exposed man. It was Krautmueller. He was shot through the throat.

"You're a good shot, Injun, I...ack!" Ewell took a bullet behind the left shoulder blade. He fell, mortally wounded. His breathing was labored and uneven. Sammy felt sad. He liked Ewell and knew the man would perish.

North saw Ewell fall but could not reach out for him. He was pressuring the Captain's bandana against the man's arm wound. It did not appear that the bone had been shattered, nor was there evidence of a severed artery. Bristol was conscious and suggested that John remove the cuffs from Elijah Johnson.

"Let me loose, John," Elijah said. "Ah can tend to the Captain's wound. Look, I'm not gonna doublecross yuh this time. Ah know ah did wrong back in Copperhead. Ah truly didn't want them folks to die. Raht now Ewell is dyin', and the Captain is hurt. You have to take out those shooters up above."

More shots were exchanged between the remaining snipers and Sammy and Charging Buffalo. John made a split decision and unlocked Elijah's handcuffs. "So, partners again, old prospector?"

"Still pahtners, Mr. North."

John was in the best position to ascend through the tall grass on the right of the trail. There were several trees and logs he could dodge behind if necessary, but the immediate advantage was a partially obscured alternative route to the unprotected path. He looked at Sammy, pointed to the area he had in mind, then pointed to the rock piles above the trail. This was a signal that he required cover while he attempted to move up around and behind the assassins.

Sammy and Charging Buffalo obliged him. They began a barrage of rifle fire that offered immediate peril to anyone foolish enough to lift their heads. Apparently, the remaining shooters were not in the mood to walk in the footsteps of Rudolph Krautmueller.

John North realized his plan would badly backfire if there were more than three or four shooters. Judging by the rhythm of shots fired, and the general positions of discernible gun smoke, he thought it unlikely there were more than two or three up there. Should he be betting his life on it? North lacked the time to mull it over.

Thanks to the heavy cover provided by his friends, North made it over to the first grove of trees. As soon as he reached the first large, fallen log, he dove behind it. Still working his way to the right, and upward, he ran towards the next cluster of trees, ferns, and weeds. So far, no one had shot at him. Cautiously, yet steadily, he worked his way further to the right and up the hill. It was quite steep, so he knew he had to be careful or he would slip down the moist earth and call attention to his location. He grabbed what appeared to be secure tree roots and pulled himself up. This was the challenge: once he reached the top, would he be exposed to one of the shooters?

John North nearly slipped as he pulled himself up over the edge. Some wet leaves caused him to skid slightly. He stayed flat on his belly but turned his head to the left and had a clear view of someone poised with a Winchester. The man looked like Arnie the bartender. Arnie started firing at someone down below. Slowly, North raised himself to his feet, looked around, saw no one but Arnie, then raised his own rifle.

Suddenly, Arnie must have felt a presence, for he turned to look in John's direction and hurriedly took aim. He was not fast enough. John fired two fatal shots into Arnie.

He worked his way over to where Arnie had been positioned and cautiously looked up. Someone fired at him with a pistol. The bullet came within a few inches of his face, but cut across dirt in a nearby embankment. He shot at the man above but missed. He then thought to rattle him a little.

"Two of your friends are already shot. I just killed Arnie, and Sammy Fivetrees killed your other partner just before that. Surrender, mister, or so help me, you will die today."

"You son-of-a bitch — you ruined a good deal!" Wesley lost his temper and started to fan his pistol at John. John retained the good cover that Arnie had employed and waited for Wesley to foolishly empty his pistol. John counted five shots, and then there was silence. He guessed the man was reloading the pistol or situating himself for a rifle shot. He started up the knoll with his own pistol drawn and suddenly found himself face to face with Wesley. They briefly stared at each other, then John unhesitatingly shot Wesley in the midsection. Horrifyingly, Wesley began spurting blood in rhythmic gushers. John had seen this sight at Gettysburg. The man had been hit in the aorta.

Not far from the expiring Wesley, John found the fatally wounded Krautmueller. The man was bleeding profusely from the nose and mouth and out of the neck wound.

"Was it worth all this, mister," John asked the dying man. "Riding with a devil like Callendar brought you this. It didn't have to be this way for you. May God have mercy on your soul."

John perused the highpoints, and the immediate areas below. There were no more gunmen. He fired a shot in the air and yelled, "It's North. I'm all right. There were three shooters, and we got them all. You may come up the trail."

Sammy and Elijah came up to greet North. "You gave me good cover, Sammy. It also helped that these men hesitated or lost their cool heads."

"You were fortunate, John. If one of the deadlier men had been up here, you might not have survived."

"I know it. I also know that these men were mediocre shots, so I was confident that Blood Hawk and Elijah's brother were not among them."

"Yes, those two, Callendar, and that one you called McAvee are all that remain. These amateurs were sent to slow us down, or reduce our numbers."

"An' on that point, they have succeeded," Elijah said. "Ah think it is high time that you give me a gun, John. Ewell's dead, and the Captain is hurt."

"I'd rather send you back to town with the Captain."

"We're closer to Fortune River. I think we should all keep going. It will be dark soon, so I think we should camp in those woods. Callendar and the others will not brave the mountain pass in the dark. Only Blood Hawk might attempt that," advised Sammy, "but even he values his own life and would not risk plunging to his death like the lawyer."

The wisdom of Sammy's words was apparent. In spite of Charging Buffalo's youthful protestation, everyone agreed to wait until sun-up. Captain Bristol's wound was not as severe as originally thought. The bullet had apparently passed through the arm and was primarily a concern due to future possible bleeding and blood poisoning. For the time being, bleeding had been contained, so Bristol felt he was more than able to continue the quest after a night of rest.

It was cool in the mountains but not freezing. A campfire was preferable but not mandatory. They had warm blankets and some whiskey, so they hunkered down and chose to wait. The Indians and North would take turns standing watch. North still would not allow Johnson to freely carry a weapon.

Darkness had now fallen. Callendar repeatedly asked Hannah to snuggle up against him to keep warm, but she steadfastly refused. He now drank some liquor and heard rustling about three or four yards away. With pistol drawn he waited until his suspicion was confirmed. Yes. It was Blood Hawk.

"You been out prowlin' around in the dark?"

"From a distance I observed the shooting that took place. The three men you left to do the ambush are all dead, as I knew they would be. Your plan was good, however. They are down to four men who can fight, and one that is wounded. Those three fools were able to kill one soldier."

"How 'bout that? Those boys did earn their pay after all! Best of all, ah don't even have to give 'em the pay they earned!"

"Four men, yuh say? Ah thought there'd just be three. Is the fourth...."

"It is your brother, the prospector. He seems to be working with North again."

"Yeah, but ah'm his bruthuh, He won't let anyone go 'gainst me. We got an inside man!"

"Don't count on it, Johnson. I think he will strike against us. If he tries, I will kill him. If you try to stop me, then I will kill you too."

"Don't threaten me, yuh bloodthirsty Bloody Bird; yuh don't scare me none!"

"Shet up the two of yuh. Get some rest. We're gonna take off befoah first light. Ah want to get us up to Fohtune Rivuh tomorrow. Blood Hawk, ah suggest you think up some ways to dispose of them folks. Ah think yoah time for action is tomorrow."

Hannah scornfully blasted, "Kill, kill, kill! What's the matter with you people? Is that all you want to do? Quit doing this! You don't have to be monsters! Stop it!"

Much to everyone's surprise, Blood Hawk responded to her outburst. "Woman, when men want to live a certain way as we do, then everything we want is for the taking. When others stand in the way, killing is the only way to permanently stop those in the way."

"And you, an Indian, why do you take orders from Callendar?"

"Because, woman, I owe him my life. I was going to be hanged, and he rescued me. Now shut up and sleep. Too bad you don't beat your women, Callendar."

28

BLOOD UNDER THE MOON LIGHT

They started to build a fire. Sammy and Charging Buffalo advised against it, but John North made the final decision. It was becoming unbearably cold, and he was concerned that Bristol's condition might rapidly deteriorate. Also, there was the hint of possible snowfall in the air. Should Blood Hawk and the others circle back and attempt to pick them off, then they would have to be ready for them.

Even Bristol disagreed with North's decision. "Actually, I am an officer in the army, and you represent local civil authority at best, so I should overrule you."

"That may be true, Captain," John stated calmly, but since I am the only legal authority still standing and walking around unassisted, then I insist that I shall outrank you tonight. Besides, I have a feeling that Callendar and the others are sitting around their own campfire. Blood Hawk would love to come down and use us as clay pidgeons, but I still think Callendar is running the show. No, their move against us will be tomorrow when they might take full advantage of the daylight."

"Now that I think of it, North may be right. Blood Hawk is sorely indebted to Callendar." Charging Buffalo added, "some of my people say he once swore a blood oathe to this Callendar because the man saved his life. No, he won't leave on his own."

"He's a queer bird staying so loyal to him this long. In these mountains he could easily leave and survive on his own," North commented.

"Maybe he said s'long to Callendar and skedaddled already," Elijah suggested.

"No. We would have been engaged by him by now. He's followining Callendar's schedule. An independent killer who's comforted by Satan's direction," Sammy said.

Charging Buffalo was sitting close to the wounded Captain. The Captain looked up at the youth and asked a pointed question. "What's in this for you, son? Yes, I know that Blood Hawk had left you for the ants, but why did you come this far?"

"It seems strange that I would be fighting alongside of someone such as you, Captain. Your army has done little except bring grief and suffering to my people. The buffalo were plentiful until a few years ago. Now the herds are thin, and your government does not seem to mind. That tells me you want the buffalo to keep dying. When they die, then so do the Cheyenne, the Dakotas, Black Feet, and other tribes."

"I'm not denying there are many who hold that opinion. I do not happen to agree with it. I am just a soldier who fights where he is told to fight. Again, tell me why you have insisted on joining us?"

"Blood Hawk must be stopped. Since he is tied to that rancid southern man, then it is clear that they both must be stopped. I too, am indebted to men who saved my life. North and Johnson saved me, so in a sense, I am in a position similar to that of Blood Hawk. No one has betrayed me. If they did, you would not see me unless you became my enemy — and if that were the case, you would only see me at the point of death."

Elijah chuckled and said, "Cap'n, ah think he's sayin' thet he's gonna do what he wants to do until it doesn't please 'im any moah." He then turned to Sammy for his response, but there was no reaction. Sammy was fast asleep.

John made a pot of coffee and drank a couple of cups to help keep him focused during his watch. By the second cup, he was the only person still awake. He sipped the hot, bitter brew and thought about poor Hannah. She was resourceful but definitely scared. First, she was abducted by ostensibly wicked men. Next, her husband, although a man she had grown to dislike immensely, fell off a cliff to his death. Finally, she was in the company of disreputable, untrustworthy men in a cold, dark mountain setting unsure whether she will lose her virtue or her life before dawn. How hideously frustrating it was for John to be so close, yet still too far away to help her.

John checked the sky for signs of clearing. Yes, the clouds were scattering. It probably would not snow, or rain for that manner. Above he gazed as if searching for a midnight miracle. All that appeared was the moon — but it was a full moon. Maybe this was the miracle. He looked at the peacefully slumbering companions and poured the remainder of his coffee near the fire. He woke up Sammy and asked him to step away from the campsite.

"You must stand watch until morning. I cannot wait any longer. Now that the moon has risen, I will use that light to help draw closer to the outlaw camp. I cannot allow Callendar or the others to bring Hannah to any harm. As a man in love with her, I cannot waste another moment allowing them the opportunity to rape or hurt her in any way. I will leave now, but you must guard the others."

"John North — you speak foolishly. Going by yourself is folly. I will accompany you."

"No! I will go with him!" Charging Buffalo had not slept and had heard every word.

"Thank you, but I don't want you to risk your life."

"None of you will stop me. I shall go. Sammy should stay with the Captain and Johnson."

North and Sammy looked at one another, and Sammy declared, "So be it. I still advise that you do not do anything rash or alone. I suppose it is better for one foolish man to go in the company of another — at least they will not have to speak of foolish things alone."

North and Charging Buffalo saddled their horses and left camp. They rode at first, but when the trail became quite narrow, they stepped down and slowly guided the animals. The moonlight was still bright, so they continued. If it clouded up or precipitated at any significant level, the men agreed to stop and wait. Come what may, they at least felt as if they were making more progress in this manner.

At the fugitive camp, Callendar could not sleep. He lay a mere two feet away from the tempting feminine prize of Hannah Olson, and it had been a long time since he had been able to entwine himself around a desirable female body. That whore, Sally, was the last woman he had taken, and she was not all that cooperative that time. In fact, she made the entire experience unpleasant. Hannah, on the other hand, would be worth the battle. She was more mature, and certainly prettier than Sally. He could see the round outline of her thighs and hips and felt a burgeoning desire for her.

Hannah rolled over on her right side. Callendar saw her ample breasts squeeze together as she shifted. This was pure heaven. He reached over and gently ran his calloused fingers through her reddish-brown hair. It felt very silky and soft. Her very presence drew him toward her like a magnet. He bent down and put his lips close to hers. She groaned and exhaled as one experiencing an uncomfortable dream. Callendar hesitated momentarily, then gently pursed his lips and pressed them against Hannah's. She groaned again, and this seemed to encourage him to repeat the action. She licked her lips, and he hungrily bent down and kissed them again.

Much to his surprise, Hannah continued to sleep but spoke clearly. "Oh, John. Kiss me again. I love you, too. I'll always love you, John."

Her dreamy proclamation actually made him pull away. Immediately angry, he felt violently compelled to just grab her and rip off her dress. Raping her would satisfy a lot of needs, he thought. Still, the thought of doing this repelled him. She was not a hooker or a cheap woman. Hannah was the kind of woman who caused a man to reach out in love rather than violence. "What? Am I falling in love with her?" he shockingly asked himself. No, not really. Taking her this way just did not seem appropriate. Being with her reminded him of the girls he used to court back in Mississippi. If the world had been different, this would have been the kind of girl he would have married and who would have given him fine, beautiful children. Ah, regrets. Not being a father — what a deep, deep regret.

"Ah think muh brain is fillin' up with hot grits," he muttered.

"Whajja say, P.J.?" inquired a groggy McAvee.

"Ah say, shet yer filthy trap, or I'll shove a fistful of coyote crap into it!" Callendar rolled over and tried to sleep.

Blood Hawk did not sleep. Like North, he had been watching the clouds disperse and approved of the ascendancy of a full, bright moon. Without looking back, he set out without his horse but made certain he was armed with rifle, pistol, and Bowie knife.

John waited until the newest wisp of clouds passed over the moon. He looked at his young companion and felt badly that he had insisted on joining him. It was one thing to risk his own life, but risking the life of this young man was wrong.

"I think you should go back, Charging Buffalo. You don't have to do this. I consider your debt to me and Johnson paid in full. Go back with the others and plan on having a long and happy life."

"You are one of the more just white men I have met, and it does me no dishonor to call you friend. Still, you are a white man and do not understand me or my people. Blood Hawk killed my own. These were his people too, and he must die the way of my people. He must be killed in an act of rightful justice. It is not right that anyone destroy him except me. Again, I thank you for saving me that day. I agree that my debt to you is repaid. You live a wonderful life with that beautiful smiling lady. I must leave now."

Like a flash, Charging Buffalo disappeared into the darkness. John North protested, even raising his voice more loudly than he should have. The path was still narrow and treacherous, so he could not ride his horse yet. He did grab the reins and walk as quickly as feasible, however. In the distance, he heard hoof beats. Charging Buffalo was riding.

Following approximately fifteen minutes of deliberate, yet careful descent down the path, Blood Hawk heard hoof beats. Someone was sufficiently foolish enough to provide the sound of his arrival. This would be the person's heralding of his own death, he said to himself. It was good he had not slept. He normally listened to Callendar because he owed the man his life and actually admired his talent for planning and getting away with profitable schemes and crimes. This time, he was a fool. He reasoned that a silly woman who needed to be beaten into submission, not coddled, compromised his leader.

Blood Hawk stood behind a thick tree. He waited for the sound of the hoofs to get louder. He grasped his rifle in both hands like a club and waited for the unsuspecting rider. Beads of sweat formed on his forehead. How could this happen? Blood Hawk never sweated before a fatal encounter. Could it be the lateness of the hour or the possibility that his adversaries might be using cunning to advantage? That was it. Every fiber in his body told him a trick was about to be played.

The horse came by quickly, and Blood Hawk stepped forward and swung the rifle as if it were a medieval broadsword. Whoosh! It should have struck a human body mounted on the saddle, but the horse was riderless. Now worried, Blood Hawk pulled back and positioned the rifle to shoot someone in back of him. Instead of finding someone down the trail, he heard a rustling in the tree above him, and out of the corner of his eye saw the form of a man — a Cheyenne — who leaped from an upper branch directly towards him. He fired the rifle, but the man fell onto him and deflected the rifle upwards. Charging Buffalo quickly pinned him to the ground and pressed a knife against his throat. Fortunately for Blood Hawk, the boy was not as strong, so the knife hand met great resistance from Blood Hawk's own powerful hand.

Charging Buffalo gritted his teeth and pressed down with all his might, attempting to slit the man's throat. The blade succeeded in cutting the skin and drawing some blood.

"You simmering, stinking rotting bag of cougar guts, I am avenging you for killing my — uhhhhh...." Charging Buffalo felt a deep pain in his side. Almost as quickly, he felt a pressure leaving his side, then enter the area between his ribs. Blood Hawk had managed to grasp the Bowie knife with his other hand and apply two very deep stab wounds.

Charging Buffalo started to feel weak, but with what strength he had remaining he plunged his own knife deeply into Blood Hawk's chest. Due to his failing strength, he could not precisely target the blade to the man's heart and set it alternatively into the fleshy area just underneath the left shoulder bone. Blood Hawk, always the calm, quiet, and sinister deadly shadow, now cried out loudly in pain. Enraged, he pushed the boy away, picked up his knife, and set out to drive it into his heart.

John North had hurried as quickly as he could once he heard that rifle shot. He arrived in time to see Blood Hawk hovering above someone with that formidable knife. Not issuing a warning or waiting for clearer identification, John pointed his Winchester and fired into the back of Blood Hawk. The man fell onto his face and was still.

Charging Buffalo groaned, and John North practically tripped attempting to reach him. Just as he saw and clearly identified the badly wounded and blood soaked body of the young Cheyenne, Blood Hawk raised himself up and lunged at him with the Bowie knife. Surprised that the renegade was still alive, he momentarily hesitated before pointing the rifle upward to fire. There was no time. All he could do was hit the man's hand boldly and knock the knife out of his grasp.

Blood Hawk was very strong; he bowled over North and pushed aside the rifle. He tried reaching for North's Colt .45, but North drove his fist into the man's ribs. This caused Blood Hawk to scream. Apparently, the blow had affected the area that had been shot. Blood Hawk reached up and tried to grab North by the throat. John rolled him over, and the two men rolled back and forth struggling for the dominant position to kill. At last, Blood Hawk pulled North's revolver from the holster. At the same time, North's hand touched the Bowie knife. He quickly brought it up and stuck it into Blood Hawk's armpit. Blood Hawk cried out horribly. His grip on the pistol weakened, and John was able to push it away.

Blood Hawk was mortally wounded, but his eyes blazed into North's like two fireballs launched from the arsenal of Satan himself. John pulled out the Bowie knife and was about to plunge it into the man's heart. Suddenly, a hand pulled onto the renegade's long hair and roughly yanked his head back. Another hand produced a knife that slid strongly and rapidly across Blood Hawk's throat. There was now more blood than predatory bird manifested by the renegade. Gore flowed copiously out of the neck of Blood Hawk. He fell backward onto the hard ground and was at last slain.

The person who finally ended the wicked reign of Blood Hawk was the young Cheyenne, Charging Buffalo. It came at a cost. The man, who would not see the wisdom of old age, learn to fall in love with the girl of his dreams, or enjoy the company of children he could teach to be warriors, fell to the ground next to Blood Hawk. John North, not experiencing such carnage since the Civil War, felt those old, terrible, feelings he had known in places such as Little Round Top and Petersburg. He labored to shake them off. Soon, he got up and sought to help Charging Buffalo.

He examined the brave yet impetuous man and listened for any remaining words he might offer. The young man was covered with blood and breathing shallowly. Tears started to well up in his eyes as he held up the young man's head and said, "You are one of the bravest men I have ever seen. May God have mercy on your soul, because you were one of the finest men I have ever known, Charging Buffalo."

Charging Buffalo said nothing but squeezed North's hand weakly and tried to smile. He gasped for air a few more times, then passed away.

John North just stood over the young man for a few minutes and shook his head. "I should not have let you come with. I knew this would end badly. Your death will be something I will carry with me forever. My own stubborn pride got you killed. I should have waited until morning."

"It's too late for thet now, pardner."

John North spun around and drew his pistol. He was ready to discharge a round but saw the form of Elijah Johnson in the shadows.

"Yuh can shoot if yuh like, but ah didn't come to bushwhack yuh, John. Ah'm afraid ah can nevah do that. Ah'm like that poor, dead boy there — ah got promises to fulfill. Ah need to right some very terrible wrongs I done."

North kept his pistol aimed at Johnson as the old prospector approached. He sized up the man and said nothing. He simply held up the pistol, set the hammer down gently, and said, "I finally believe you. I can't continue to be a one-man avenger. I need your help, partner. Can I rely on you?"

"John, I swear to God Almighty I'll help yuh. Ah just won't personally kill Chahlie."

29

---•---

LIKE IT OR NOT, LAW HAS ARRIVED

Abby Franklin spent a long, miserable, relatively sleepless night. When she finally awoke from a mere two hours of sleep, she realized the nightmare was true: her beloved Johnny was gone, and she would be solely responsible for bringing up the two children. Sure, Sammy Fivetrees said he would return and help the family at the ranch, but what if he changed his mind? Also, did Abby and the children know this man well enough? Worst of all, what if he ended up getting himself killed just like Johnny? The thought vexed her greatly. Instinctively, she liked Sammy and knew he would be a man of his word. She did, however, fear the possibility of his death. After all, didn't death visit Johnny? Wasn't everything spinning out of control?

Abby shuddered to think too much about a "what might be even worse" scenario. She promptly understood there were many things worse — and they all involved her and the children. Sammy had to return — he simply had to return.

This woman, Sally, is supposed to be a terrible floozy, Abby thought. Still, ever since they met her, Sally had shown her and the children nothing but kindness and tenderness. Many of the townspeople did not even inquire about her and the boys. Certainly, the Masons were caring people and Doc Brandt was showing a lot of compassion. Anyway, nothing seemed right. Johnny was dead — so everything was twisted ugly.

"Abby, I made breakfast for you and the children. Your youngsters both seem better today. Ruthie is getting over her cold, and Harold claims his leg is a lot more improved. How about you — did you get any sleep?"

"Not much, Miss Sally. Ah kept thinkin' about muh poah Johnny getting gunned down by that cracker. That McAvee — who looked like he really enjoyed causin' all that harm. How can a man be so hateful? What did Johnny ever do to him? Why is there so much poison in these white folk?"

Sally started to wipe away some tears from her eyes. She looked at Abby, who was on the verge of breaking down completely, and simply held out her arms. The two women fell into an embrace and sobbed. As soon as she determined her voice would function through all the moisture, Sally said, "I quit tryin' to understand mean folks a long time ago. They made me go along with things I'm too ashamed to talk about.

Killin' hard working, decent human beings is not something to make anyone superior. It makes them more like an animal — no, worse than an animal. I despise those people."

"Sammy Fivetrees said he would not rest until he found and brought in that McAvee person. Marshal North said they would round up or kill the bunch of them. Ah just hope to God that he's able tuh save thet pretty young Hannah. He loves her so…"

The ladies heard a knock on the door. Sally answered and saw the smiling face of Roberta Mason. "Abby and Miss Redmond, you ought to know that a stagecoach just pulled in. The passengers are a judge and a U.S. Marshal. Kirk suggests you ladies get presentable and meet over at the marshal's office in about an hour."

An hour later, Abby and Sally did as they were asked. Roberta's offer to look after Abby's children was accepted, so Abby could stay with the judge or U.S. Marshal as long as necessary until interrogations were finished.

They entered through the door cautiously. The women feared that Mr. Foster's body might still be sitting at the chair. It wasn't. Instead, there was a tall, thin man leaning down, apparently examining the remains of dried blood on the floor. Standing next to the leaning one was a middle-aged, fairly stout man wearing a black suit and string tie. He sported bushy sideburns, a thick, white mustache, and white fringes of hair around the temples. When he saw the ladies, he said, "Hello. I am Judge Milford Quartz, and this is United States Marshal Anthony Marconi. We just came in from the city of Cheyenne, and we want to get as many statements as possible."

"Yoa honor," Marshal Marconi suggested. "If it is all the same, ah think ah could be of more assistance getting on the trail of the badmen and helpin' out the town marshal."

"Let's not jump to conclusions, Tony. First, I will speak with this redheaded lady. You may send your black servant back to her quarters."

"I am no one's servant, Mistuh Judge! What is this — Mississippi justice all ovuh again?"

"Easy does it ma'am," Marconi cautioned. "The judge and I just don't have all the facts."

"One major fact," Kirk Mason interrupted, "is the wrong that has been done to this lady. Your honor and Mr. Marshal, this is Abby Franklin. Her husband was severely wounded along with her son, Harold, by former Marshal Callendar and his deputies. One of those deputies, a man named McAvee, murdered her husband."

"Wait, I thought one of you said that the man, Johnny Franklin, killed your mayor. I don't take kindly to negroes rising up against white authority, Mason."

Sally exploded, "That authority figure tried to rape me, and her husband saved my life! He could only stop him by shooting him! We are the wronged people, judge!"

Marshal Marconi calmly asked the two ladies to be seated. The ladies got a good look at this man. Aside from his tallness, he was a handsome, dark haired, about forty years of age, and well groomed. His hair was cut to a respectable length, as was his full, black mustache. He wore a clean, bright green shirt, cowhide vest, and fairly new looking leather boots. He wore six guns in the style of a gunfighter — butt first. He was an unusual entity of the west at that time: an Italian-American from Virginia. His good, cultured southern manners must have showed, for the ladies felt comforted by the man's demeanor. The judge, on the other hand, kept making offensive statements, and exuded an aura of intolerance and slant for confrontational deportment.

Soon, the two women, Kirk Mason, and Doctor Brandt told all that they knew. They emphasized the readiness of John North to bring law and order to the town and to track down and apprehend or kill the criminals who brought bloodshed to so many in the community and region.

"Well," Judge Milford Quartz muttered as he kept readjusting the fat lapels on his copiously thick suit jacket. "It bothers me to hear that this John North seems intent upon hunting down and killing those five men who allegedly killed his family. Of course, you are all just taking his word for that. Where's the evidence? Maybe he is just some sort of maniacal killer himself. As for the army going along with this, well…that does speak well for North. After all, that Major at the fort did send a telegram ordering Captain Bristol to pursue and bring in Callendar and his deputies dead or alive. I can't say that I would trust those two savages that accompanied them. Hmm…I guess Bristol knows these redskins better than I do."

Abby and Sally were primed to blow up at the biased judge, but a calming expression on the face of the U.S. Marshal told them such a move would be ill-advised.

"Your honor and Marshal Marconi, we are delighted that you made it to Copperhead so soon," Mason flattered. "We thought we would not see you for another week at least!"

"Luckily, I was in the city of Cheyenne meetin' with Judge Quartz on some other federal business when those alarming telegrams came in." Marconi, an eduated man, spoke in a curious combination of Virginian and Italian accents, but due to his purposeful elocution, appeared to be working diligently at suppressing both. "Look, ah know that this man, Callendar, is wanted for many crimes. The fact that federal authorities weren't aware of his roostin' in Copperhead was either a credit to his ability to keep his corrupt position quiet or oah feeble ability to find a bad man like that. In any event, I think it's proper that Marshal North pursued Callendar as he did. That deadly renegade, Blood Hawk, is a one-man slaughterhouse. If any or all of them are brought in alive, I'm sure that there will be ample chahges that will help guide them to the end of a rope. However, even if they come back as corpses draped over saddles, den the world'll be better off."

"Hmmmph," the judge grunted with some perturbation. "Yes, you have a point, Tony. Of course, your instincts are usually right about matters. I enormously hate seeing people running around trying to be judges. After all, I went to law school a long time to learn what I did about the law. This fellow, North, he's probably an illiterate sheep man."

This time, Doctor Brandt interjected. "Mr. Marconi, I can detect a bit of ol'Virginia in your voice. I hail from Tennessee myself but lost the twang in medical school. A number of eyes gazed curiously at the physician upon hearing of his confessed southern origin. "Anyway, I spoke with North. You might say that he could challenge any of us in an intellectual discussion. It is remarkable that he showed as much linguistic restraint as he did. Many folks aren't half as smart."

"May we go now, Mistuh Judge?" asked Abby.

"Yes, yes. Just don't leave town yet. After this North and whoever was with him returns, we will hold a legal hearing. At that time, I will need testimonies in court. You might actually help prevent this John North from getting hanged."

A collective "What?" echoed in the room. Immediately afterwards, Judge Quartz said, "Come on, people…do you think I was serious? Ha! Unless the evidence existed, I wouldn't hang the man. In fact, I don't even believe in hanging. I just want to send the bad people to prison — for life, in many cases. However, if in about ten years or so, they seem to have seen the error of their ways, then I say they should get paroled. Who knows? This fellow Callendar was probably a nice man at one time. I know he probably owned slaves and all that, but didn't a lot of people? Sorry, Mrs. Franklin, but you knew how it was. Hell, my own grandfather owned about twenty slaves in Georgia. Personally, I never cared for slavery because I was born in Michigan. Still, a fella like Callendar must have had good qualities before the Civil War. We have to believe in the basic goodness of the white race. If we don't, then evil shall prevail."

Abby had had enough. "Sir, ah don't feel well, and muh children need me. May I go?"

"Yes. The pretty redhead may go as well. By the way, Sally, is it? Are you married?"

Sally shook her head, then went out the door with Abby. As soon as they were out of earshot they both laughed.

"Sally, are yuh laughin' cause the pompous ol' judge doesn't know 'bout your past?"

"No. I'm laughin' that he would ever think I'd ever be interested in a jackass like him. Captain Bristol, on the other hand — now there's a man I wish would call on me some time. I doubt it though. He's a gentleman — and you know what I am."

Abby grabbed her arm and literally stopped her from walking. "Ah know exactly what yuh is — you is a big hearted gal and wunnerful friend to me an' muh kids. Ah thank the Lawd thet you came into oah lives when yuh did." The ladies smiled, put their arms around their waists, and walked back to Doc Brandt's office. It was time to look after the children.

Back in the marshal's office, Judge Quartz asked, "Tony, what do you think?"

"Ah think that the townspeople ought to go ahead and hold funeral services for the dead, and I oughta take off right away and join up with North and his posse in either helpin' them bring the crimes to an end or assistin' them in bringin' home the prisoners." The sudden passion in this conviction seemed to exude more Virginia than usual.

"You are a federal marshal, Tony. Do as you see best. I always trust you implicitly."

"Thanks, judge. You know, that is how I am starting to feel about this John North."

Later, outside Dr. Brandt's office, Marshal Marconi was abruptly stopped by the doctor. "Marshal, I am sure that you are quite busy at the moment, but I wanted to just let you know that it is quite refreshing to find a fellow southerner in the territory who is not some alcoholic, thieving murderer of some variety."

"Is that why you keep yoah identity as a Tennessee boy hidden from the folks, doctor? Or are yuh just ashamed to be known as a states rights fella among all these northerners?"

"Ashamed? Nonsense. I love Tennessee and my people. I just can't brag that there are many tolerant people when it comes to proclaiming southern roots. People are still mad at southerners. Haven't you found it to be the case?"

Marconi glanced at his well-polished boots, then looked Doc Brandt squarely in the eye and said, "When you are Italian and Virginian in a place run by the northern victors of the war, then you really learn the meanin' of 'tolerance.' Ah helped bring a whole bunch of those vulgar Ku Klux Klan bastards to justice a couple years aftuh the war, so a few Yankees showed me respect, but ah nevah did cotton tuh the idea of Lee surrenderin' to Grant — who's now the President! On the othuh hand, yuh gotta change with the times."

"I know what you mean."

"Do you, doc? Ah'm not ashamed of bein' either an Italian or Virginian. If someone don't like it, then tough. I got a great answer for 'em."

"What is it, marshal?"

"Screw you! I'm an American. I also wear a badge, so mind your manners."

The doctor laughed and said, "Well said. I'd be honored to buy you a cup of coffee, sir."

"Offer accepted, physician. I was thinkin' of buying some supper. I'm partial to burnt steak or possum stew."

Doctor Brandt smiled slightly, then tried not to think too thoroughly about what he judged as loathsome culinary preferences.

30

PAYBACK

Charlie Johnson could not believe his eyes. John North and the young Cheyenne brave had done the impossible: they killed Blood Hawk. If Blood Hawk could die at the hand of these people, than anyone else could and probably would as well. Charlie, for the first time since he could remember, felt genuine fear. It did not occur to him that it would simply be easy to raise his rifle and pick off North from behind. Besides, Elijah had entered the scene. Charlie reasoned that if he shot North in the back, then Elijah might turn against him forever. Maybe he had already! No, that was not possible. Confusion was taking hold! Pain in the head! Better to go back to Callendar and let him make the decisions. First, all the deputies except McAvee got killed, now Blood Hawk. Was this Judgment Day? Callendar had always made the final decisions — he had to do so again!

The man scurried up the hill and nearly fell over a ledge. He gained control, then deliberately set out to keep either positioned in the center or to the extreme right of the trail. He had to rejoin Callendar and McAvee. It would take the three of them to deal with North and his helpers. But what if Elijah was in on the kill? Johnson thought, "Could I kill my own brother? Not likely. Furthermore, Callendar can't kill him either! Hurry, hurry…return to the camp — talk this over with Callendar right away. Damn!" The headache was worsening. Anytime the confusion set in, the headaches returned. This always made the confusion worse.

Finally, he smelled the horses. Soon, he saw them and, thanks to the moonlight, found his way over to where Callendar and the girl were sleeping. When he located them, they were not sleeping. The girl was sitting with her arms crossed and looking down on the ground. Callendar was smoking a cigarette and reloading his dragoon colt.

"Well, did Blood Hawk finish 'em already? Is he still huntin' 'em? Yuh know he likes to take his time — like some kinda damn panthuh. It thrills 'im to death to cat-stalk 'em. Well? Why ain't yuh answerin' me, yuh stupefied moron?"

"Blood Hawk ain't stalkin' no one, boss. He went an' got hisself stabbed with his own Bowie knife. Thet John North stuck him hard."

Callendar tossed down the cigarette, then yelled, "*Then* he killed North, RIGHT?"

"Not exactly. Yuh see, thet Cheyenne kid got up behind and cut his throat. Blood Hawk is dead. The two of them kilt Blood Hawk!"

"Damn it, damn it; SON OF A BITCH, DAMN IT! How in hell...."

"Ah know...ah can't believe it muhself!"

"Tell me that you killed the two of them!" P.J. had never been this disoriented.

"Well...Blood Hawk and thet Cheyenne more or less kilt each othuh...."

"More or less? Are you retarded, man? Then *you* killed, North, RIGHT?"

"Wrong! Ah got so rattled, ah came back here tuh see what we oughta do next!"

Callendar's every cell spattered ferocity, and he flew toward Charlie and struck him hard in the jaw with a right cross. Charlie fell back and his shoulder struck a tree. A branch tore his shirt and cut a gash in his arm.

"Yer outta yer mind, yuh cotton pickin' simpleton! Whadda yuh mean 'see what we outta do next?' Ah'll tell yuh what yuh outta do next: plan on gettin' a belly full of lead! If thet man was able enough to kill Blood Hawk, then oah advantage is very badly reduced. Didn't ah always tell yuh about people like thet? If they're too tough, fast shootin', more clever, or surely blessed with holy water, yuh always shoot 'em from behind! Of all the times to forget muh advice, yuh had to forget it tonight!"

"Ah'm con-confused again, boss. Just like ah was thet time in Denver. We was robbin' a bank, and ah didn't seem tuh know where we were or what ah was goin' to do next!"

"Ah remembah Denver! That's when yuh hauled out yer pistol and shot thet little girl and her mama! We had all we could do to keep oah distance from yuh aftuh that! Confusion! Yer nuthin' but a damn, stupid, feeble minded weasel!"

"Ah don't think yuh should call me names, P.J. It ain't fair. Yuh know ah have helped yuh many times. Ah earned yoah respect!"

"Yuh make me choke! Wake up thet slumberin' sot, McAvee, and make sure you two saddle the horses. We gotta head out of here right away. Already ah can see the sun startin' to rise, and North ain't gonna wait 'til we have mornin' coffee and flapjacks. He's out for ouh hides right now. Now MOVE YER WUTHLESS ASS!"

Of course, Hannah had heard the entire conversation. Her silence was an intentional effort to collect as much information about John as possible. What she heard was sufficient: John had obviously survived the attack by the deputies, had slain Blood Hawk, and was pressing to rescue her. No, she would not say a thing unless it might impede the progress of the remaining outlaws. It was risky, but she would give it a try.

"Mr. Callendar, I cannot travel unless I get some food. I implore you, sir, let's at least eat a cold breakfast."

Callendar's earlier attempts to engender a field of gentlemanly decorum were sorely absent. "Mrs. Olson, ah don't care if yer belly eats itself — we are ridin' now! Give me any trouble, an' so help me, ah'll rip thet charmin', sweet face with muh pistol barrel!"

Callendar raised the weapon in a believably threatening manner, so Hannah quickly complied with the order. Charlie was obviously sinking into madness, Callendar would destroy anyone resisting his commands, and McAvee — well, the look in his eye had always bothered her. He constantly eyed her as if he owned her. Hannah had seen him give her lascivious stares on the trail and in camp. Only Callendar prevented this filthy pervert from openly attacking her. He was the man who apparently enjoyed killing Abby's husband, so why would the feelings of a vulnerable woman mean anything to him? She knew he would probably attempt rape at the first available opportunity.

"I think we ah gettin' fairly close, John. Ah can hear voices. In fact, it sounded like Chahlie was gettin' that confusion voice again."

"Confusion?"

"Yeah. Evah since the War, he had episodes of gettin' confused when he was under a lot of pressure. Pressure from things he could not control. A doctor once examined him, 'nd surmised thet he had one of them things growin' in his brain — a tumor."

"A 'tumor?' Charlie has a brain tumor? That's a cancerous growth."

"Ah know. Now maybe yuh see why ah tried to be protective. None of this bad stuff was really Chahlie's fault. But the bad stuff kept gettin' worse and worse — ah started runnin' outta ways to protect him."

North stopped and looked Elijah in the face. The sun was rising, so there appeared to be more light than shadow in the man's expression, and there was a deep understanding of the pain his brother had caused so many people. "And by protecting him, you were unleashing him to inflict more and more horror on everyone else. You know that it all has to stop here and now."

"Ah surely do."

"Elijah, I mean it. You cannot stop me. This is non-negotiable. He will be stopped today. I will try to bring him alive though. I promised you before, and it is a bargain I will try to keep — *if possible.*"

"Now we find out, Mr. North. There they are."

Callendar was helping Hannah mount her horse. He helped put her foot into the stirrup, then assisted her in swinging her other leg across the back of the horse. In a sliding gesture, he ran his hand across her derriere and down her right thigh. North could see the man's smirking, pronounced teeth and Hannah's discomfort over this familiarity. Still, he did not want his jealousy to endanger her life. He waited for Callendar to step up to his own horse before taking action. Charlie and McAvee were now mounted on their horses.

Both Elijah and North had dismounted and gotten down on their stomachs at the edge of a ridge overlooking the four riders. Both men aimed their rifles at human targets and waited. Then, John broke the silence by firing his Winchester about two feet from Callendar's head.

"Drop your weapons! We have you covered. Release the girl, and I may let you live. If you don't release her, I will kill you as I did the men you sent to murder us."

McAvee panicked and bolted off. He didn't get far. Elijah kept him in his sights and then fired. McAvee fell, but his foot caught in a stirrup. He was dragged off.

Charlie saw Elijah and rode directly toward him with pistol drawn. He screamed crazily and shouted, "IT'S TIME TO DIE! TIME TO DIE! LET'S DIE, BIG BROTHUH!"

North hesitated and instantly learned the consequence of such hesitation. Charlie shot Elijah and hit him in the chest. North then put Charlie in his sights and tried to wing him in the shoulder, but the horse's hoof stepped into a hole in the ground, and Charlie careened to the left just as John fired his rifle. The bullet pierced Charlie in the heart.

Not wanting any sort of delay, Callendar let loose of Hannah's horse, turned, and galloped away. North quickly got onto his mount and pursued Callender. As he passed Hannah he shouted, "Look after Elijah, Hannah. I will be back!"

Hannah wanted to plead for him to remain, but she knew such a plea would be futile. John had to finish the job. Only Callendar remained. The thing she could say in response was, "I'll wait for you — be careful!"

Callendar had never been in such a situation. His men had always been with him in a swift and fatal attack against his intended victims or dispatched to successfully ambush them. John North had finished off all of his men — including Blood Hawk and Charlie Johnson! This had to be a nightmare! There was a sense of disbelief. This was going to be a warm, July day in the mountains, and it was not clear if he would live to see the end of it. "No!" he self-admonished. "My life was not supposed to end this way!"

North was riding faster and rapidly approaching Callendar. P.J. Callendar reverted to his usual, calm, cool calculating thought process and looked for a way to gain another advantage. He suddenly stopped his horse. John North figured he would run directly into the backside of Callendar's horse, so he swiftly turned to the right and avoided the collision. Instead of riding past Callendar, he jumped off his own horse and pushed Callender off the saddle of his own. The two men landed near the edge of a cliff and did their best to avoid going over the edge. Callendar rose to his feet first and turned to kick John in the face.

John anticipated the attack, grabbed Callendar by the boot, lifted the man's leg into the air, and caused him to lose balance and fall back. Callendar did not fall to the ground but had to flap his arms like an awkward buzzard to prevent himself from falling. This gave John North enough time to rise up, crouch low, and make a headfirst run toward Callendar. Callendar tried to dodge him but was not sufficiently quick. John's head struck P.J. Callendar in the stomach and nearly knocked the wind out of him. John rose up and savagely struck Callendar in the face with alternating jabs from his left and right fists. Callendar was tough, however, and blocked a fourth jab with his own right arm and pasted John in the mouth with a left hook. He then hit John in the abdomen and in the jaw.

North fell back — the blows from Callendar were severe, since the man was very tall and muscular. John North, however, was a seasoned fighter and had rarely lost a fist fight. The men were fighting for keeps, so Rules of Distinguished Gentlemen were not on the table. John kicked Callendar in the right shin and smashed the flat of his right fist against Callendar's right ear. Stunned, Callendar fell to his knees and fumbled around for his pistol. Before he could draw it, North kicked him in the face, then kicked him in the ribs. North quickly removed Callendar's pistol from the holster, then cocked back the hammer.

"You dirty, filthy, pus-headed maggot! You killed my parents! You and your people were responsible for killing all those soldiers, Mr. Foster, and yes, even poor young Charging Buffalo. Now your 'leadership' has lead to the deaths of McAvee and Charlie and probably Elijah as well. Give me one good reason why I should not blow a hole the size of Yellowstone Park in your unnatural teeth!"

Callendar spit blood and a loose tooth from his mouth, caught a deep breath, and replied, "Ah can't think of a single reason, Yankee. You done turned muh life into dung. Yuh killed all muh friends and beat hell outta me — an' ah'm only hopin' yuh slip up, so's ah can get thet gun and blast yuh with it. Since ah don't think thet likely, ah'm guessin' ah got nuthin' else to say 'cept ah'm sorry ah evah met you or yoah family. The experience has not been rewardin', Mistuh North."

The moment John North had been working for had finally arrived. First, he shot Baker. Then he wounded and captured Chapeau, who died miserably from infected wounds. Blood Hawk tried to destroy him but was himself destroyed. Then the moral dilemma concerning Charlie and Elijah came to an end when Charlie madly shot his own brother; thus making it easy to pick off Charlie. Now the leader of the wolf pack was cornered. He was within close proximity and well within his power. Snuffing out the man's dreadful life would be a relatively routine execution. Retribution was a trigger squeeze away.

If retribution was a routine action, then why was there hesitation? The other four were dead — he killed them all. The main perpetrator, P.J. Callendar, was the most deserving of swift capital punishment. All right, then: why was he still breathing?

John North remembered the last conversation he had with Hannah back in Copperhead. He recalled her words, "There has been so much bad feeling and cruelty...," and even more important, "We have to keep telling each other there is more to life than just hating these people."

Callendar looked up at North and said, "Well, Yankee, what're yuh waitin' foah? Shoot!"

John showed no emotion as he walked up to Callendar and said, "You're not getting off so easily. There is more to my life than just despising yer rotten guts." John then struck Callendar across the face with the man's own dragoon colt. P.J. was out cold.

He quickly took a rope and bound the man's hands. Subsequently, he draped the man across the saddle of his horse, tied up his feet, and used additional rope to fasten him around the saddle. It was highly unlikely that P.J. Callendar would escape.

John heard someone approach. He turned and saw that it was Sammy Fivetrees. "Hannah, is she...."

"She is fine. Captain Bristol is with her, and the two of them are trying to help Elijah Johnson. I am afraid he does not look very good. I think that your prisoner will only escape if you ride him and his horse down the cliff to visit the lawyer. You truly know how to tie one on, white man!"

"Very funny, Cherokee. Actually, that wasn't half bad, or half good. I must be feeling better. I'm even willing to start laughing at a lousy joke! C'mon, let's rejoin the others."

At Sammy's insistence, John North rode ahead. It was obvious that he very badly needed to take Hannah into his arms. Meanwhile, Sammy took the reins of Callendar's horse and led the animal with its heavily bound cargo behind John.

As the two riders passed the body of McAvee, it was not evident to either man that anyone had even bothered to check on him. McAvee knew for certain that no one had investigated his condition. Since he was alive, he snickered that it was his triumph that everyone had ignored his fate. Ever since that meeting in the Fortune River bar this John North had complicated the lives of people wanting to exercise their personal freedoms. So what if a few colored people, no-good Indians, stupid sodbusters, and other worthless settlers got killed? The west was for people like Callendar, Blood Hawk, Charlie Johnson, and Nate McAvee. The soldier boys, Injun scouts, and do-goody marshals like John North were taking away the freedoms to drink, go whoring, rob stagecoaches, shoot non-white people, and do all the other fun things a good ol' boy loved doing.

Now it was payday! John North's back was a target bigger than the front door of a church. It was time to throw lead into that door. Even the damned scout wasn't looking in his direction. Slowly, meticulously, Nate McAvee lifted his head and upper body. It was not easy. After all, that damned Elijah Johnson — Elijah Johnson, a man he had prospected with and broken bread with at campsites — had the audacity to put a Winchester slug into his ribs. Well, sure, it hurt, but at least the slug missed the lung. It was easy enough to breathe. There, he sat up enough to get a clear shot at North's back. If there was time, then maybe he could also kill the scout. He pulled back the hammer, aimed, and then…

Crackkk!

"Sorry…your turn to die, not mine." Actually, Sammy was aware of Nate and swiftly turned and pistol shot the man through the right eye and through the brain. "You were loud, McAvee. Your death avenges Johnny Franklin and his family."

"Thanks, Sammy," North said.

"You are welcome. However, I think we are getting too old for this line of work."

North laughed and added, "I hear you. It's time to retire from this vocation."

North got off his horse and raced up to see Hannah. She ran into his arms before he made it half way up the knoll. She pressed her mouth to his and embraced him long and passionately. Their embrace filled his heart with joy and soulful satisfaction he had never felt previously. His reason to go on living was there — the love of this woman.

Hannah broke away long enough to state, "Do you…know about Edward?"

"Yes. We found him. I am sorry, Hannah. Witnessing his death must have been terrible for you. I did not like the man at all, but I did not crave his death."

"Neither did I. I saw Charlie and the other man fire at you — and saw Charlie die. It was awful — and especially for Elijah."

"How is Elijah?"

"You better come up here and see for yourself, John," Captain Bristol replied.

John took Hannah by the hand, assisted her up the small hill, and walked to the prostrate form of Elijah Johnson. Elijah's chest wound had been bandaged, but it was clear that there had been major blood loss. Remarkably, he was lying there awake, yet struggling for breath.

"Hey, old prospector — I see you pulled through. I knew you were tough."

"Not…that tough. Did…did yuh get Cal-len…," Elijah tries to finish the name but coughed several times instead.

"Yes. I whipped the tar out of him. Beat him within an inch of his life, then roped and tied him like broken heifer. We finally stopped him and his men in their tracks."

"But yuh didn't kill 'im?"

"No. I didn't."

"Why not?"

Before responding, John looked into Hannah's eyes which communicated a mutual understanding. There was more to life than….

"I am not God, Elijah. I set out to be judge, jury, and executioner and pretty much fulfilled those roles. God help me, I even killed your Charlie. In the end, when I stared into the face of the devil's apprentice I knew I had to face a tribunal for my actions. It would have been easier to kill Callendar than turn him over to society for judgment. I had to do this right."

Johnson coughed some more, and John North wiped away some of the blood coming from his mouth and held up his head in an effort to assist the man in breathing better.

"Then…you finally understand."

"Understand?"

"Love is strongeuh than revenge. You an' Hannah love each othuh. You have thet to live foah. Ah loved muh bruthuh, Chahlie — ah tried muh best to save and stop him, but ah could only stop him by l-lettin' him kill me. Odd, isn't it? Someone had tuh end his torture, and you did, John. Problem is — if Chahlie hadn't shot me, ah nevah woulda let yuh shoot Chahlie. Ah guess it was a mighty queer kinda wheel spinnin' 'round."

"Elijah, you better not talk so much. We have to get you well."

"Ah am gettin' bettuh — no more cold nights outside, bad gold pannin' days, or worries 'bout catchin'cholera. You two be happy together." He then coughed heavily enough to turn his face blue. After stabilizing and breathing surprisingly easier, he virtually whispered, "Ah envy you gettin' such a purty gal. I admire her an awful lot."

Hannah smiled, bent over, and kissed the dying man on the cheek. Elijah smiled, uttered, "Very sweet lips…," then died.

John repressed tears as they formed in his eyes. Hannah began to cry sufficiently for the two of them. Elijah Johnson was gone, and in spite of his many faults, including some dreadful decisions breeding horrible consequences, he would be missed. His death signaled the end of an era.

Captain Bristol patted John on the back and said, "Look!"

Riding up to the gathering was a tall man on a strikingly handsome white horse. It was Marshal Marconi.

"Ah see that ah finally found you boys. Ah am the U.S. Marshal you sent for, and ah see you have at least one live prisoner among all the dead bodies lyin' on the trail."

"Yes. We tried to bring in more prisoners, but events just didn't pan out that way."

"Understood. Ah have participated in a few similar events myself. Once deputied for Wild Bill Hickock who had a way of getting into situations where a lot of people ended up under the soil. It sometimes happens. Brought a few folks from town who will help us pack up these dead ones and take 'em down to Copperhead for proper burial."

One of the folks brought to assist the U.S. Marshal was Doctor Brandt. He quickly went to work on Captain Bristol, redressing his wound and certifying him safe to travel. After seeing that the fight wounds on North and Callendar were understandably painful, yet ultimately superficial, he did clean the more severe cuts on Callendar. Hannah insisted on caring for similar lacerations on the face of John.

Soon, the party was traveling down the trail and before nightfall had recovered and picked up all the bodies — including Edwards'. It was difficult retrieving him from that area off the cliff, but there were enough ropes and men to handle the task. All of the bodies were loaded onto horses except for two: those of Charging Buffalo and Blood Hawk.

Hannah asked, "Why did we bury the two Indians where they fell, instead of taking them back to town?"

Sammy gave the reason. "Both of these men lived in nature. They were very much different, yet they felt they were extensions of nature. It was only fitting that they remain in the mountains where the greatest meaning to their lives was expressed."

"I think I understand, but go ahead, Sammy," John interjected.

"Charging Buffalo's finest moment occurred when he successfully vanquished the unrelentingly evil life of Blood Hawk. Blood Hawk's finest moment was leaving the earth he ruined and disgraced. Did you notice that we buried Charging Buffalo on the ridge above the undistinguished grave we dug for Blood Hawk? Charging Buffalo will always be seen above Blood Hawk. He shall forever be superior to his mortal enemy."

The party did not return to Copperhead until nightfall. As John helped a weary Hannah down from her horse, he considered her first words might be, "I need a hot bath and a comfortable bed." Instead, she said, "Ironic, isn't it? We were so close to Fortune River and never set foot in town. Mother knows I'm late to arrive. What might she be thinking at this hour?"

31

TRIAL AND VERDICT

Judge Quartz deemed it "impossible" for Hannah to leave Copperhead, even for a few days, to go see her mother in Fortune River. He said "all relevant actors in the drama" must be detained in Copperhead until the trial of Callendar commenced and concluded.

One of the young men in town, Liam O'Sullivan, was hired by Hannah and John to deliver a handwritten letter to Naomi Fjord, Hannah's mother, explaining Hannah becoming an unexpected widow and the details concerning the criminal events and forthcoming trial. Five days had passed since O'Sullivan had left to deliver the letter, but he returned with a reply from Naomi. This was the reply:

Dearest Hannah:

I am so very, very relieved that you wrote and apprised me of the reasons for your delay in coming to visit me in Fortune River. There were so many potential reasons for such a delay — illness, Indian attack, bandits, or accidents. As you indicated, some of these — bandits and the tragic accidental death of Edward — were extremely elemental reasons for your delay. Above all, let me express my deep love and affection for you, daughter, and my relief that you are personally safe and well. Also, I want to convey my deepest sympathy for the loss of your husband, Edward. I am so sorry that you had to go through something like that at such a young age. I never met him, and you told me little about him, but I am sure that you loved him — since you had married him.

As for the matter of meeting and befriending John North, I am not at all surprised that you think so highly of him. In the brief time that I spoke with John earlier this month, I learned to like and trust him as well! He is a man who is serious about keeping promises.

Your uncle must stay and look after the hotel, but I intend to take a trip to Copperhead accompanied by my good friend, and I am happy to admit, husband-to-be, Phinneas Pleasance. We should arrive by Friday, if not before then, and will be with you when you sit in that courtroom.

With Love,
Mother

Hannah read and re-read the letter in the two days since she had received it. In the meantime, Judge Quartz had sent for an attorney in Laramie to come up and defend P.J. Callendar. The trial, he said, would not begin until Callendar was represented by court approved counsel.

The day after the survivors had returned to Copperhead, Elijah and Charlie Johnson were buried next to each other. Kirk Mason officiated separate Christian memorial services for Johnny Franklin, and Elijah and Charlie Johnson, as well as Abel Foster, Edward Olson, and Charging Buffalo. The young Cheyenne probably would not have approved of such a service for himself, but Roberta Mason insisted that "the nice young man be assisted into heaven." The killers, outlaws, and accomplices were all buried as well. Mayor Agee, Hubert Wesley, Rudolph Krautmueller, Nate McAvee, Arnie Mitchell, Brad Fulton, and Laura Roscoe were also interred in what Doctor Brandt described as a "group good riddance" ceremony, that nevertheless asked the Lord Almighty to have more mercy on "these tarnished souls than they ever had for righteous people on this planet."

O'Toole and the other unfortunate soldiers who had perished were loaded into wood coffins and sent back to Fort Green per command of Major Vincent Jacobs, whose squad had arrived in Copperhead the day after the posse returned. Captain Bristol immediately telegraphed Fort Green requesting that he and the recovering Trooper Warshinski return right away. Bristol's request was denied due to a direct order from the major that he remain and cooperate with the civilian judge until criminal matters involving the murdering of civilians and army personnel were legally resolved.

On the eighth day after the posse's return, many were feeling quite anxious.

"John, do you think Judge Quartz will begin the trial tomorrow?"

"I hope so, Hannah. We are all pretty much stuck in purgatory until that trial starts. For all I know, he might take a notion to indict me for some crime. Kirk Mason warned that this judge is not a scintillatingly tolerant cuss."

"I have had to deal with a lot of needless paperwork and inexplicable delays in my army career," added Captain Bristol. "But this time I have to follow the whims of a civilian authority who seems half-crazy at best. How did your personal interview with the man turn out, John?"

"Like a Salem witch trial." John, Hannah, and the Captain were seated in the aafé drinking coffee and becoming increasingly annoyed over Judge Quartz's delays and interrogations.

"Witch trial?"

"Hyperbole, as Mark Twain might elucidate. Even so, I told him about Callendar and his men ambushing me and my family, and he kept returning to the question, 'Did you plan the murder of Callendar and the others, young man? Are you any better than former Marshal Callendar?'"

"Your reply?"

"Hell, yes! These people were like rabid wolves running in and out of communities biting, hurting, destroying, and taking spoils. I said I didn't seek them strictly to satisfy my own anger but to stop them from hurting the public in general."

"He must have liked that answer, John," Hannah declared.

When John raised an eyebrow, Hannah added, "After all, he didn't arrest you once you said that."

Suddenly, U.S. Marshal Marconi entered the café and said, "That defense lawyer — a Mr. Alex Suthern — just came in on the stage. Ah told the judge, and he said Callendar's trial starts tomorrow morning at ten AM. All three of you gotta be there. John, you've been directed tuh make sure that Abby Franklin, Sally Redmond, the Masons, Doc Brandt, and the Cherokee fella show up in court. Since this town doesn't have a courthouse, Fulton's saloon will be the facility."

"Is it his honor's way of setting up easy access for thirst quenching?" Bristol muttered.

"Thanks for letting us know, Marshal. We'll be there. By the way — I know that Callendar is in your custody in the city jail, but I would like to have your permission to speak with him privately today."

"Not possible. His lawyer, Suthern, ruled out any visitors."

Marconi left, and John said, "It's just my luck that Callendar's lawyer is named 'Suthern,' and my last name is 'North.' I wouldn't be surprised if this Judge Quartz had problems with "North' verses 'Suthern.' After what Abby told me about this guy's biases, he might let Callendar go due to nostalgia for them Mason-Dixon Line days."

"I hope not," Hannah said. Mr. Marconi *is* southern, but he seems without prejudice."

"Yes, I admit he is a good man." Then, with unexpected solemnity, John said, "I swear, so help me, I will never allow Callendar to harm or kill anyone again."

The next day, the trial convened. Marshal Marconi represented the people of the territory as prosecutor, and Alex Suthern represented P.J. Callendar. Mr. Suthern stood a mere five feet six inches tall, sported a long, gray beard, wore thick eyeglasses, and showcased two gold teeth in place of his original front incisors. He did not look like an aggressive type but soon demonstrated that he performed against stereotype.

Suthern, who was from southern Vermont, implied in a high, squeaky, irritating voice that John North was "A bloodthirsty, vindictive man," solely bent on personal vengeance that "incipiently ignited a chain of violent events leading to the unnecessary deaths of not only the beloved mayor of Copperhead but individuals such as Mr. Chapeau, Blood Hawk, and Charlie Johnson who had been deprived of their civil rights."

Upon hearing sympathetic descriptions of poor, persecuted Pierre Chapeau, Deputy Wesley, Nate McAvee, and others, Kirk Mason literally fell ill and puked on the saloon floor. Judge Quartz cursed him for "willful desecration" and ordered Abby and Sally to clean up the mess. The two women refused and were fined ten dollars each.

The following day, Captain Bristol was called to the stand. He told the court about Callendar's willful murdering of his men and the senseless killing of the Scottish farmer and his hired hands. This was all circumstantial evidence, Suthern objected. However, when Bristol produced the piece of broken mirror that matched the other little mirrors on Callendar's hatband, the judge rubbed his heavy jowls, and groaned, "Hmmm-mmm...."

Much to Suthern's chagrin, Callendar insisted on testifying on his own behalf. Under examination from Marconi, he denied ever seeing, let alone killing John North's family. He also denied wounding Johnny and Harold Franklin, ambushing the troopers, ordering Blood Hawk and the other 'deputies' to ambush anyone, and stoutly denied the abduction of Mr. and Mrs. Olson. Edward came of his "own volition" and made the wife "obey."

During a key moment of testimony, Marconi asked Callendar, "Under risk of committing perjury, are you denying that you abducted Mrs. Hannah Olson? Remember, several people said they saw you forcibly take her out of town."

"Natcherly — I deny it all. The woman is a lyin' trollop. There ain't nuthin' she wouldn't do to protect John North. Them two was lovers all along — even when her husband was alive. Besides, its her slutty word against that of her dead, gentlemanly lawyer husband."

Judge Quartz interrupted, "John North and this woman were lovers? That kind of adulterous behavior is unacceptable!"

Unexpectedly, Sally Redmond interjected, "Not as unacceptable as P.J. Callendar makin' a hooker out of me and Laura, God rest her soul. Callendar and Mayor Agee used us all the time. They were filthy, sinful, and European-like."

Callendar started laughing. He sensed that Judge Quartz had sympathized with him from the beginning and figured this biased man was his ticket to freedom. For this reason, he looked up at the judge, expecting him to wink and nod as if to say, "Sure, this woman is just a whore. Whores have no credibility." Instead, Callendar looked up at a face contorted in anger. The judge gritted his teeth, raised his gavel into the air like Thor's Hammer, and shouted, "I have heard enough! This man is a vile, perverted Sodomite! I find him guilty of sin!"

"Er, your honor," Marshal Marconi cautiously objected. "I don't think that is a specific crime."

"How about at least six counts of murder, then? There were uh, what, at least four soldiers killed, that black, that Elijah Johnson character — yeah. Six! I say this P.J., or Pierce Justin Callendar is guilty of six counts of murder. Anything to say before I pronounce sentence, you plantation-loving trash?"

Absolutely stunned and barely able to mouth any words whatsoever, Callendar managed to say, "I kilt some uv um, but not all uv um…an' they had it comin'!"

Suthern protested, "I object! I object! This is all highly inappropriate! I demand a retrial, your honor!"

"I demand that you shut your hole, Suthern! This man is a whore lovin', thievin', murderin' scandalous Johnny Reb. Keep quiet, lawyer, or I'll hold you in contempt. As for you, Callendar, due to your many, many improprieties, I order you to be taken out to the nearest strong tree limb, where you will be forcibly removed from being seated on a nag and hanged by the neck until you are absolutely dead. This trial is over!"

John North looked at Hannah, and the two of them looked at Callendar. The man had been convicted after all. Clearly, the judge did not care about John and his family, or Hannah's terrifying abduction, or the needless killings of so many people. What mattered most was punishing the man for his sleazy, hedonistic appetites. Apparently, Sally Redmond said the right thing at the right time and pushed the Judge's flammable self-righteous prude button.

After the trial, Captain Bristol asked if the saloon were to remain closed forever or if it would reopen. North said the town leaders figured the drop in visitors' revenue would be disastrous, so the saloon would reopen. Odie Rawlins, the sole surviving employee of the late owner, Brad Fulton, inherited the business by default and was eager to start selling bad whiskey and stale beer to whomever desired it.

"Captain, may I buy you a drink?" inquired a demure yet flirtatious Sally Redmond.

"Young lady, that would be delightful. What about you, John?"

"Thank you, but Hannah and I…wait! I see a couple of familiar riders!"

Hannah looked over to the riders, jumped up and down excitedly, and screamed, "It's mother! My mother! She did get here after all!"

Following many embraces and kisses, Naomi stood and held the right hand of her daughter and the left hand of John North, put John's hand on top of Hannah's, and said, "This is Wyomin', kids. Let's get to the point. I see that you love each other. You're both available, and you look like a gorgeous set to me. I give you my blessing for a long and happy marriage!"

Overjoyed, John and Hannah hugged, kissed, laughed, then repeated the cycle several more times until Naomi said, "Hey! Enough of that for now. I thought I heard someone say something about a saloon somewhere!"

That evening, John North was granted his meeting with P.J. Callendar. He wanted to speak with him alone.

"Ah understand yuh wanted to talk with me befoah the trial, North. Ah couldn't see the point of it then or see it now. What duh yuh want, Yankee?"

John walked closer to the bars of the cell, grasped one of them with his right hand, and asked, "I wanted to ask you if it was worth it. All the stealing, injuring, and killing you either ordered or personally perpetrated — was it worth it to you? You're going to hang tomorrow, so I wonder now if you have anything to say?"

Instead of telling John to leave, as he half expected, Callendar propped up his pillow, sat up a little higher in his bunk while still maintaining a reclining position, and said, "Muh life is not what yuh'd call the sort of thing fairy tales are made uv — 'nless yoah talkin' about Beauty and the Beast, with me bein' the Beast while imaginin' he's the Beauty. Ah always thought ah was doin' the right thing 'cause ah always held muhself in pretty high regard. Ah nevah thought most folks were half as talented or as worthy as me. Muh pappy told me we were a special family, so ah always comported muhself in thet way. Hey, do you always pick the brain a of man on the eve of his death?"

North did not reply but went on to ask, "Are you sorry about what you did to my family? What about the Franklins, or the Olsons? Regrets over even getting your own men killed?"

Callendar started smirking with those personality-defining teeth and said, "Them people stood in muh way. Ah really am sorry thet Chahlie killed thet little bruthuh of yours. Ah have always liked kids, and it is not right thet a child should be shot. Chahlie was difficult to regulate, if yuh get muh meanin'. As for the othuhs yuh mentioned, better them than me."

"How much did you get from selling the goods in my mom and dad's wagon? Forty, maybe fifty dollars? Did Dad have ten gold pieces in his pocket? Was it worth taking their lives? What if someone had done that to your family?"

"Keep muh family out of it. Since yuh seem obsessed, ah'll tell yuh plain thet the answer is 'no,' I would not have wanted muh family to be ambushed. Listen up, Yankee — muh entire country was ambushed. Lincoln, Sherman, you, and them uthuh blue bellies attacked oah land and buried oah way of life! What's a few families compared to a country, John North?"

"Your value system is repugnant. You can't rationalize murder like that. In the end, you are still a barbaric killer. There is no excuse for what you and your men did."

Callendar jumped up from his bunk and tried to attack North, but North grabbed him by the throat and squeezed off his air supply. Callendar then struggled to reach for

North's Colt .45, but North grabbed three of the man's fingers and roughly bent them backwards. Callendar screamed and slumped toward the floor. North pushed Callendar further back in the cell, then stepped back at a sufficiently unreachable distance.

"What's goin' on in there?" barked Marshal Marconi.

"Nothing important," North replied. "Callendar was just expressing grief for Blood Hawk and his other pathetic friends."

"You dare tuh mention muh men? They were loyal, and all lived brave lives as ah did. None of us evah talked about the risks we took, but we all knew we'd be bitten by a bullet or rope some day. When yuh live hard, yuh die hard. Thas all!"

"That's fine, Callendar, except for one thing."

"Whazzat?"

"Tomorrow, I am going to go on living with a lovely woman who will marry me. The two of us plan to bring up a loving family. You are going to be executed. In our own different ways, we are facing a reckoning for the choices we made in our lives."

"A reckoning, you say? The North Reckoning is more like it. If it hadn't been for yoah damned *reckoning*, none of this would have happened. Good night, sir."

"Good night, Callendar. Your suite in hell awaits you."

32

RETRIBUTION

On the evening of Callendar's conviction, he was granted the final meal he desired. He ordered a two-pound beefsteak, fried potatoes, corn bread drenched in butter, hominy grits, two eggs over easy, coffee with cream, and fresh apple pie. He savored every single mouthful and asked Marshal Marconi to compliment the café's cook for preparing such a splendid feast.

There was no minister in town, but Kirk Mason, being a righteous Quaker, offered to read prayer for Callendar prior to the hanging. Callendar said no, declaring he did not believe in any deity and considered him a fool for believing in one himself. On the other hand, he did thank him for considering his feelings in the matter of his imminent passing.

Early the next morning Marshal Marconi placed the rope around Callendar's neck while Doctor Brandt steadied the condemned man's horse. Only a few people came to witness the execution: the two men conducting the hanging, John North, Sammy Five-trees, Sally Redmond, Captain Bristol, and Cornell Dustin, the undertaker. Judge Quartz and Mr. Suthern had both decided to sleep in that morning. North was asked if he wanted to do the honors but declined. The law was dispensing the justice — that was sufficient.

"Any final words, Callendar?" asked the U.S. Marshal.

P.J. Callendar looked at John North, then into the faces of the other witnesses, and said, "Ah thought it ovuh, an' ah don't hold any grudges 'gainst any of yuh. Ah also say thet ah'm sorry for killin' anyone thet didn't deserve killin', but still sorrier thet ah didn't kill John North when ah had the chance. Marshal Mahconi, ah'd like tuh be buried with muh fancy hat on muh head. It is some comfort that muh hangman's from Richmond and not Detroit. There's nuthin' else 'cept ah'm gonna miss good food and hot female bodies."

Marconi slapped the horse on the rear end, and Callendar danced in mid-air. The rope's knot had been tied properly, so Callendar's neck broke instantly. He convulsed for a moment or two but died quickly. The dreaded outlaw leader passed into irrelevancy.

As he had requested, Callendar was buried with that hat containing the little mirrors hatband. Moreover, the black clothes he had always worn served as interment wardrobe.

Everyone concluded it would be excessively troubling to contact the various next of kin of all those outlaws, so they did not bother. Whatever cash the men had on them paid for their coffins, burials, and grave markers. Should anyone want to look for them in the undertaker's grave register book, or actually seek their graves, then the names were identified both in the book and on the simple wooden crosses stuck into their plots.

33

TIME GOES ON

Subsequent to the execution of P.J. Callendar, life gradually returned to something of a normal level. Law and order became the norm, and people dedicated their lives to commerce, general survival, and happiness where it might be cultivated.

Judge Quartz and U.S. Marshal Marconi had wasted little time in returning to southern Wyoming. About a year later, Judge Quartz enraged some Chinese Tong suspects in his courtroom as being "sub-human foreign interlopers," thus causing a general riot in his court. Seven people, including the bailiff, were hospitalized. The following day Judge Quartz was found dead in an alley with a deep hatchet chop in the back of his neck. The suspects jumped bail and were never seen again.

Marconi, on the other hand, ran for the office of District Attorney and was elected. From there, he continued to build a political reputation and attained his greatest success years later working in the Theodore Roosevelt administration in the Attorney General's office. He was vacationing in England in 1912 but died in his sleep two nights before he was supposed to sail on the Titanic's final voyage.

Captain Edgar Bristol returned to Fort Green with Trooper Warshinski. The trooper went on to serve a successful twenty years in the army. Problems occurred between Cheyenne, Sioux, and other Indian nations in the Wyoming and Montana areas following the discovery of gold in the Black Hills of South Dakota. It all came to a head in 1876 when Colonel George Armstrong Custer and his men were wiped out in the Battle of the Little Bighorn. Fortunately, Warshinki was under the command of Major Reno, so he narrowly survived with Reno and many others.

Bristol, on the other hand, escaped all that trouble. He had followed Sammy's example in 1875 and opted for retirement. As soon as he could be discharged, he returned to Copperhead and ran for mayor. He was elected almost unanimously. Furthermore, he wooed, and ultimately married, Sally Redmond whose wanton past was never again brought up in polite conversation. Living in Denver in 1900, Edgar and Sally bought an a automobile that Edgar found difficult to drive. On one icy evening in December, his vehicle skidded out of control and crashed into a fire house. Only Edgar was killed. Fortunately, he was heavily insured, so Sally ended up financially secure. The two had no children. She took up painting and became generally interested in the arts. She assumed the life of an honored elderly art museum philanthropist in Denver. She lived to be ninety-eight.

Odie Rawlins ran a successful saloon that he named "The Coppermouth." He was not allowed to provide prostitutes, but he did provide a lot of gaming tables. Some say the rowdy fights and outrageous behaviors of many of its disagreeable patrons added fuel to arguments favoring temperance and ultimate prohibition.

Kirk and Roberta Mason eventually convinced a Methodist minister to permanently start a church in Copperhead. They were unable to get a Quaker congregation set up, so by 1888 they were desperate to have any Christian church. The Methodist minister marveled at the large number of apparently premature deaths in 1875 and wondered if some sort of plague had swept through the area. Kirk wryly replied, "It was a terrible lead storm that blew in." The Masons longed for the east coast in their autumn years and moved to Pennsylvania where virtually everyone lost contact with them.

Sammy Fivetrees kept his word to Abby and the children. He helped them not only maintain their ranch but expand it as well. Soon, the ranch specialized in raising prize hogs, chickens, and eggs, as well as corn, cabbage, and potatoes for sale. Within three years of his arrival, Sammy and Abby were married in a quiet ceremony. Harold Franklin did what many considered unthinkable at the time — he continued to read more and more books and ended up attending a fine college in the East. He became a physician, and a widely respected one at that. Ruthie continued to have some respiratory problems, but when she turned seventeen, she met and married a black cowboy. The two of them settled in Arizona where she recovered from chronic respiratory ailments.

John North and Hannah Olson were married in August, 1875. It was the custom of widows to wait a year or so before remarrying, but Hannah heeded her mother's advice and chose to spend as much time with John as possible. Sammy Fivetrees stood up as best man, and Sally Redmond was matron of honor. The wedding took place in Fortune River, and about a month after they were married, Naomi finally married Mr. Pleasance.

John and Hannah North moved to Fortune River and remained there until 1878. John became the first town marshal of that little town but grew weary of law enforcement and the lack of income it provided. In the summer of 1878, following the unavoidable tuberculosis death of Naomi, John and Hannah moved to California where John opened a dry goods store and Hannah taught grade school. She specialized in teaching English and arithmetic. In 1879 they took a trip to Lettuceville, California and met the widow and offspring of Abel Foster. John and Hannah recounted Abel's integrity and bravery during that troubled summer of 1875. The family thanked John and Hannah for being such a good friend to Abel. Hannah graciously added that Abel was the truest of friends.

In 1883, Hannah gave birth to a healthy son. John and Hannah named him Marcus Nathaniel, in honor of their respective fathers. The happy family lived in California until 1890 when they uprooted and moved to Seattle, Washington, where John North resumed duties as a law enforcement official. He quickly rose to the rank of police captain and continued in that capacity until his retirement in 1910.

During the Spanish American War, in 1898, John argued that it was his duty to join the army and fight for America. No one wanted John to serve at that time insisting that at fifty-three, he was probably too old.

Over the many years that passed, the North family succeeded in revisiting Copperhead as well as Fortune River a few times. Those visits always included visits to the Franklin Ranch. John treasured the times he went hunting and fishing with Sammy. Both John and Hannah loved visiting with Abby and the children. Sammy and Abby ended up with a child of their own, a girl they simply named, "Princess."

The Norths had constantly invited Sammy and Abby to come up to Washington State and visit, but they never came. In 1906, Sammy wrote and said they were "Really going to catch the train up there this year," which was exciting news. Sadly, Sammy died of a massive stroke that same week while feeding chickens. Abby passed away from cancer two years afterwards. By all accounts, their years together were rich and wonderful.

During the summer of 1909, John and Hannah received a telegram from Dr. Harold Franklin. It stated that he had been offered a job working in a Seattle hospital, and he had accepted the offer. John eagerly wired him back and told him he and his family could stay at the North home until they got settled. By September, the Franklins had arrived and soon became neighbors. Some of the other neighbors objected to the idea of a black family moving in their neighborhood, but John persuaded in them "to mind their own damn business."

Hannah was troubled that their son, Marcus Nathaniel, had not yet found a girl and married her. In 1910, he was twenty-seven and still living the life of a bachelor. Marcus was starting to achieve some success in selling those "crazy horseless carriages" many had laughed about a few years before. Now, no one was laughing. It was clear the automobile was not going to go away, and the day of the horse as the primary means of transportation was coming to an abrupt halt. John's comment was succinct, "It's just as well. My bones are getting too brittle to be riding those animals any longer."

Then, in July, Marcus met and fell in love with Mary Beth Cooper, a pretty blonde he met waiting on him in a Woolworth store. They were married in time for Thanksgiving.

Certainly, by 1910, the focus of everyone was the promise of a better life in the twentieth century. Cold nights out on the trail, fears of Indian attacks, and protecting oneself from roving gangs of gun slinging outlaws were concepts one read about in pulp novels and not identifiable as everyday experience for most people.

In fact, John and Hannah North found themselves talking about the old days less and less. This was quite true until the subject was heartily resurrected from a couple of unexpected sources in the years that followed.

34

MASTERING HISTORY

On a cool, sunny April morning in 1915, John North walked down a busy Seattle city street personally content, but somewhat annoyed by the presence of so many smelly, noisy cars everywhere he gazed. Still, at age seventy, he felt there was so much to be grateful for in his life. His son was successful, married, and had provided him two lovely grandchildren, Johnny and Amanda. They were loaded with zest and gave him added energy each time he was lucky enough to spend time with them. Best of all, he was still with Hannah, in spite of her recent bouts of rheumatoid arthritis and heart disease.

John approached a newsstand and noticed a stack of books propped up featuring a photograph of the Rocky Mountains on the cover. Intrigued, he picked one up and examined the title. It read, "Killers that Escaped the Law," by Odie Rawlins. Odie Rawlins, Odie Rawlins. "Who in hell is Odie…the name sounds familiar…Rawl…," then it hit him. That bird who took over Fulbright's — I mean Fulton's putrid saloon back in Copperhead! Could this guy still be alive?

He leafed through the book, and sure enough, there was the photo of a scraggly, white bearded, bald, old goat who looked just as ugly as an old man as he did a young one. Well, who were these "killers" he so expertly wrote about? Turning to chapter two, there was Billy the Kid, chapter three, Wild Bill Hickock — Hickock? He was a difficult man, but he was a peace officer! Chapter four, Jack North. Whoa!

He immediately went to work reading chapter four. According to Odie Rawlins, the *expert* on western history, "A rogue marshal named Jack North forced his will upon the town of Copperhead, Wyoming in 1876. Frustrated after he was prevented from selling Winchesters and ammunition to the rebellious Cheyenne nation, he sought revenge on his one-time commanding officer, Mortimer Agee, and shot him dead. He then ran existing Marshal P.U. Callendar out of town along with the man's deputies."

Exasperated, John had to force himself to read more. "Once on the run, P.U. Callendar and his law-abiding deputies felt safe from the murderous North and his Indian and negro accomplices, but they tracked him down in the mountains and shot and killed them one-by-one. Callendar alone was captured and hanged in Copperhead without benefit of receiving a fair trial. Once North was through with what he considered a "piss ant of a town," he married a saloon prostitute, moved west, and opened up a notorious cathouse in San Francisco where he died of the flu in 1899."

"Son-of-a bitchin' liar. Although he was appropriate with the P.U. name change...."

"Hey, you can't go away without payin' for that book, old man."

North gave the vendor a dollar, then said, "I pay this money only to enable you to earn your living, my good man, not to give profit to the worm who wrote this garbage."

"Garbage? Hey, it's a best seller! Don't you like to hear the truth about the west?"

"I do now! And I intend to let others know about it too, 'young timer.'"

The incident seriously raised John's blood pressure and made him hopping mad all night. Hannah, worried that John might pop a blood vessel in his head, called their son Marcus and asked him to talk to his father. Marcus came over and heard his father's complaint, and looked at the fiction generating that complaint.

"Well, Dad, there is only one thing left to do: sue the old coot! For years you have been telling me about the Civil War, and the story of what happened in Copperhead, so I don't blame you for getting riled. We don't want you to get a stroke over it! Let's get our version of events out there for people to examine!"

The Norths then hired a lawyer, Abraham Fichtner, who filed a suit against the author, Odie Rawlins, and his publisher, Bigg-Peabody Press. There was no response to the suit until a year later, when Abraham Fichtner called John and Marcus into his office for a conference.

"It has come to my attention that Bigg-Peabody Press is guilty of fraud, as well as slander. Its shadowy publisher, Stanley Chapeau, paid one thousand dollars to Mr. Rawlins in a nursing home for the rights to his story. Chapeau took the bewildered man's rantings as gospel and published them as verifiable history. Mr. Rawlins is now deceased and really had not approved of all the material published, according to his daughter."

"Did you say Chapeau?"

"Yes. In fact, this publisher, whom I have spoken with over the telephone, claims he was an actual descendent of a man murdered by Jack North."

"It figures. A man like that would have to be a bastard. The Chapeau I knew was a skulking bastard too."

"Now the good news," Fichtner said. "Once I notified Mr. Chapeau that Jack North, a.k.a., John North, was still alive and offended by the lies, he said he was sorry and would immediately withdraw all books from the newsstands."

"He gave up that easily?"

"Not exactly. Our lawsuit asked for fifty thousand dollars in damages, unless he pulled the books off the market and sent us eighteen thousand dollars instead. He opted for the latter, Mr. North. Congratulations."

John North thanked Mr. Fichtner and shook his hand. During the ride back home, John told his son, "Who would have thought that my old enemies would strike back all these years later?"

"Well, at least it's over."

"Not by a long shot! I intend to write a tale myself. It will tell the world what really happened."

During the next two years John North wrote his own version of events that fateful summer in 1875. He called the story, "Between Copperhead and Fortune River." It was published in late 1917, but most people had their minds on the Great War, so not many copies were sold. Regrettably, the book disappeared from circulation and memory in general. At least the Bigg-Peabody book disappeared as well.

The second unexpected source of reviving vivid memories of the old days occurred in 1919. Marcus, Mary Beth, Johnny, and Amanda came over to pick up Grandpa and Grandma and take them to the movies. There was a western playing called, "Justice in Wyoming."

"I don't know about these flickers about the old days, Marcus. You sit in a dark show hall, stare at a bunch of black and white moving pictures of a bunch of overfed, cornball California actors pretending to shoot and kill each other. One man gets shot, clutches at his belly like he just ate a raw onion and pig snout sandwich, then falls down hoping you'll believe he's dead. Personally, I think the people making up these stories are dead from the neck up, if yuh know what I mean."

"You are incorrigible, John," Hannah scolded. "The kids just want to take us out for some entertainment."

"I know…and I appreciate it." Suddenly spry for a seventy-four-year-old man, John promulgated, "Here's a better idea! Why don't we go out and see one of those slapstick comedies! You know, Charlie Chaplin, the Keystone Cops, or that Fatty Arbuckle. Ha!Ha! He reminds me of someone I once saw gobbling candy in Minneapolis. Anyway, Arbuckle has that new kid working in his films now — that really funny guy, Buster Keaton! I think he'll end up the funniest one of all. It's better to laugh than dwell on suffering and shooting."

"Grandpa," Johnny interjected. "Don't you like cowboy movies? I like to wear my guns and cowboy hat and shoot the outlaws! You don't like the outlaws, do yuh?"

Marcus took Johnny to task and said, "Johnny! Don't speak to Grandpa that way. As a matter of fact, Grandpa knows all about being a cowboy. He really was one once."

"Really?" Johnny's eyes popped, and his mouth dropped open in total admiration. "Grandpa! Did ya ride a horse, rope cattle, and kill a bunch of outlaws?"

John nervously glanced at Marcus, who put a hand on Johnny's shoulder and said, "Your Grandpa was a real western marshal in 1875. He was like a policeman and tried to keep people safe."

Having been provided such an excellent opening, John added, "This is true, Johnny. It was all about keeping people safe, so they could do their jobs, take care of their families, and do the good work expected of them by the Lord. All that other stuff about fighting people and handling a gun was not as important. Want to know what was most important to me then, Johnny?"

"What was that?"

John put his arm around Hannah and says, "Meeting your Grandma and marrying her. Of course, I had to save her from some rotten pears at first. That's a story I can tell you later. Right now, let's go to the movies."

After returning from the movies, Marcus, Mary Beth, and the children said good night and went home. The movie they had gone to see did turn out to be a slapstick comedy, but the earlier conversation John had with his grandson still percolated in his mind. He looked troubled, and even a little disoriented. Worried, Hannah picked up the telephone and called Harold Franklin.

Harold lived a couple blocks away, so he soon arrived at the house. He took John aside and said, "John, I am still your doctor, and I am still advising you to work a little harder at keeping calm. Your blood pressure remains a problem. Hannah also tells me you still eat too much salt. My other patients have cut back on salt and fatty foods like butter, and they're doing better. Will you listen to me?"

"Yes, yes, yes. Harold, you know I trust you. I can't begin to thank you enough for all that you've done for Hannah and me. I know I'm wearing out faster than I want to admit, but I still feel good in so many other ways. I am still eternally grateful that you got Hannah well after her last spell in the hospital. God works through your hands, son."

Harold closed his medical bag, sighed, and looked approvingly at his geriatric patient. "I am the one who is eternally grateful, John. If it weren't for you and Hannah, I wouldn't have been accepted by this community — well, at least most of it. Quite a few still don't like seeing a Negro doctor. Anyway, I'm grateful for your support and for even more than that."

"What's that, doc?"

"Eighteen seventy-five. Yes, I remember those days. I recall my ma, pa, and all the violence and heartbreak of that time. I also remember people of character. When it counted, you and Hannah stood up for me and my family and accepted us for who we were, not what we looked like. Sammy was the same. He was my second father."

Tears started to well in John's eyes. "You are like another son to us, Harold. I knew you loved reading that large old book — I knew you'd go far. I just didn't want people like Callendar and those other brutes to prevent you from succeeding. You are grateful to me? Son, because of me, your father was killed! How did you ever forgive me? I should have saved him!"

Harold gently grabbed North's hand and replied, "I also wish you could have saved him. I wish I had been old enough and strong enough to fight Blood Hawk and McAvee. But you weren't there when my pa got killed, and I was too young to stop his death. What we ought to think about is what we did save. Think about that instead."

Dr. Harold Franklin thanked Hannah for the glass of milk, bid the elderly couple goodnight, then walked home.

After closing the door, John turned and showed Hannah a scratched, worn-out, silver music box. He opened it, but the music would not play.

"You still have your mother's music box! It is amazing that you have it after forty-four years!"

"Yep. If I value something, I'm plenty stubborn about letting it go. I've made a decision. I want our little granddaughter Amanda to have this. It should stay with women folk."

"She will cherish it."

"I think…I still want to hang onto it for a little while longer. Do you think she'd understand?"

"What a silly question! She doesn't even know you are planning to give it to her yet! Of course."

"I mean…it is hard to let go. Hannah, you have to stay with me as long as you can. I won't let go."

"I'll stay as long as I'm permitted by the Lord and no longer. That's all any of us can promise, my love. Let's go to bed. It's late."

John and Hannah went to bed, but John did not sleep well that night. His failures and violent behaviors came back to haunt him in his memory — as they periodically would through the years at moments when he least expected it. However, Harold's words, "…think about what we did save," seemed to give him comfort this time. Not only that, Hannah's pledge to stay as long as she could gave him inner peace.

35

FINAL RECKONING

About two days later, Hannah stood washing dishes in the kitchen sink and saw her husband stroll in looking for a slice of bread to nibble. She said, "John, it's been a superb life with you. We've had many, many happy times together. When I look back at our lives, I know we have had ups and downs, sunny days and rainy ones, but nothing ever compared to those days in 1875. Do you ever think a lot anymore about those dark, dangerous times in '75?"

John looked at the white-haired, wrinkled face of his wife and realized he loved her as much today as he did when he first saw her on that stagecoach getting robbed by Blood Hawk and Chapeau. Ha! Those were two names it would be nice to forget, along with that fiend, Callendar. He carefully weighed her words, smiled, took her hands into his, and said, "Every day, Hannah. I think about them every day. I may not fully remember what happened five, or even fifteen years ago, but those days are embedded in my brain as if they had been seared in by a hot branding iron. What makes their memory bearable today is one little thought that I think is pretty significant. Those days were awfully rough, but thank God, my son and grandchildren will not have to experience those days. As you know, we have consistently tried to make them a better world than that one."

"Yes, John, but it will always be one of the best times for me because I met you then and there."

"Me too." John rested comfortably in a kitchen chair and said, "You know, the night before Callendar was hanged, I went to his cell to speak to him directly about all the terrible things he had caused."

"You never told me that before!"

Visibly surprised, John added, "I didn't? I have to wonder why not. Maybe I wanted to spare you any more thoughts about that villain. Anyway, he said something that night that has stuck in my craw ever since. After I told him he would be facing a reckoning for his evil deeds, he said it only happened because it was a *North Reckoning*. Would you be so kind as to give me your opinion on the meaning of such a statement?"

Hannah shook her head, and said, "He must have meant that it was all your doing. The judgment against him and his men happened because of your persistent stubbornness and determination."

"That's what bothers me, Hannah. Did I play God? Was it right for me to do everything that I did?"

"Only the Lord can answer that, John — you should know that by now. If it makes you rest easier, I think you had better look at things in another way. Consider what might have happened had there had not been a *North Reckoning* as that unrepentant man put it. You were one man — only one man — who did his best to make a difference, a very, very *good* difference. As far as I am concerned, you did all right, Marshal North."

"Hannah, you have no idea how much that means to me." John leaned over and softly kissed her on the lips. "It's a warm, sunny day. Let's take a nice, romantic walk down to the park. Ouch! I think I'm starting to feel arthritis coming on. What the heck, let's head out anyway!"

THE END